Sophie's
DRAGON

SUPERNATURAL BONDS

Jory Strong

ELLORA'S CAVE
ROMANTICA PUBLISHING

What the critics are saying...

ॐ

"Yet again, I am blown away by the sensuality and intricacy of a Jory Strong book. The *Supernatural Bonds* series has been magnificent and as always I can only hope that secondary characters will be given their own books. Sophie was a treat to read about. Her love of the arcane and her acceptance of things not quite normal made her the perfect pairing for Severn. And Severn? Oh my, it was truly a treat to read about him. The man oozed sexuality and was just Alpha enough to make me swoon a few times. This was definitely a keeper." ~ *Fallen Angel Reviews*

"*Sophie's Dragon* is part three of the Supernatural Bonds series. While I intend to read the first two, this book easily stands alone. The plot is hot, steamy and delightful. I like reading about dragons, elves and things of quixotic fantasy. This is not a short story yet I couldn't put it down. [...] The book came alive in my hands I could see the story as it unfolded. Jory Strong is an extremely talented author; I will be looking for more of her books. I highly recommend this one to all fans of erotic romance." ~ *Reader Views*

"This was a fantastic story! Sophie and Severn have a lot of chemistry, and I particularly liked how Sophie wouldn't just give in and let Severn have everything his way. [...] I thought all of the characters were very well drawn, and the story drew me in and kept me reading until I was through. Great story!" ~ *The Romance Studio*

An Ellora's Cave Romantica Publication

www.ellorascave.com

Sophie's Dragon

ISBN 9781419957093
ALL RIGHTS RESERVED.
Sophie's Dragon Copyright © 2007 Jory Strong
Edited by Sue-Ellen Gower.
Cover art by Syneca.

This book printed in the U.S.A. by Jasmine–Jade Enterprises, LLC.

Electronic book Publication April 2007
Trade paperback Publication September 2007

Also by Jory Strong

∞

About the Author

&

Jory has been writing since childhood and has never outgrown being a daydreamer. When she's not hunched over her computer, lost in the muse and conjuring up new heroes and heroines, she can usually be found reading, riding her horses, or hiking with her dogs.

Jory welcomes comments from readers. You can find her website and email address on her author bio page at www.ellorascave.com.

Tell Us What You Think

We appreciate hearing reader opinions about our books. You can email us at Comments@EllorasCave.com.

SUPERNATURAL BONDS: SOPHIE'S DRAGON

Dedication

ം

For Sue-Ellen Gower – thanks for being there. I count myself lucky to have you as an editor and friend.

Trademarks Acknowledgement

ം

The author acknowledges the trademarked status and trademark owners of the following wordmarks mentioned in this work of fiction:

Mustang: Ford Motor Company

Starbucks: Starbucks U.S. Brands

The Twilight Zone: CBS Broadcasting Inc.

Victoria's Secret: Victoria's Secret

Chapter One

❧

Severn Damek's grip tightened on the steering wheel as he pulled to a stop in front of Inner Magick. Heat radiated from him and threatened to damage the interior of the expensive sports car. Dragon fire fought to escape through human nostrils and mouth.

He had an infinite amount of wealth at his disposal and yet he hadn't been able to obtain the one artifact that was priceless, essential to his kind, the one item that would be worth his very life. Severn smiled slightly—not that he intended to pay with either his life or his fortune. He was a dragon prince, almost impossible to kill in this mortal realm. And dragons took what they wanted, especially when it rightfully belonged to them.

Nothing would stop him from recovering the cup. No one would stop him from taking it. Let the Wizard Enos burn through all eternity for creating the chalice and tying the fertility of the dragons to it with a powerful spell. Let the faerie queen Otthilde perish in a cold storm for gaining the Chalice of Enos then losing it in the human realm. Let mortals and fey both beware. He would cut a path through them and leave nothing but smoldering ash if any tried to keep him from finding and possessing the Dragon's Cup.

The smell of heated leather forced Severn to curb his anger and his fire. Given his state of mind, it wouldn't amuse him to have to explain the spontaneous combustion of his car.

By The Great Shared Ancestor! To have been so close, only to have the chalice disappear when Carl VanDenbergh was murdered! It would test any dragon's temper and patience!

He'd thought the policewoman Storm O'Malley would lead him to the chalice. But she was a homicide detective and her leads had led to death, her responsibility limited to pursuing the ones responsible for it.

But the policewoman, or rather the necklace she wore, had inadvertently made him contemplate something even a handful of years ago he wouldn't have—using Elven magic to find the chalice. Severn grimaced. Elves, they were a snobbish lot for the most part, with their caste-system and their obsession with the purity of their blood.

They had been the first to see a future where the humans not only walked in the same world as the rest of the supernaturals but would one day take it over. They were the first to flee, to carve a home for themselves in an alternate realm with only a few necessary overlaps to this one. The dragons followed later. And then the faeries, which probably explained why the faeries so closely resembled the humans they liked to scorn.

By all accounts Aislinn Windbourne Dilessio, the half-elf owner of Inner Magick, was psychic as well as talented in the working of stones. She was heartbonded to a human policeman and used her skills to aid those humans the magic allowed her to assist. She appeared to be different from the rest of her kind. That was the reason Severn had shed his suspicion and dislike of the Elves and come in person to speak with her. Perhaps she would be willing and able to assist a dragon.

Severn slid from the sports car. Surprise gripped him when he got to the shop door. There'd been no reason to think anything of great value would be found at Inner Magick, but as he touched the glass, heat and energy filled his chest. Every instinct insisted something priceless waited inside to be claimed.

* * * * *

Sophie Alexander smiled as she unwrapped another set of runes and examined the workmanship. She felt like a kid left to play in the toy store though officially she was filling in while Aislinn and her assistant Marika were away for the day.

Warmth flowed into her with thoughts of her best friend, Aislinn Windbourne Dilessio—owner of Inner Magick and psychic, though Aislinn downplayed that part of her extraordinary talent the same way she downplayed her amazing skill at making jewelry and working crystals into artistic creations.

Out of habit Sophie's hand strayed to the heartmate necklace Aislinn made for her. It was a pendant of finely wrought leaves cradling a dark blue crystal with hints of red. According to Aislinn the stone would come to life in the presence of the man Sophie was supposed to share her life with.

Sophie laughed softly. *Number of dates, ten. Registering on the heartmate crystal, zero.* But she wasn't about to give up or start doubting Aislinn. No way, especially not now, after witnessing what happened to her cousin Storm, once Aislinn gave her a necklace. Storm ended up with two men, not one!

It still boggled Sophie's mind that her homicide detective cousin was living with two men, even considered herself married to them! It was a good thing Tristan and Pierce were cousins who looked like they were twins. The color of their eyes was different, but a pair of shades or a comment about fashion contact lenses and no one was the wiser. Amazing! She'd have thought the other cops would pick up on the fact there were two men, but so far only Aislinn's husband, Trace, and Storm's partner, Brady, seemed to be aware of *both* Pierce and Tristan's existence.

Sophie closed her eyes and concentrated on the dark crystal in her own necklace. It definitely seemed warmer than it usually did. She didn't think she was imagining it and when Aislinn looked at the stone before leaving with Marika, she'd said, "Soon."

Soon. How many interpretations could there be to that word?

Sophie opened her eyes and grinned. Well, it all depended on the species probably. Soon to one of the dragons or faeries she created in her fantasy novels might be a decade or even a century. Soon to a detective in one of her mystery novels might be an hour or a month. But as far as she was concerned, soon couldn't be soon enough, especially now that Storm had Tristan and Pierce in her life and Aislinn had the super macho Detective Trace Dilessio in hers.

"Soon," Sophie whispered, though she couldn't suppress a shiver of nervousness.

Sometimes the vision of finding someone to share her life with was a cherished dream. Other times, usually in unguarded moments of sleep, having someone who loved her turned into a nightmare.

Sophie tightened her grip on the pendant and felt its comforting warmth against her palm. *I am not like my mother. I don't need to be rescued. I'd rather have no man than the wrong one.* Years of practice and the distance of time allowed her to keep the horror-scene images of her mother's murder from surfacing.

She took a deep breath and turned her attention back to the rune sets. So far she'd managed to unwrap—and put aside for herself—three sets of them. Her innate sense of humor and optimism returned. She could easily picture Storm's raised eyebrows and often asked question. *Don't you ever get enough of that stuff? Can your apartment hold another item?*

Sophie laughed as she imagined her response. *Well, it's not like I have any rune sets. Crystals, yes. Crystal arrangements, yes. But rune sets, no. And besides, these will make great gifts.* She snorted at her own lie. "As if."

She *could* give them away but once she'd "collected" an item it was hard for her to part with it. In fact, it was nearly impossible, but she *could* do it, if absolutely necessary.

Sophie tucked the necklace under her dress so she could feel it against her skin. It was something she'd felt the need to do lately. "Which probably explains why the crystal seems warmer," she chided, knowing there were plenty of people who'd think she was nuts because she actually believed there was magic in the world.

But she needed to believe, even now that she was an adult, she still *needed* to believe. Because otherwise, it would be too easy to see only the ugliness and the horrible things people were capable of doing to each other.

She frowned as she thought about her newest project and the man she'd be pitted against, Severn Damek. She wondered if he was truly as ruthless as he was rumored to be. She'd researched him. She'd even used parts of what she'd found to form villains in several of her stories. But the truth was, no one knew much about the elusive billionaire. There were rumors he was the head of an organized crime family. There was speculation he'd fled from another country, wiping out the treasury before he'd done so. There was even talk about him having a price on his head. He was an intriguing mystery.

Storm had toned down some of her dire warnings about him. Still, it was only after hours and hours spent badgering her cousin with questions as well as threatening to drag her to psychic fairs that Storm had finally given Sophie a strictly unofficial copy of her case notes on the Carl VanDenbergh Senior murder. The murder itself was solved, and one of the items stolen from VanDenbergh's estate the day he was killed had been recovered, but the Chalice of Eros, or more correctly, the Chalice of Enos—The Dragon's Cup—was still missing.

Thinking about the cup sent excitement racing through Sophie's body like a car on a NASCAR track. The chalice had been insured for five million dollars, which would mean a nice finder's fee from the insurance company if she could locate it, though it wasn't really the money that motivated her to search for the chalice. It was the story she'd write, whether she found the Dragon's Cup or not.

According to a fairytale in one of the centuries old books in Storm's collection, the Chalice of Enos was created by a wizard who was envious of the dragons because they had so much treasure and wouldn't share any of it. He cursed them and made them barren. But a dragon could get around the curse by giving the wizard some of his or her treasure. In exchange, the wizard would let the dragon drink from the cup, which would restore fertility, at least for a while.

Somewhere along the way, the wizard Enos died or the chalice was stolen. Eventually it came into the possession of a faerie queen who used it for orgies, and then it disappeared. End of fairytale, which was fine with Sophie. At the moment she was planning to write a mystery instead of a fantasy, though she'd weave the back-story of the Chalice of Enos, also known as the Dragon's Cup, into her story.

Over time, if Storm's husbands Pierce and Tristan were to be believed—which Sophie did, absolutely—the original legend of the Dragon's Cup was lost and the Chalice of Enos became misnamed the Medici Chalice of Eros. It got the reputation of being a cup of orgies *and* sexual stamina, which was why Carl VanDenbergh had been after it for years, the old goat.

Sophie's mind was already whirling with possible characters and plots. And though Storm had warned her somewhere in the neighborhood of a thousand times to be careful, to stay below the radar screen *and* to watch out for Severn Damek who was also pursuing the cup, Sophie was already hooked on the story.

The chimes announcing a customer sounded in the front room. Sophie looked longingly at the box of unwrapped rune sets before she rose to her feet and turned toward the curtained doorway leading to the display area of the shop.

Severn's body tightened as soon as the redhead stepped into view. Fire raged through his cock and smoldered in his testicles. In the span of a heartbeat it became nearly impossible to contain the magic and remain in human form. His nostrils flared, taking in her scent, knowing immediately she was fully human and unmated. *Mine*! The word resonated from deep within, a dragon's battle cry he had no intention of ignoring.

The woman's eyes widened slightly, as though she heard the claim. Her hand went to cover a necklace hidden from view by her sundress.

Severn's nostrils flared again. He scented the Elven crystal and vowed to examine it carefully before he held this woman underneath him and took her body.

"Can I help you with something?" she asked, the husky sound in her voice licking over his skin and forcing him to close the distance between them in order to bathe in her scent.

She backed up a tiny step, a small show of feminine fear and submissiveness that only sharpened his desire for her. "I'm looking for Aislinn Dilessio."

"She won't be back until tomorrow."

"You're not her shop assistant Marika."

"No."

"I don't know who you are."

His voice was a growl that stroked low and deep inside of Sophie. It heightened her awareness of him. The heartmate necklace burned against her skin. She shivered in reaction. Her stomach tightened and twisted. Her palms grew sweaty and her courage tried to flee. This could *not* be her heartmate.

He stepped closer, claiming her personal space as his own. His heat and scent swamped and invaded her senses. "Give me your name," he ordered, his manner arrogant, confident, as though he was used to being in command, used to being obeyed.

Sophie licked her lips and his eyes followed the movement. "Marie," she said, using her middle name because she felt safer putting a flimsy barrier between them.

His eyes narrowed and his nostrils flared as though he could scent she was thinking about hiding from him. "Have dinner with me."

He cannot be my heartmate, she told herself again even as the stone burned against her skin and confirmed that he was.

True, she'd fantasized about having a husband like Aislinn's, one who was dominant and possessive, protective and yet amazingly loving. But next to the man in front of her, Trace-The-Caveman looked like a Renaissance man and Storm's husbands, Tristan and Pierce, looked like faeries!

"I don't even know your name," Sophie said.

Severn's eyes narrowed further. His mind was wary even though razor-sharp sensation and hot need twisted inside him like a writhing dragon. "Makar," he said, yielding his middle name because he didn't want her to be swayed by his reputation or by the mystery surrounding his first and last names in the human world. "Have dinner with me," he repeated, gentler this time, preferring to lure her to his lair rather than simply take her there.

He considered himself above human law but he wasn't ignorant of it. And beyond that, Marie was friends with the half-elf Aislinn. Until he knew whether or not the half-elf could help him find the chalice, he didn't want to alienate her by fighting with this woman, *his* woman. "Have dinner with me, please. We can dine nearby, within walking distance if you prefer."

Sophie knew she'd never forgive herself if she chickened out now and didn't at least spend some time with Makar. She glanced at her watch. "It's late enough. I can close the shop now."

She retreated to the back room in order to double-check the door there. Her gaze lingered on the rune sets she'd been unwrapping. If only she knew how to read them…

Sophie took the necklace out from underneath her dress. She stared at the dark blue stone with its shifting, swirling hints of red. She remembered the day Aislinn gave it to her, the day Aislinn almost died.

"Among my mother's people, there are certain clans who use a crystal to find their husbands and wives," Aislinn said.

"It doesn't make someone feel something they wouldn't feel without the necklace does it?"

"No."

"How does it work?"

"If you mean how does the magic in the crystal work, then I don't know the answer. But the crystal will come to life and glow when you're around your perfect mate."

"And the catch is…I'm the only one of us that'll know we're perfect for each other. Right? The guy may have no interest at all."

"The crystal wouldn't lead you to someone who's wrong for you."

"So even if it never glows, at least I'll know from the start if a guy isn't Mr. Right?"

"The magic demands that you give up something if you want to gain something."

"Maybe we should test it out on you first. You could make yourself a necklace and see if Trace is right for you. Then if he is, you could pass the crystal on to me."

"When I left my mother's home, one of her servants gave me this crystal, but it never responded to me. Ready?"

"What do I have to do?"

"Walk out into the surf. When your mind is clear and open, dip the crystal into the ocean, then put it on."

"Shouldn't I visualize Mr. Perfect while I'm out there?"

"What's in your heart is already known."

Sophie rubbed her finger over the strange stone. She felt the same mix of hope and longing, anxiousness and nervousness she'd felt before—along with something more— fear that the man waiting out front for her was more powerful, more potent, more dominating than she could handle.

I am not like my mother. I won't lose myself and then my life like she did, Sophie told herself as she climbed the stairs to the apartment that used to be Aislinn's but was now on loan to her until she got her current edits finished. She sighed as she stepped into the tidy, Spartan apartment. She longed to be in her own apartment, surrounded by all the crystals she'd collected. "Soon," Sophie muttered, sensing a theme emerging and smiling despite the aggravation that always surfaced at having her apartment building turned into a war zone of blaring music and screaming parents, compliments of the neighbors above and below her.

She removed the necklace. She felt naked without it but she forced herself to place it on the nightstand next to the bed and leave it there. She wanted to face Makar without the crutch of the stone, without the magical influence of the heartmate necklace.

Severn glanced in the direction of the curtained doorway and scowled. It made him uneasy to have Marie out of his sight. It made it harder to maintain the human illusion.

He flexed his shoulders and the dragon on his chest writhed in tandem with the beast that was his true form. He'd been too long in this realm, he thought, rubbing a hand over the tattoo hidden underneath his shirt—a raging dragon, dark blue with hints of red woven throughout it.

Footsteps sounded. Severn's cock jerked and protested its confinement when Marie stepped into view. How could he not be drawn to the long, dark red hair that matched his own? To the emerald-green eyes that were a perfect offset to his own sapphire-blue ones? Satisfaction rippled through him at the thought of the children they would produce together.

"There are a lot of good restaurants around here," Sophie said, her breath catching as his eyes moved downward. She knew he was seeing the way her nipples pushed against the thin fabric of her dress, hard, tight points that practically shouted for a man's attention. She licked her lips and his eyes moved immediately to her mouth as though he was hyperaware of her every movement, her every reaction to him. "There's Mexican, Italian, Chinese, all within walking distance."

Makar's gaze met hers. Her stomach fluttered at what she read in his eyes. He'd prefer directions to her bed instead of directions to a restaurant.

She smoothed her hands over her hips. It was harder than it should be to stop the invitation to skip dinner and move right to dessert in the form of lovemaking.

The silence grew heavy, charged, an unspoken conversation taking place between his will and her survival instincts. His eyes narrowed slightly when she didn't say anything further. Finally he yielded. "Which do you prefer?"

"I'm always game for Italian."

"Italian it is then."

Makar moved closer. His fingers encircled her wrist in a possessive shackle that sent heat and need and primitive fear pulsing through Sophie's veins.

They paused at the front door only long enough for her to set the alarm and lock up, then they moved down the street, weaving through tourists also answering the call of internal dinner bells. Sophie's stomach dropped and twisted with nerves when they got to the small Italian diner she favored. Mama Lancione was at her usual position, greeting her family's customers and guiding them to booths and tables.

"Would you mind Mexican instead?" Sophie asked, realizing that as soon as they walked in, Mama Lancione would hug her and greet her by her first name.

Possessive fury boiled in Severn as his gaze moved over several of the men on the other side of the window. His grip tightened on Marie as her tension vibrated through his skin and fed his suspicion that a boyfriend or lover was inside the restaurant.

He studied the most likely candidates and committed their faces to memory. They would never get near her again. A dragon prince didn't share even the least valuable of his treasures, much less a mate.

"Mexican is fine," he said when Marie's efforts to pull away from him forced his attention from the pathetic human rivals inside the Italian restaurant. He allowed her to lead him to the restaurant of her choice. He told himself that if his suspicions hadn't been stirred and the possessiveness of his dragon nature brought to the surface, he *might* have slowed his courtship.

It was a convenient lie.

In the end he made no attempt to temper the mesmerizing allure his kind was capable of when they were in this realm. She was his mate and he had no intention of letting her escape her fate.

Chapter Two

ဢ

Dinner was a conversational dance held in a fog of lust. It was a torment to the senses that left Sophie brutally aware of her tightened nipples and wet, wet panties.

Aislinn had told her once that she felt beguiled by Trace, that she'd known as soon as she saw him that he was her heartmate. Sophie had mistakenly assumed beguiled was only another name for lust. Now she knew better.

She'd lusted before. She'd loved before. But she'd never felt the depth of attraction, the aching, all-encompassing need she felt as she and Makar approached Inner Magick. Her mind was filled with fantasies and her body craved his touch.

The magic demands that you give up something if you want to gain something.

Sophie wondered now if she'd put too narrow an interpretation on what Aislinn said. She'd assumed the price for using the heartmate necklace was that she might end up alone because it had never reacted to any of the men she dated. Now she thought the true price might be steeper, and yet she had no choice but to pay it.

"Do you want to come in for coffee?" she found herself asking as they walked around to the back of the shop where a stairway led to an outside entrance to the apartment. She knew even as she issued the invitation that she would never get as far as making the coffee she was offering. She felt as though a hurricane had rolled in from the ocean, pelting her with forces beyond imagining, tearing up the landscape around her and reforming it into something straight from one of her fantasy novels.

"Yes," he said. His voice was a purring growl that made her squeeze her legs together. She was in his arms as soon as the apartment door closed behind them, her front molded to his as his hands moved down her spine.

His moan of pleasure hummed through her. His lips were flames against her neck as he kissed upward. She was whimpering by the time his tongue forged into her mouth in an aggressive claiming.

There was no fighting the desire. There was only yielding to it and burning with it until finally the need for air forced their lips to separate.

Sophie was panting, desperate for breath. Her heart beat wildly as her womb fluttered at the satisfaction she read in Makar's face.

His hand trailed over her cheekbone. His thumb brushed across her swollen lips before moving downward. He hesitated at the rapid beat of her pulse. His eyes darkened. She didn't protest when he pushed the strap of her sundress off her shoulder.

"Beautiful," he said as the dress slipped to reveal the curve of her breast. *His,* her body translated and her cunt clenched in reaction.

Her nipples were tight aching points and had been from the moment she first saw him. Now the weight of the dress was almost painful.

She closed her eyes against the sensations rushing through her. Underneath the exquisite need lurked a fear she didn't want to confront. She was no stranger to sex but she'd never experienced desire like this. She'd never met a man like this one.

Makar's knuckles smoothed over the tops of her breasts. She opened her eyes when they reached the remaining strap and pushed it off her shoulder. She wasn't as well-endowed as Storm but she'd never feared her breasts would disappoint a man. His sharp intake of breath as the dress dropped to her waist, taking the sewn-in bra cups with it, was heady praise.

"Beautiful," he said again, his voice huskier now, his body radiating tension and making Sophie feel more feminine than she'd ever felt. "Take the rest of it off." It was almost a growl.

She flushed with arousal and embarrassment, primitive woman at odds with modern woman. The latter won. Her hands moved to the buttons of his shirt. She wanted to bare some of his skin before she bared more of her own.

His hands stopped her before she'd gotten the first button undone. He shackled her wrists and pulled her arms behind her back so her body arched helplessly. He punished her for not doing as he'd commanded. His lips teased over her breasts, biting and sucking and licking everywhere but where she needed it the most.

"Put your mouth on my nipples," she begged as she fought his tight hold and tried to thrust an engorged areola against his lips.

He ignored her whimpered pleas. His mouth moved up her neck. His bites became more aggressive, as though he wanted to mark her.

She was wet and swollen, so flushed with need that she could barely stand by the time his lips finally covered hers. Sophie opened her mouth and welcomed his tongue into her depths in the same way she wanted to welcome his cock. He moaned in satisfaction. She swallowed the sound and craved more. He deepened the kiss, extended it until her only thought was to yield to him, to please him and be pleasured in return. When he left her lips he moved to her ears, her neck, her breasts. She felt boneless, completely submissive by the time he stopped his assault.

Makar held her away from him and steadied her before letting go of her wrists. She shivered in front of him, a prisoner of lust.

"Take the rest of it off," he said.

Sophie released a couple of buttons, freeing the sundress to fall to the floor. Hunger flashed in his eyes at the sight of her standing in sandals and a dark blue thong.

The bulge in his pants grew more pronounced but Sophie didn't dare reach for him again. Instead she stood in front of him, vulnerable, waiting for him to make the next move.

Makar's knuckles traced an imaginary line from the pulse point at the base of her neck to where her breasts met to form her cleavage. "You were wearing a necklace earlier. Where is it?"

Sophie sensed the question was important to him. She knew instinctively that there was no use in denying him an answer. She shivered, anticipating where the answer would lead them.

"In the bedroom."

She didn't resist when he pulled her against his body. A moan escaped when he brushed his fingertips along her spine.

"Take me there," he whispered, an order, but gentler than his last. There was a promise of pleasure and completion in his voice.

Sophie led him into the bedroom. The necklace was where she'd left it on the nightstand. She picked it up and wasn't surprised when Makar extended his hand.

"Let me put it on you," he murmured, as close to a request as she'd heard him offer.

She hesitated for only a second before yielding the necklace to him.

Heartstone. The Elven crystal burned against Severn's palm—deep blue with threads of red, the colors of his lair. Its presence affirmed what he already knew. This woman was his mate.

Joy made Severn's magic shimmer and fight against the form he was required to maintain in the human realm. He wanted to lift his face in dragon song.

It had to be an omen that the Chalice of Enos, the Dragon's own cup, was within his reach. Why else would he come here, seeking the half-elf's assistance, only to find his mate? A mate he could get with child if the chalice was found.

Despite being a prince, he was no different than the majority of dragon males and especially those who chose to dwell in this realm. He'd prayed for a human mate, one who would be as soft and submissive as a female dragon was tough and controlling.

True, there were males who found pleasure in battling with dragon females for supremacy, just as there were males— like his father—who accepted being dominated. He was not one of them. Not only did he want a human mate who would desire to please him and who would yield to him without a struggle, but where all young belonged to a female dragon and her word was law, with a human as a mate, all offspring would belong to him.

Severn touched the heartstone to his lips then placed it around Marie's neck. He wished he could strip out of his clothing and cover her body with his. He wanted to thrust into her sheath as his eyes held hers.

It was too late for that now.

What had started out as a shield had become a trap. She would find out soon enough who he was. But this first time, he couldn't risk her seeing the dragon on his chest and knowing he hadn't given her his more common name. He couldn't risk that she'd try to reject him.

He turned her so the delicate line of her spine was facing him. His hands went to her sides and then around to her breasts. His palms covered her nipples before his fingers took control of them, squeezing and tugging, driving her body once again into a maelstrom of desire.

She writhed in his arms, whimpered and pressed her buttocks against his erection. He kissed her neck, her shoulders. He gave in to the temptation to mark her, to grip her with his teeth as his hands left her breasts long enough to sweep her thong down and then free his cock.

When she would have turned in his arms he growled and clamped down harder on the soft skin where her shoulder met her neck. One hand went to her breast. The other stroked her abdomen then pressed between her legs. He cupped her mound, raked his fingers through her curls and rubbed over her clit before delving into her wet slit.

Her breath came in pants. Her body shivered continuously under his assault. Her whimpered pleas tore at Severn's control.

He wanted to replace the fingers between her legs with his tongue. He wanted to replace the fingers grasping her nipple with his mouth. But he'd left it too late. Despite the desperate need to taste her, to plunge his tongue into her channel and suckle at her breasts, Severn couldn't afford to let her see him now.

His testicles burned with the need to fill her with his seed. His cock was engorged past what any human male was capable of, the twin rings of thick cartilage circling beneath the head of his penis clearly visible, their sole purpose to stimulate the female of his species into ovulating.

With a low growl he urged Marie forward, onto the bed. He controlled her movements, positioned her so her chest was on the thick comforter, her buttocks in the air, her thighs spread to reveal the plump folds of her swollen labia.

The sight of it sent a rush of dizziness through Severn. His cock thickened and lengthened to its true size regardless of which form he was in. The skin on his penis stretched so tight it was almost painful. He circled it with his hand and a jolt of exquisite agony rushed up his spine when his palm touched the ridges beneath the head. He couldn't resist. He couldn't stop himself from leaning in to run his tongue over and through her wet folds.

She cried out and started to twist as though she intended to roll to her back and spread her legs. The movement cost Severn the last of his control.

He mounted her then. His body covered hers completely and left no doubt who was dominant and who was submissive.

His weight and strength held her completely immobile as his cock lodged at her entrance. His lips pulled back in carnal triumph as he began working himself into her.

The feel of her small human channel clamping down on his penis and making him fight for every inch drove him into a frenzy of painful pleasure. He was panting, wild for her, completely obsessed with her by the time he was lodged all the way in.

The veneer of being a human male was almost completely stripped away and yet in some part of his mind he knew he needed to regain enough control to make sure she was all right. Slowly he released her wrists and lifted off her body far enough so he could press kisses along her shoulders and spine.

He covered her breast with his palm then stroked over her abdomen until he found her fully erect clit. Her channel tightened on him as he fondled the swollen knob. Her buttocks rocked backward and his touch became more commanding. Satisfaction roared through him at the way she quivered under him, at how she moved to the rhythm he set as her husky whimpers and moans urged him to claim her completely.

Nothing he'd ever experienced felt as good as pumping in and out of her tight channel. Nothing felt as satisfying as holding her down while the rings on his cock brought her so much pleasure that she thrashed underneath him and begged him to let her come.

Magic gave ground against the force of his desire. The hollow spurs at Severn's wrists extended from their sheaths and filled with serum. They were an ancient adaptation that left human females unconscious—a necessity in the days when dragons lived in rocky lairs that could only be reached by flying. But more importantly, the serum altered human females, changed their chemistry so they could conceive a dragon's young.

Anticipation rushed through Severn, fierce and hot. He pressed his mouth to Marie's shoulder. He tasted her and took her scent deep inside himself. He bound himself to her completely.

The bed shook with the force of his thrusts. His body screamed with the need for release. His strokes grew faster, harder. Without conscious thought his hands went to her shoulders and raked downward over her back. The spurs broke her skin and the serum flowed into her.

She convulsed underneath him in orgasm. The tight fist of her inner muscles made him shout and pump furiously as his seed roared from his body in a lava-hot eruption that left him dizzy and weak, unable to do more than shift to his side and cuddle around his mate.

* * * * *

Sophie woke up groggy and disoriented. But when she would have forced herself to sit, a heavy arm tightened around her waist. A husky voice murmured, "Sleep a little while longer."

Makar. Instinctively she reached for the heartmate necklace.

A masculine chuckle sounded. A male hand covered hers. Makar's skin was as warm and alive as the crystal in her necklace.

"The heartstone doesn't lie." Velvet-soft lips brushed across her shoulder. "You belong to me. Sleep now, we'll get up later."

Sophie yielded to temptation. She drifted into a light sleep but woke again when the absence of masculine warmth coupled with the hushed sound of a conversation filtered into her consciousness. Her heart jerked in alarm when she opened her eyes and took in the unfamiliar dresser against the wall—a priceless antique, its legs ending in clawed feet, the woodwork surrounding the mirror a dragon.

"I would have warned you when I first learned you'd brought a female here, Severn," a male voice whispered. "But until a moment ago, when the deliverymen began arriving with your mother's favorite foods, we had no warning she was coming. We still don't know how many she's bringing with her."

"When will she get here?" a familiar voice asked and shock whipped through Sophie. Dismay and a touch of fear followed. Memories of the previous night rushed in and she was afraid her heart was beating so loudly he'd hear it.

Now she knew why Makar had grabbed her wrists when she went to unbutton his shirt. Now she understood why he'd forced her onto her hands and knees and taken her from behind. He'd been afraid she would see the dragon raging across his chest and realize he was Severn Damek.

He might not know Storm was her cousin, but he did know Aislinn had created a necklace for Storm, and Storm had seen the dragon tattooed on his chest. He probably guessed that Storm had mentioned it to either Aislinn or her. And she had.

Or maybe his thoughts had been even simpler and he'd guessed that like hundreds of others who were curious about him, Sophie had seen the beautiful dark blue dragons carved in bold relief on either side of the heavy gates leading to his estate, the threads of red woven through them glowing hot like embers among coal. She should have guessed who he was when he appeared at Inner Magick. Storm had described him perfectly. She'd even captured his attitude.

The sudden silence at the doorway drew Sophie's attention. She forced her breathing into a slow and steady rhythm as Severn moved back into the room. He dressed quickly then left. She lay still for several moments longer before getting up. All her thoughts were centered on escaping.

Sophie's stomach churned as her presence in Severn's home took on an ominous meaning. Suspicion gained a firmer grip as she looked around the unfamiliar room. Her heartbeat tripled in her chest. She'd never passed out during sex before, much less passed out long enough to be taken somewhere in a car.

An icy finger trailed down her spine and chilled her to the core. Had he looked at her driver's license after she'd passed out and found out who she was? She wasn't hugely famous, but the town was proud of their hometown author. Over the years there had been a number of articles in the local paper about her, most of them mentioning how she often investigated on her own in order to make the background for her stories authentic. Had he guessed she was looking for the Dragon's Cup, the Chalice of Enos, too? Or maybe he knew because his cousin co-owned Drake's Lair with one of Storm's husbands. It was possible Pierce had said something to Tielo in passing about her interest in the cup.

Sophie bit down on her bottom lip. She closed her mind to the churn of unanswerable questions and chaotic emotion. She slid from the bed and found her sundress and purse on a chair. The shoes and panties were missing but she didn't care. She would have wrapped a sheet around herself if she'd needed to.

Adrenaline surged through her as she left the relative safety of the bedroom. She eased down the hall and prayed she wouldn't encounter anyone. Most of the doorways were open. The rooms she passed were empty save for priceless antiques and artifacts. More than once Sophie's breath caught in awe at the splendor of the items Severn owned, but then the rumors about him whispered through her and her gut churned as she wondered where the items had come from and how he'd acquired them.

She guessed the kitchen would be at the back of the house. She assumed that given the size of Severn's estate it would have a delivery entrance. She prayed whoever was bringing supplies for his mother's visit would provide a means of escape.

Luck was with her…or more accurately a great bustle of activity along with a panicked, "She's arrived! She has another female with her along with their servants!"

The announcement sent people scurrying from the kitchen long enough for Sophie to emerge from her hiding place and head for the exit. Her heart jumped when a brown-uniformed man looked up. She forced a confident smile. His attention returned to the boxes he was unloading from a dolly.

She escaped, too hurried to stop and appreciate the dreamscape of Severn's elaborate gardens and beautiful statues, too panicked to do more than climb into the delivery van and find a hiding place. Her pulse was still pounding in her throat, the blood still roaring through her ears when moments later the man in the uniform appeared.

She held her breath. Imagined conversations raced through her mind as she anticipated him finding her. But instead of unloading the boxes she was hiding behind, she heard him lift the empty dolly and secure it to the wall. The blissful sound of the back doors being closed and locked followed.

When she was younger being locked in the back of a truck would have been the seed for terrible nightmares. But years of dealing with her terror by incorporating it in her stories and having the heroine escape had served as therapy—of a sort. Sophie shivered in the darkness and tried to keep old memories at bay as the van rumbled to life and began moving.

She'd driven by Severn's house before. She'd seen the dragons guarding the entrance but had no idea how far back the house was set. The van slowed and stopped.

Fear washed over her. What if Severn had noticed her missing and ordered the van to be held at the estate's entrance? She realized too late that with so many priceless possessions, he probably had a security system that included cameras.

There were voices. She envisioned the road outside the gate and knew the chance of flagging down a passing motorist was slim.

Relief poured into her when the van moved forward again. She slid to the floor and braced her back against the wall. Her arms hugged her knees to her chest.

Sophie closed her eyes and pictured the road. She drove it in her mind. When the van stopped again she was ready. She jumped out as soon as the door opened.

The deliveryman stumbled backward.

"Sorry," she mumbled, quickly looking around and recognizing the location.

Euphoria filled her and made her giddy. She was not only close to the beach, but she was near Madame Fontaine's home.

Sophie set off toward the psychic's house. She was almost there before she remembered Madame Fontaine was on a date with Storm's partner Brady. A double date, actually, since Storm, along with Tristan and Pierce were also spending the day on the water, cruising in a boat Pierce had won in a poker game at Drake's Lair.

Sophie stopped in her tracks and dug through her purse. The image of her cell phone sitting on the passenger seat of her car flashed through her mind. "Damn." For a minute she felt completely and utterly alone. For a minute the past overlaid the present and old fears tried to surface.

"Okay, let's get a grip here," she muttered, finding strength in the sound of her own voice. "You're not really afraid of Severn, are you?"

The necklace burned against her skin. Need fluttered through her belly. Her traitorous body tightened and ached for his touch. Her hand moved to clasp the pendant. *The magic demands that you give up something if you want to gain something.*

Sophie shivered. Her cunt lips were flushed and she felt arousal trickling down her inner thighs. Sensation bombarded her as she relived those moments with Severn's cock filling her. She yearned to have his body covering hers, heavy and dominating, possessively masculine.

No, she wasn't afraid of him in a pour-on-the-concrete-boots-and-get-tossed-into-the-ocean way. It was a much more feminine fear. After sex with Severn, she knew no other man would ever come close to pushing her buttons. *I'd say I definitely paid the price. But that doesn't mean I'm willing to pay it again, or pay a higher one.*

Her mother had been weak and helpless. She'd gone from man to man until finally finding one who was completely controlling. When she'd tried to leave it had cost her life. It would have cost Sophie's as well if she hadn't managed to hide from her stepfather's murderous rampage.

Sophie pulled the necklace out from under her dress and let its warmth keep her memories at bay. The heartstone Aislinn had given her was a small piece of magic that was all her own.

Sophie resumed walking. The rumors about Severn could be sorted out later. For the moment she had to figure out the safest place to go.

Chapter Three

𝕊𝕆

Severn's anger could be felt though the entire estate. His bellow of rage could be heard by everyone within the compound. *Gone! She was gone!*

The air burned in his lungs. For several long moments he feared he would need to return to the dragon realm in order to regain control and avoid torching everything in his path. By The Great Shared Ancestor he wanted to incinerate something!

He moved with deadly purpose toward the control room for his security system. One of those in liege-service to him had already hurried ahead to view the tapes.

"She left as your mother was arriving," Xanthus said. He stepped away from the monitor so Severn could watch it. A recorded segment looped continuously, showing Marie slipping through the kitchen door and into the back of a delivery van. She was followed a few minutes later by the uniformed driver.

Severn's eyes narrowed as he stopped the playback. He compared the man's face to the ones he'd seen through the window of the Italian diner. Next to him Xanthus said, "I don't think he knew Sophie was hiding in his truck."

A fresh burst of rage moved through Severn. His focus shifted from the screen to Xanthus. He pinned the other man in place with a gaze full of feral menace. "Sophie?"

Xanthus' eyes widened slightly. His surprise only fueled Severn's anger. He'd never before brought a female to his estate to bed her. That the female who'd escaped now appeared to be a stranger to him, someone he'd picked up… Menace rolled off him. "Sophie?"

Xanthus stood his ground. "Sophie Alexander. She's best friends with Aislinn Dilessio, the half-elf owner of Inner Magick. She's also the cousin of Pierce and Tristan's wife Storm, the policewoman you allowed Pierce to bring here."

"The writer?" Severn asked, his voice little more than a growl.

Xanthus nodded. "You've got a few of her books in your library."

Anger at his own carelessness and lack of attention burned in Severn's gut as he envisioned the hotel-like room above Inner Magick. He'd been caught up in the heat and scent and incredible allure of his mate. He'd ignored the obvious — that a room so barren of personal effects couldn't possibly belong to a female as vibrant and beautiful as Sophie.

"She stays at Inner Magick?" Severn asked, knowing Xanthus had developed an interest in the half-elf's assistant Marika.

"Sometimes, when she writes."

"Do you know where she lives?"

"No."

"Find out."

Severn turned and strode away. His emotions raged hot and fierce and dangerous.

He considered the possibility that the Elven heartstone had been enchanted and Sophie wasn't his true mate at all. But as quickly as the thought stroked the flames of his fury, he dismissed it.

In the old days, when all of the supernaturals lived in this realm, the magic had been potent enough for an Elven crystal to enslave a dragon's heart. But that was no longer possible. Now only the strongest of dragons and those serving them could visit and stay in this magic-weak realm.

Sophie was his and the presence of the heartstone that burned in the colors of his lair was only a coincidence. Every cell in his body recognized the truth of their relationship. Every particle of his being demanded he find her.

A muscle twitched in Severn's jaw. His errant mate would soon learn an important fact. She belonged to him and he guarded what he owned with a dragon's possessiveness. She'd be very lucky if he allowed her out of the bedroom.

* * * * *

Sophie called Inner Magick from the home of Madame Fontaine's next-door neighbor. She hoped to find Aislinn there but it was her assistant Marika who answered the phone.

"How'd it go at the show you and Aislinn went to yesterday?" Sophie asked.

"I'm not sure if Aislinn's going to be in today," Marika said and the off-kilter answer sent instant alarm through Sophie.

"Is everything okay?"

"You might want to try her cell phone. Do you have the number?"

The fear in Sophie's chest deepened. "Cell phone?" Aislinn was probably the *only* person she knew who *didn't* have a cell phone.

Marika rattled off Aislinn's home number and Sophie's gut tightened. Her fear escalated when she heard a man's deep voice growl, "Who is that?"

"Should I call 911?" Sophie asked.

"No. Not at all." In response to the male voice Marika said, "It's a client, Xanthus." To Sophie she said, "I don't know when Aislinn expects those tarot cards to arrive. You might want to give her a call. And definitely call before you swing by here. I'd hate for you to make a trip and be…and not find what you're looking for."

"Are you sure you're safe?" Sophie asked, not knowing what to think. She'd met Xanthus before and liked him. He had to be pretty damn trustworthy for Trace to have once asked him to serve as a bodyguard for Aislinn.

"Absolutely. No problem at all. Like I said, call Aislinn's cell. She'll be able to tell you when to come by." The click of the phone indicated Marika had hung up.

Sophie shivered. She shot Madame Fontaine's neighbor a smile she hoped didn't reveal how wildly her stomach was churning.

The man's eyebrows were drawn together. "Is everything all right with your friend?"

"I think so." And she did...still, it was unnerving. "Is it okay if I make another call?"

"Make as many as you need to."

She dialed Aislinn's number. "Are you alone?" she asked when her friend answered the phone.

"The Caveman is gone," Aislinn said, using the name Sophie most often used when referring to Trace. "He's at work."

"Would it be okay if I come by?"

Even though Sophie had tried to keep her voice light, she knew she hadn't completely succeeded.

"Something's happened?"

"Yes. I'll tell you about it when I get there. I'm at Madame Fontaine's next-door-neighbor's house but I don't have my car. I've got to call a cab, then I'll head over."

"I'll come get you."

Sophie opened her mouth to say that would be great, then worried Severn Damek already had someone watching Aislinn's house. It'd be better if she took a cab and made a run for the front door when she got there. Aislinn had a good security system, plus she was married to a cop. Even Severn wouldn't crash into her house. He'd wait until...

Sophie reeled in her imagination. *I've been reading too many of my own books!*

"If it's all the same," she said, "I need to think some things through before I get to your place."

"You'll leave now?"

"As soon as the cab gets here."

"Okay."

* * * * *

Severn waited in a limousine parked within sight of the half-elf's house. His cock throbbed and his temper had warmed the luxurious interior several times.

He'd have preferred to be in one of his sports cars. But the limousine and driver were a necessity because he couldn't think of an easy way to secure his wayward mate in broad daylight.

A growl smothered the lie. He amended his thought. He *could* think of another way. He could fuck her as he had the night before and inject more serum into her.

Unfortunately he didn't anticipate the opportunity arising. He'd have to settle for a less physically satisfying method in order to get her into the limousine quickly and efficiently. He couldn't afford to have anyone guess at the tenuous nature of his bond with Sophie.

His mother ruled a fiefdom where all she saw belonged to her and where everyone—be they servants of the lesser races, dragons or even her own mate—was commanded by her. Severn had no doubt that she, and Audriss, the female she'd chosen for him, would try to interfere before he took Sophie to the dragon realm and sealed the magic of their bond.

Severn thanked The Great Shared Ancestor once again for the blessing of a human mate. Despite Sophie's disappearance he had little doubt who would be in control. He would. And rather than having to battle a female before mounting her or wait until his female summoned him—as was the lot of many male dragons when dealing with the females of their species—

he would shove his cock into his submissive mate's tight channel whenever, wherever and however he chose.

Heat once again filled his lungs. He wanted to roar and let the fire of his need and frustration escape in a blast of incendiary flame.

"Go around again?" the driver asked as the temperature in the car soared.

When Severn nodded, the limo pulled out into street and traveled the roads leading to and around the half-elf's house. He'd hoped Xanthus would track Sophie down to her true living quarters and trap her there until he could reclaim her. But apparently the human female Xanthus was drawn to had evaded his questions and grown suspicious when a call came in while Xanthus was at Inner Magick. It was that call which had Severn guessing Sophie might be on her way to see the half-elf.

He shifted position in a pointless attempt to get comfortable. His cock screamed for one particular feminine channel. It pressed angrily against the front of his pants and warned there would be no relief until it was buried in Sophie's slick, hot depths. When he got her back to his bed he would fuck her so long and so thoroughly she wouldn't be able to walk, much less run!

A low frustrated growl filled the car. Of all the times to find a mate and have her escape him! Of all the times for his mother to arrive!

When he returned to the house—*his house, his by right of possession*—his mother's spies would have heard rumors and informed her about Sophie. Even if Sophie were Dragon, his mother would label her inferior to the female she'd selected. His mother cared only about how a mating—made more important now that the Chalice of Enos had resurfaced—between Audriss and him would consolidate *her* power.

The limo turned the corner almost at the same moment a taxi pulled into the half-elf's driveway. There was no chance of intercepting Sophie as she slid from the car and quickly disappeared into the house.

"Park in the driveway?" his driver asked as the taxi vacated the spot.

"No. Pull to a stop at the end of the block," Severn said, not wanting to give the half-elf a reason to involve her policeman husband. Seeing Sophie and knowing where she was had eased much of the fire that threatened his control of the magic.

He didn't worry about what the half-elf would tell Sophie. The ancient covenants governing them all in this realm forbade revealing the existence of other supernaturals to any but a mate.

Severn settled back in his seat to contemplate his next move. Perhaps it would be better to let Sophie have a few minutes with her friend before he reclaimed her.

* * * * *

Sophie knew Severn was in the limousine parked down the street. Her entire body told her though she hadn't seen him with her eyes.

"What's going on?" Aislinn asked as she keyed in the alarm code.

"I think I found my heartmate," Sophie said and winced at how panicked she sounded.

Aislinn grasped the chain of Sophie's necklace and pulled the pendant into view. Her eyes widened before her gaze met Sophie's.

"It's Severn Damek, Aislinn."

"Did he hurt you?"

When Aislinn's spine stiffened and she glanced at the panel next to the front door, Sophie suddenly felt foolish for telling her to set the alarm. She had definitely been reading too many of her own crime stories. She'd let all the rumors she'd collected about Severn turn him into a boogey man. The last thing she wanted was for Aislinn to think she needed protection and get involved.

"No. It's not that. It's just… He came to the shop yesterday while I was unpacking the rune sets. He told me his name was Makar. We went out to dinner and ended up… This morning I woke up in his bedroom and I don't know how I got there."

The tension left Aislinn. She laughed softly. "He's your heartmate, Sophie, and I believe Makar is his middle name. Of course he'd want to take you to his home. And there's no way you could resist him, not any more than I could resist Trace when I first met him."

Some of Sophie's natural humor reasserted itself. "And that was shocking, Aislinn. You went into Trace's arms for a dance and then straight out onto the beach for a moonlight fuck!"

Aislinn's eyes sparkled. "And we haven't slowed down since."

Sophie laughed. She knew Aislinn was telling the truth. The heat between Aislinn and Trace was impossible to miss.

"Why don't we go into the kitchen?" Aislinn said. "I've been experimenting with making mocha frappachinos. I think mine are almost as good as the ones at Starbucks. Or I could fix hot coffee if you'd rather have that."

Sophie peeked out the window again. "I'm pretty sure he's in the limo parked at the end of the street."

"You're safe here, Sophie. You can stay with us."

"Trace would love that."

Aislinn grinned. "He'd grumble about having to confine the sex to the bedroom, but if you're worried about your safety, he'd offer to protect you. You're my best friend."

Emotional tears rushed from Sophie's chest and clogged her throat for a moment. She gave Aislinn a hug.

"I'm okay," Sophie said. She knew she'd have to face Severn sooner or later. She didn't intend to spend a lot of time hiding out or looking over her shoulder. It wasn't her style — which was *not* to say she was stupid about danger. Deep down she didn't really believe she'd end up a victim like her mother.

When she was younger she might have confused dominant and possessive with controlling and obsessive. Not now. It'd been a shock to wake up in a strange place and find out the man she knew as Makar was someone else, but she hadn't been completely honest with him either. He was probably wondering why she'd told him her name was Marie.

Sophie startled when Aislinn touched her arm. "Sorry," she said, "you know how I can get when I'm thinking."

"I can go out and invite him in if you want, Sophie. This house would serve as neutral territory."

"I'm not sure I'm quite ready for that."

She let Aislinn lead her to the kitchen and fix her a frozen coffee drink. While they sat at the table, she found herself telling Aislinn everything.

Desire and heat curled in Sophie's belly the more she talked. She thought about that blissful moment when she'd woken up with Severn curled around her and he'd said, "The heartstone doesn't lie. You belong to me."

How was it possible a man like Severn believed in such a thing? And yet *he* was the one who'd walked into Inner Magick... And what did she really know about him, other than what Storm had told her and what she'd discovered as part of her own research?

"I've never passed out like that from an orgasm," she repeated, not quite willing to let go of the belief that something devious, strange or out of the ordinary had occurred.

Aislinn actually laughed. "But you've never been with a man like Severn Damek before."

Sophie's nipples tightened. Aislinn had *that* right. Severn was an addiction after only one encounter.

"So you're saying I overreacted when I ran?"

"No, from what I know of him, he's like a prince who rarely has anyone challenge or defy his will. It's probably a good thing you made your stand right away so he knows you're capable of holding your own against him." Aislinn reached over and picked up Sophie's empty cup. "But I still think it'd be a good idea to invite Severn in and talk before he catches you and hauls you back to his bed."

Sophie's cunt clenched in reaction to the idea of being back in bed with Severn. She closed her eyes and squeezed her thighs together. She had it bad. "Okay. Would you mind asking him in for coffee?"

Aislinn laughed. "Not at all. If you go he'll probably pull you into the car before you get the first word out."

Surprise made Severn lean forward in his seat as the half-elf emerged from her house and walked toward the limo. He smiled at her courage. She was safe enough from him, though she couldn't be sure of it.

There were ancient compacts that governed the supernaturals when they were in this realm. But he doubted those in the Elven realm would intercede on her behalf. Even though her grandfather was a king, she was still an exile. She was an unwanted half-breed judged unworthy to live among her kind.

Severn slid from the limo. He found Aislinn beautiful despite her Elven blood. "You offer sanctuary to Sophie?" he asked, not bothering with the formalities of introduction.

Aislinn's laugh and smile threw him off guard. "I offer a choice of frappachino or hot coffee." Her expression grew serious as she added, "Plus a chance to talk to Sophie on neutral territory."

Chapter Four

ဢ

His mate didn't look the slightest bit sorry she'd snuck out of his bed, escaped his house and made him spend his time, energy and patience searching for her. And yet his cock didn't care. It felt as though it would claw its way out of his trousers if he wasn't fast enough in getting rid of the barrier separating it from Sophie's cunt.

"Let's go," Severn growled, knowing it was the wrong thing to say but unable to keep himself from saying it.

Sophie inhaled sharply. Her body reacted to his words despite what her mind supposedly wanted. An eyebrow arched in response but heat raced through her nipples at the way his face went taut at her silent refusal to jump up and do his bidding.

Heartmate he might be—not exactly the one she would have asked for, but the one she'd apparently ended up with all the same—and she was willing to accept *some* of the responsibility for what had happened between them, but he had some things to learn too.

"You might as well sit down and stop acting like a fire-breathing dragon," Sophie said and nearly jumped out of her skin when glass shattered at the kitchen counter.

She turned in her chair and saw Aislinn picking large pieces of a fancy mug out of the sink. "You need help?"

Aislinn hesitated for only an instant. "Severn's coffee is ready. Why don't you get another mug and pour him a cup while I deal with this."

Sophie rose and moved over to the coffeepot. A bolt of panic hit her when Aislinn finished at the sink then left the room with the shattered remains of the cup, as though somehow they warranted a trip to the outside garbage can rather than a hasty drop into the kitchen trash.

Severn followed Sophie to the counter and used it to trap his mate. His palms settled on the smooth ceramic surface so his arms rested against her sides. His chest touched her back. His cock ended up in a torturous heaven, pressed against her buttocks and separated from its home by her thin sundress and his summer trousers.

"You learned who I was and so you ran?" he asked, deciding to take a different tack with her now that he was close enough to feel her heat and smell her arousal.

He'd purposely left her underwear behind when he'd carried her to his car the previous night. Now he thought about what he'd find if he lifted her dress.

His nose told him she would be slick and wet and swollen. His imagination saw her without panties, available for him as she should be.

Sophie shivered. She only barely managed to keep herself from moaning and leaning over the counter. A fantasy of begging him to lift her dress and pierce her with his cock flickered through her thoughts. *He's your heartmate, Sophie. Of course you couldn't resist him*, Aislinn had said but this went way beyond anything she'd ever expected or experienced.

"I ran because you drugged me or…something…then took me to your house without asking my permission *and then* I learned who you really are."

His mouth found her neck. This time she couldn't restrain her whimper.

"You belong to me, Sophie *Marie* Alexander." His voice had a sharp edge to it. "You belong in my house, in my bed."

"I know you're used to getting what you want and ordering your little kingdom of employees around, but a night of sex, Severn *Makar* Damek, does not give you ownership rights to me."

A low growl sounded in his chest. Sophie tensed. She had only a second to worry that she'd pushed him too far before his hand was at the front of her sundress and jerking the heartmate necklace into view. "Do you deny what the heartstone says? You are my mate, Sophie. Mine! You knew it last night before accepting my invitation to dinner. You knew it when you invited me into the apartment. You knew it when I shoved my cock in you."

He pressed closer and the heat of his erection seared through their clothing and sent a flood of arousal to Sophie's inner thighs. He was outraged male and rippling masculine power, yet his aggression fed desire and not fear.

She wanted to turn in his arms and press her lips to his in appeasement. She wanted to whimper and plead and feel him inside her. But she fought the urge to give in without first finding a safer middle ground on which to begin a relationship. She needed to be sure she could really handle his dominance without losing herself.

"I know the necklace responded to you," she admitted, keeping her voice low and steady, proud of herself for sounding so calm. "I know the crystal is supposed to come to life and glow when I'm around my perfect mate. But that doesn't mean I have to accept the man. And it certainly doesn't mean I *belong* to him like a piece of property."

Fire threatened to erupt from most of the orifices in Severn's body, but in particular from his mouth and cock. By The Great Shared Ancestor, his mate was trying his patience. If she weren't very, very careful, she'd soon feel the erotic edge of his temper. He already longed to fuck her so thoroughly she couldn't rise from his bed. It took no effort at all to add the fantasy of punishing her first then tying her wrists and ankles so she lay spread-eagled on his sheets.

He had claimed her. He had coupled with her as a male dragon takes not just a willing human female, but a chosen mate. He had injected his serum into her. Her body was even now adapting, changing so she could one day bear his young.

His cock ached. It was already engorged. The rings beneath the head of his penis were exposed and the brush of his trousers against them was excruciating. Yet she dared to pretend she had the option of refusing him!

"Let's go, Sophie," he growled again, close to pulling her skirt up and mounting her in the half-elf's kitchen.

Sophie closed her eyes against the need rippling through her. In another second she'd lean further over the counter and pull her dress up herself. "I'll leave with you on one condition," she said, somehow managing to force the words from a body that was in meltdown. "We don't go to your house. We go to my apartment."

Severn's nostrils flared but his instant denial died before it could take the form of a bellowed, *No.* The rational part of his mind quickly overrode dragon instinct. *Yes.* He would let Sophie take him to her lair. Doing so would serve several purposes. She would feel more comfortable there and it would allow him time to more thoroughly mate with her before they returned to his home and faced his dragon mother and Audriss.

"Agreed," he said. His mouth went to Sophie's neck. His hands moved around to cup her breasts and massage their firm, pouty tips. The heat of his aggravation became a fiery burn of satisfaction as she responded to his touch and melted in his arms. "Will it anger you if I carry you to the limo?" he purred against her skin.

"I can walk. But you need to stop touching me."

The breathless quality of her voice made Severn's cock jerk in warning. His teeth gripped her neck lightly and he couldn't stop himself from pressing his erection more tightly to her buttocks. *His.* She was his and he would never allow her to escape again.

Severn closed his eyes and savored the feel of her in his arms. He inhaled deeply and filled his lungs with the scent of her. His cock pulsed and he could feel the moisture gathering on its tip. His hands slid downward until he found the warm skin of her thighs. The urge to lift her dress and free his erection was nearly impossible to resist but somehow he found the strength to do it. "Let's go."

Sophie was glad Severn had the limo. It was ostentatious, especially as a surveillance vehicle, but the moment they were in the back of it she was in his arms.

"Give me the address," he said, his fingers spearing through her hair and holding her mouth a small distance from his own.

She gave it to him.

Sophie felt drugged in his presence. It was almost like being in heat. She was burning up, needy. Her entire body screamed for one thing. Severn. His cock. His seed. The feel of his body on hers.

It was worse than before. Much, much worse.

Severn was struggling for breath by the time Sophie led him into her apartment. He was beyond finesse. He was almost beyond control and yet he needed to maintain enough of it to bury his cock in her tight channel without her seeing it. One hard fuck and the magic fabric that held him into a human shape would slip back into place. But at the moment his cock was dragon-ridged.

He covered her lips with his as soon as the front door was closed and locked. He thrust his tongue into her mouth as he swept her into his arms and moved toward the open doorway of the bedroom.

In the apartments above and below Sophie's the sound of electric guitars and indecipherable lyrics vibrated the floor and ceiling. In his current state Severn was grateful for the noise. There would be no chance of anyone hearing her screams and calling the police as he took her.

He stopped kissing her just long enough to jerk Sophie's dress off before putting her on the bed and immediately coming down on top of her. His fingers fisted in her luxurious mane of hair and held her head to the mattress as he once again covered her mouth with his. She writhed underneath him. Her hands clawed at his back, pushed at his shoulders and made him shiver in anticipation of feeling her nails scrape against his skin.

He hadn't taken his shirt off the previous night. He hadn't been able to risk her seeing the dragon raging across his chest. But today he no longer had to worry about her discovering who he was.

Severn raised his head and growled, "Unbutton my shirt, Sophie."

Shirt. Pants. Shoes. All of it. She was so desperate she would have removed them with her teeth if it would mean bare skin could touch bare skin and his cock would tunnel into her cunt.

Some other time she would tease him, slowly undoing each button, savoring each inch of exposed flesh, but not this time. She was so anxious for the feel of his chest against her breasts that it was almost impossible to concentrate long enough to manipulate the buttons on his expensive shirt. But when she finally succeeded…

He was smooth, flowing muscle and skin so hot it almost seemed as though the dragon on his chest was alive and breathing fire. She ran her fingers over it and wanted to trace it with her tongue. But when she nuzzled a tight male nipple he grabbed her wrists and pinned them to the bed.

"Later." It was a growling pant. He shifted so a single hand held both her wrists while the other one pushed between their bodies and freed his cock.

"Please," Sophie said, opening her legs and canting her hips, making it easy for him to guide himself into her.

"Mine," he said, using the hand circling his shaft to prevent anything more than the head of his penis from lodging inside her.

Sophie whimpered. She knew what he wanted but she fought the urge to give in without making him work for it.

"Please," she said again, moving her body, rubbing her arousal on him, tempting him with her wet heat.

His face tightened further. "Say the words, Sophie. Admit you belong to me."

"Fuck me first."

Severn's buttocks clenched in reaction to her words. The movement made him pump through his closed fist and nearly spew his seed across her pussy as the ridges on his shaft pressed against the band of his fingers.

By The Great Shared Ancestor, Sophie was killing him with her resistance.

He allowed more of his cock to slide into her. Enough so the dragon ridges tormented not only him but her as well.

"Please, Severn," she cried, arching against him, the mouth of her cunt trying to clamp down on him and suck the rest of his penis into her body.

"Say the words, Sophie," he panted, forcing his own out. "Admit you belong to me."

She was desperate with the need to feel him deep inside her. Her reason for resisting was lost in a haze of desire. "I belong to you, Severn," she said as her mouth sought his.

Satisfaction roared through Severn, a hot flame that joined with his lust and consumed him from the inside out. He released her wrists and plunged his cock into her. He claimed her with his penis as his mouth covered hers. He breathed his fire into her and grew wild with savage pleasure when she scratched his back and buttocks as he fucked her mercilessly.

The first wave of release brought only a moment's relief from the fire raging inside Severn. The dragon desire to mate was on him. He wanted to fuck until he could do nothing more than collapse upon his female and guard her until he had enough energy to resume mating again. Mine! Every cell in his body screamed it, claimed it, rejoiced in it. Sophie was his. His!

He smiled as he looked at her. The soft, sleepy, sexy expression on her face told him without words that he'd satisfied her despite his roughness, despite being completely out of control.

Severn couldn't resist leaning down and pressing his lips to hers. He traced along the seam of her mouth with his tongue, gently asking for permission to enter. She made a sound somewhere between a sigh and a whimper as she opened for him, her tongue twining with his, letting him lead the dance.

Submissive. The word purred through Severn. His cock stiffened to its true size inside her though the ridges were no longer present.

Sophie made a small sound but didn't try to dislodge him. She didn't protest as his hips began moving, driving his penis into her depths.

When her neck arched, her eyes fluttering shut, Severn growled, "Watch. Watch while I take you."

Sophie whimpered when he lifted himself off her. The muscles on his arms and chest rippled as he held himself above her so they both could see his cock as it pumped in and out of her. The sight of it, wet and glistening, bold and beautiful, powerful, made Sophie need it even more.

"Please," she whispered when his slow strokes became torturous.

She was covered with a sheen of sweat, shaking by the time he finally gave in to her pleas and lay so his chest was against hers. She wrapped her legs around his waist and her arms around his neck. She locked her lips to his.

Their tongues were equally aggressive this time. They rubbed and pressed against each other in the same rhythm as their lower bodies ground and pumped and fought for release.

When orgasm came they swallowed each other's cries. Fire spewed like lava into Sophie's womb and she writhed in Severn's arms as he shuddered above her in exquisite ecstasy.

Afterward they lay tightly entwined with his cock still inside her. Severn would have liked to spend hours cuddled in that manner but the noise he'd welcomed earlier—the screaming electric guitars and crashing drums, the out-of-tune, indecipherable lyrics—suddenly made it impossible to linger and get to know his mate better. By The Great Shared Ancestor, now that his cock wasn't speaking he could barely hear himself think!

"Surely you don't consider this music," he said, wondering how Sophie could remain so peaceful when he felt like incinerating something.

She laughed. "I could tell you it gets better the longer you listen to it but that would be a lie."

His nipple went instantly hard when her fingers passed over it on the way to the dragon on his chest. She traced the tattoo before shifting so she could study it more closely.

Severn smiled despite the noise. Apparently all it took was a thorough fucking to make his mate relaxed and playful. "Let's gather your things and go back home now," he said.

Sophie's head lifted with a jerk. The surprised expression on her face was the only warning he had before she pulled away and rolled off the bed. He grunted at the loss of her warmth. He silently cursed at having somehow mismanaged the situation.

"I am home," Sophie said. "And I don't intend to pass out and wake up in a strange bedroom again."

His eyes narrowed as he took in her stance. She was wary and suspicious and determined to put up a fight if he tried to physically remove her from the apartment.

It was tempting. He would enjoy having her squirming and naked in his arms. Unfortunately such a course of action would hardly go unnoticed.

His instinct was to pounce on her then retreat to his lair as quickly as possible. The sight of her standing in front of him, naked in her challenge, fed the desire to force her onto her hands and knees in order to cover her body with his. He could scrape the spurs down her back and send her into oblivion as she screamed in climax. The thought of it heated his blood but his rational mind argued against it. He'd gained ground with Sophie. He'd gain further by giving her some time to accept the inevitable.

Severn growled in frustration. He rolled from the bed but rather than try to get his hands on his recalcitrant mate, he strode out of the bedroom and began prowling around her apartment.

His mood lightened when he noticed how little room there was for anything beyond all the crystals she'd collected and hoarded. A smile chased away his aggravation. She was a true dragon's mate!

Sophie escaped to the bathroom and took a shower. The blast of the water drowned out the music. It soothed her frazzled nerves until she remembered what was on the table next to her computer.

Shit! She'd promised Storm she wouldn't let anyone else see the case notes on the VanDenbergh murder and the missing Dragon's Cup.

Sophie streaked out of the bathroom, wrapping a towel around her as she went. But it was already too late. Severn was leaning against her desk with a smile on his face. She could tell at a glance he'd already gone through not only the folder but the notes she'd made detailing her own thoughts and plans for looking for the missing artifact and writing about it.

He closed the distance between them. His movements were smooth and the pleased expression on his face stroked over her. She didn't resist when he pulled her against him and kissed her shoulder, her neck, her ear.

"The Fates are truly smiling on us, Sophie. You plan to search for the Chalice of Enos as research for one of your books and my family has hunted it for centuries. I am hunting it now," he bit her neck, a sharp, quick, erotic pain that shot straight to her nipples, "as you already know. You have admitted you belong to me. So there is no reason for us to search for the cup separately. We can make it our joint project. It'll be a way to spend time together and get to know one another better."

His voice was so full of good humor Sophie didn't feel the slightest desire to pull away from him. She shifted so she could study the dragon on his chest.

Joining forces with him made perfect sense. He had a lot more resources when it came to pursuing the chalice. And if his family had really been chasing it for hundreds of years then he'd know more of its history. That interested her almost as much as actually finding the cup.

Sophie smiled. She liked the idea of spending time with him, of getting to know him as they pursued something they were both interested in.

She leaned in and rubbed her cheek against his chest. She kissed his nipple and laughed when he growled.

"I was going to turn the chalice over to the insurance company," she said. She knew he had no such intention.

Severn chuckled. "Sophie, they have insured it for five million dollars. I once offered the same amount for it. Which do you think they would prefer if given a choice? The money they've had to pay out, or the chalice itself?"

She looked up to meet his gaze. She knew the answer but still found it nearly incomprehensible. "Do you really have so much money you can spend five million on something because it's called the Dragon's Cup and is featured in a fairytale about dragons and wizards?"

"Yes." He hugged her. "I know Storm is your cousin and she is sworn to uphold the law. The Chalice of Enos will be mine. But as a gift to my beautiful mate, I will promise to pay for it when I find it."

Sophie laughed despite herself. "Then I guess I'd better search with you so I can hold you to your promise."

His mouth swooped down to cover hers. His hand pulled the towel from her body and dropped it to the floor.

Sophie moaned when naked flesh once again touched naked flesh. She shivered at the feel of his cock pressed hard and firm against her belly.

"Stay with me while we search for the cup," Severn said, cupping her buttocks and rocking his aroused penis against her abdomen.

It would be easier if she did. It made sense. Still, Sophie hesitated—until the teenagers from Hell and their parents erupted into a screaming match in the apartment above hers.

She laughed when Severn jerked and cursed. There was no way she could ask him to stay in her apartment, even if it was only for every other night. *She* couldn't even stay in her apartment.

"Okay, I'll stay with you," Sophie said, some instinct making her add, "as long as I can come and go as I please."

His immediate frown told her he didn't like her condition. She tried to pull away but he wouldn't let her.

Sophie's spine stiffened. She met his frown with one of her own.

She could deal with ending up in the *exact* same place she'd escaped from earlier in the day, but it was going to be on *her* terms this time.

Emotion chased through Severn like a young dragon after its tail. A low rumble sounded in his chest. The thought of her leaving his lair without him was almost intolerable but he could see no way around the condition set down by his mate.

He fought against his instincts to possess and guard. She had said only that she desired to come and go as she pleased. She'd said nothing about his sending those in his service to protect her when he couldn't be with her.

"Agreed," he said, tangling his fingers in her hair, holding her in place. His kiss was punishing despite his acceding to her demand.

It was only later, after Severn had parked her restored Mustang in his garage full of sleek, expensive sports cars, that Sophie remembered how it was she'd been able to escape from his estate in the first place. Her footsteps slowed as they approached a side door. Their clasped hands forced Severn to either turn and look at her or drag her after him.

"Maybe we should put this off for a while," she said. "Didn't your mother just get here for a visit?"

Chapter Five

🕉

A low growl sounded in Severn's throat. Sophie wasn't sure whether it was because she'd mentioned his mother or because she'd suggested putting off her temporary move to his estate.

He turned and his gaze swept down her body in a blatant gesture of ownership and possessiveness. She found it hard to swallow but she didn't retreat or try to take her suggestion back when he crowded her aggressively.

His hand cupped her face then trailed downward to curl around her neck. His thumb brushed across her rapidly beating pulse in a stroke that was both a warning and a promise of security.

"Do not think to leave me again, Sophie. I take care of what's mine. Every inch of you belongs to me. Every inch. For now and for always. You are my mate. Mine and only mine. Whatever my mother or the female she's brought with her might tell you, remember this, only I have the right to either pleasure or punish you. No other may touch you or command you. You belong completely to me." His voice was whispered menace and sultry promise.

Deep, deep in the recesses of her being she knew she should protest. She should draw a line in the sand here and now and tell him she wasn't a possession or a woman who could be ordered around or punished. But fire roared through her body.

It started where his lips touched hers. It flowed into her as his breath became her breath.

Lust pooled in her womb and rippled out on heated waves to her flushed cunt lips and erect clit. His tongue tangled with hers and tolerated no resistance. The hand that had been against her neck moved to cup her breast. His fingers claimed her nipple so fiercely she might as well have been naked for all the protection her clothing gave her.

Sophie arched into him. She closed her eyes, unable to focus on anything but his touch, his taste, his scent.

Her nipples burned with painful pleasure. His grip on them was so commanding she could only arch into him and beg with nearly animal sounds for him to finish what he'd started.

Severn growled again. The need to mate was overwhelming.

He walked Sophie backward in the garage until they reached the sleek metal hood of her Mustang. Without lifting his lips from hers he jerked her dress up and pushed her panties down. He freed his cock before crowding her, positioning her on the hood of the car and impaling her with his penis.

She screamed in pleasure when he shoved himself into her roughly. She clawed at his back.

The spurs at his wrists pulsed, ready to descend and inject her with serum so he could finish bonding with her by taking her to the dragon realm. *His.* It reverberated along every nerve ending. It became his sole thought as he pounded into Sophie.

He swallowed her cries of excitement. He cursed the presence of his shirt and how it protected him from the stinging punishment of her nails as she fought, not to get away from him but to get closer. He wanted to stop long enough to strip out of the garment so she could rake him with her talons but he couldn't stop fucking her. He couldn't force his hands away from her body.

With a keening sound Sophie came and her thrashing stopped. Severn began panting, thrusting wildly. He was lost in the sensation of wet heat, of slick feminine flesh caressing the ridges of his cock and sending fingers of unbearable ecstasy through its head.

He ripped his mouth from hers and roared as his buttocks clenched and seed jetted through his shaft. The exquisite release left him dizzy and weak, unable even to pull his penis from his mate's body when the last of his semen filled her.

He kissed her again, gently now. He rejoiced in having been blessed with a human mate, a soft, submissive female who wanted to be cuddled and held after the mating act, who could be touched at will, fucked at will.

"I'm not a possession," Sophie said, her voice slurred, drunk from the intensity of the orgasm he'd give her.

Severn smiled. He was so relaxed that her small defiance slid off his good mood in the same way water slid off his scales when he was in dragon form. He stroked her breast, pulled down the neckline of her dress and the bra so he could smooth over her nipple and admire it before picking up the Elven crystal. It burned against his palm in recognition of who and what he was to her.

"You are my heartmate," he said, using the Elven term for their bond.

"Maybe," Sophie said. She looked at him through lowered eyelashes as she took the necklace from him. Her subtle show of submission sent joy and warmth straight to his heart, her small challenge made his cock fill again.

Reluctantly Severn stepped back. His gaze lowered to take in the sight of her pussy as his penis emerged, wet and hard and ready for another round of fucking.

"We will continue this conversation when we get to the bedroom," he said.

His fingers combed her pubic hair. His thumb brushed over her clit.

She whimpered and widened her legs. Her feet braced on the bumper of the car as she arched into his caress.

Severn inhaled deeply as he looked at her cunt lips, flushed and full, coated with arousal and spent seed. He filled his lungs with their mingled scent then bent and rubbed his cheek against her mound. He nuzzled her engorged knob with his nose. He licked it and tasted himself as well as her. He had never felt so completely satisfied, so utterly fulfilled.

He couldn't stop touching her. He couldn't resist the urge to kneel at her feet when she slid from the hood of the car and stood.

He kissed her inner thighs. He once again filled his lungs with the scent of their mating. It was pure torture to draw the panties up her legs and reposition them over her mound and ass. He hated the thought of her wearing them. He *wanted* their mingled juices to be obvious to both his mother and the female dragon she hoped to mate him with. But he knew it was too soon to involve Sophie in such a primal display.

Severn pressed a kiss to Sophie's now-covered cunt. He stood and gently brushed his mouth to hers. He licked over her lips lightly and shared their combined taste.

He hoped they'd be able to get from the garage to his bedroom without interruption, but suspected they wouldn't. The fuck had delayed them and though he'd had little time to speak with his mother before discovering Sophie's escape and going after her, he didn't doubt she was already fully informed about his involvement with a human female.

Like all female dragons, his mother would resent his taking a human mate. Her displeasure would be intensified by her desire to have an alliance of her choosing. Though he had reached maturity and was no longer governed by the laws that allowed female dragons to determine the course their offspring's life would take, in her eyes, he was little better than treasure to be offered in the hopes of gaining something of greater worth.

Severn growled softly. The Wizard Enos had succeeded in tying much of the creation magic necessary for his kind to produce offspring to the cup, enough so that births were rare and who would be so blessed, unpredictable. His mother would no doubt have preferred a daughter, one she could raise in her own ruthless image—a female she could groom to one day take over as head of their lair. But sons had their uses, though his mother would soon learn he was not a son who would easily bow to her wishes, especially when it came to the taking of a mate.

She had placed a lesser value on him at his birth. She had left him in the care of those who owed her fealty while she spent her time fighting and ruling and hoarding what wealth and territory she could in the realm that now belonged to the dragons. No doubt it was because of her inattention that he'd grown up stronger willed than many of the males of his kind.

As soon as he'd been able to do so he'd crossed the threshold into the mortal world. He'd built his empire on lost treasure and hard work, on loyalty and complete obedience.

His mother might make a grab for influence and power here, but she would find out soon enough that this was his territory, not hers. And if she had any hopes of one day benefiting from the Chalice of Enos, then she would be a fool to challenge him.

Severn cupped Sophie's cheek again. He rubbed his thumb across lips still swollen from his kisses. His chest tightened as he imagined her mouth on his cock, her tongue exploring the head and the ridges circling underneath it. His penis throbbed as he imagined her moans as she sucked him into heated wet depths, her eyes pleading with him to fuck her, to come as she swallowed him down.

When she whimpered he gathered her into his arms and locked his lips to hers. He thrust his tongue into the very place he wanted his cock to be and ate hungrily at her mouth.

He would speak to Sophie later about the necessity of complete obedience. He was a dragon prince and this was his kingdom. His mate would obey him as all those in his service did. Never again would she openly defy him or run from him.

With a groan Severn finally ended the kiss and separated himself from Sophie. Satisfaction raged through him at her soft features and passion-clouded eyes, at the way she swayed slightly as if barely able to stand after his assault on her senses.

"If we should encounter my mother or the female she has brought with her, let me do the talking."

Sophie blinked like a well-petted cat. Her eyes met his and slowly cleared. She rubbed her hands over her dress as if ensuring it was completely down and her panties up. Shy heat moved into her face and Severn's heart thrilled even as his cock urged him to get her to the bedroom.

He took her hand. Unaccustomed tenderness filled him. "If we are lucky, we'll avoid my dragon of a mother altogether," he said, amusing himself with the play on words. "That would be my preference. I'd like to spend what's left of this day in bed with you."

His gaze dropped to encompass the soft outline of her nipples. The head of his penis pulsed when her areolas became tight points under his scrutiny.

Reluctantly Severn forced his attention away from Sophie though every cell in his body was attuned to her scent, her heat, the rightness of her presence at his side. Tomorrow would be soon enough to resume the hunt for the Dragon's Cup. Though no doubt he'd have to deal with his mother before he could enjoy his mate further.

Thoughts of his mother and Audriss sent irritation rippling along his back like an unpleasant sensation across the scales of his dragon form. In the space of a day he'd lost control of his mate and his estate. The first had been rectified but the second had yet to be dealt with.

By dragon law the house and grounds belonged ultimately to the head of his line—his mother. It was a fact she would be wise not to draw attention to. He had carved out a place for himself here and she benefited by the treasure he tithed to her. But he could easily separate himself completely from her and claim a lair in this realm. The temptation to do so was even greater now that he had a human mate.

The truth of the matter was that his mother, like many of the old dragons, preferred their new realm to their old one. She preferred to live in a place where kingdoms were carved out of rugged mountains high above earth and sea, where the plains between were wide open and full of prey, the oceans well-stocked with schools of beasts that could be swooped on to serve as dinner.

Human civilization and technology had progressed too far. The human population had expanded beyond the point where dragons could fly and live unhindered and unthreatened in their true form. Most of the ancient dragons hated the limitations, what they saw as the sheer insignificance of a human shape—except when it came to mating. Then even the oldest and most powerful of the males would gladly take the form of a man in order to fuck a willing woman and hopefully find she was his true mate, the female who might one day bear his young.

Severn drew Sophie through the door. Pleasure flooded him at having her in his lair, at seeing her against the backdrop of his treasures.

Technically the estate might belong to his mother but possession was nine-tenths of dragon law. He had little doubt that should he recover the Chalice of Enos, the house and grounds would become fully his.

His. The word purred through him as he glanced at Sophie. She had cost him much of the day and no small amount of aggravation, but she was at his side now and he would ensure she remained there.

His mother emerged from the drawing room and blocked their progress down the hallway. Audriss, the ultra dominant female she'd brought with her, took up a position at her side. Both of them radiated distaste and animosity. Their nostrils flared. Their attention went immediately to Sophie as the scent of spent sex reached them.

"So this is your new plaything," Audriss said. "Perhaps I will challenge her to a fight and see what she is made of. She is a pretty thing and pleasing to the eye, but she is no match for one of our kind."

"You forget yourself, Audriss," Severn said. Dragon instinct stirred inside him and filled his lungs with fire. "You are on my territory now and I will not allow you to either insult my mate or harm her."

"So you admit she is inferior to our kind?"

"Hardly." Severn pulled Sophie into his arms. He held her back pressed to his front. "Sophie is everything I have ever dreamed of."

Audriss opened her mouth but before more poison could spew out, Severn's mother said, "Enough."

Sophie shivered. She couldn't have said it better herself. She'd had enough all right and as soon as she could make an exit, she intended to do it.

Severn's mother hadn't spoken a single word to her yet, but her expression said it all. Distaste. Disgust. Sophie hadn't imagined it and she wasn't going to bother trying to convince herself that she had. Reading people was her forte. It was a skill that came to her naturally but one she also practiced frequently because it made her a better writer.

Sophie tried to move but Severn's hold on her tightened possessively. A low growl sounded in his throat.

"Do not think to run again, Sophie," he whispered in her ear. His hand moved to rest above her pubic bone. It burned through her clothing. "I have been lenient with you, but the next time I will not be so forgiving."

Arousal flooded her channel as images of what happened in her apartment and in his garage filled her thoughts. She clamped her legs together and he tightened his grip on her.

Severn nuzzled her ear and neck. It made her forget for an instant that they had an audience. But then like a bucket of cold water, his mother said, "If you are finished taunting

Audriss, *my son*, then perhaps you could send your current…companion elsewhere. No doubt she would welcome the opportunity to shower and cleanse herself. And while she is busy with that task, we have important things to discuss, matters that cannot be discussed in front of an outsider." An arrogant, haughty eyebrow lifted. "Or have you shared *all* of your secrets with this female you claim is your mate?"

Sophie tensed when Severn tensed. Her imagination ran wild with his mother's reference to secrets. All the speculation about Severn and the source of his wealth congealed in a wad of fear and worry at the pit of Sophie's stomach. She wouldn't be the first woman to be attracted to a deadly mobster with a reputation for ruthlessness.

She swallowed and forced the thoughts away. She corralled her wild imagination with logic.

Storm had backed off on her warnings about Severn. One of Storm's husbands was partners with Severn's cousin. He wouldn't be if the club was tainted. Storm was too honest a cop to go for that and Pierce was too much in love with Storm to ruin her reputation by being involved with gangsters.

"I'll speak with you in the drawing room," Severn said. "After I've seen Sophie to our bedroom."

"Do not linger unnecessarily." Severn's mother didn't bother to look in Sophie's direction before turning on her heel and retreating into the room she'd stepped out of.

Audriss made a show of glancing down Sophie's body. Her perusal made Sophie think of prison bathrooms, of inmate rapes that had nothing to do with sexual orientation and everything to do with domination. Then Audriss also turned and disappeared into the drawing room.

"Do not trust either of them," Severn said.

Sophie shivered. "I think that's a given."

Severn's arms tightened on her momentarily. He kissed her neck and then her ear. His hand slipped downward from its position above her pubic bone. He covered her mound possessively, protectively while his other hand covered her breast.

Sophie shivered again, this time with need instead of fear. "Stop," she whispered, afraid that if he kept going she'd let him fuck her in the hallway where the sound of it would carry to his mother and Audriss.

He laughed as if he guessed what she was thinking. The husky masculine sound made her want to lift her dress and impale herself on him.

"You make it nearly impossible to stop," he said, but released her. The slowness of his movements telling her it was difficult for him to do.

Out of habit she clasped the heartmate necklace and felt its heat through the fabric of her dress. Severn took her free hand and led her to the bedroom suite she'd woken in earlier and escaped from.

Her luggage sat near the foot of the bed. Severn closed the door and pulled Sophie into his arms. His lips covered hers. His tongue slid into her mouth. It teased hers until the slide and thrust of it, the needy emptiness between her thighs and Severn's nearness became Sophie's only reality.

She whimpered when he lifted his mouth. She clung to him until he sighed and once again put her away from him. His cock was a rigid, noticeable presence against the front of his trousers.

"I will make the visit with my mother as quick as possible. In the meantime, bathe or unpack or amuse yourself by exploring the contents of the room." He pointed to a pair of antique chests, both inlaid with jewel-encrusted dragons. "You'll find the keys in the drawer of the nightstand but I won't ruin your surprise or your pleasure by telling you what's in them." He leaned in and kissed her again before he left.

Chapter Six

ဢ

For a long moment Sophie stood where Severn left her. Her thoughts ranged over the full spectrum of what had happened since she woke up in a strange bed and learned that the man who was her heartmate was Severn Damek. She felt bemused and slightly shell-shocked by the events of the day. His nearly nonstop physical attention since finding her at Aislinn's house was enough to leave her in a sensual coma.

Sophie laughed and shook her head. She'd better not let him guess his effect on her. The man already had way too much confidence when it came to his sexual abilities. She didn't doubt for a minute he'd use any weapon at his disposal when it came to her.

Had she really agreed to live with Severn and hunt for the Dragon's Cup with him? Her womb fluttered in answer as a ripple of anticipation spread outward. It was a response that had as much to do with spending time with him as it did with doing research for a new book.

Sophie's attention shifted to the chests. She had to smile.

Severn had repeatedly told her she'd better remain in his home. He'd mentioned the word punishment several times. The timbre of his voice and his expression promised a sexual retribution that very nearly tempted her to disobey so she could experience it. For all that, it was his casual reference to the chests and his invitation to explore them that served to chase any lingering thoughts of leaving from her mind.

Her smile widened. She remembered Storm telling her how Pierce had warned her not to touch any of Severn's treasures when he'd brought her here in connection to the VanDenbergh murder. While Storm was telling the story, she'd rolled her eyes over Severn's tattoo and the dragon statues in his office. She'd commented more than once on how he seemed to take the whole dragon thing very seriously. Now Sophie could second that opinion—only she knew firsthand exactly what it felt like *to be* one of Severn's possessions.

She shivered in remembered pleasure. Her cunt clenched and her body burned with need. With a shaky sigh she made her way to the bathroom. She decided to pamper herself with a nice soak in the sunken tub before she settled in front of the jeweled chests and explored their contents.

Severn strode down the hallway. His cock raged at being separated from Sophie before it could plunge into her wet depths again. His balls were full and heavy and chafed at not being allowed to hang free beneath his erection. The combination made his temper short.

He paused at a phone discreetly hidden among priceless antiques. He punched in a number. "Sophie is in my bedroom. Ensure she does not leave and that no one else enters."

"Of course," Xanthus said.

Severn dropped the receiver into its cradle. A low rumble escaped as he saw again the look Audriss had given Sophie before following his mother into the parlor. He had seen female dragons mount other females in a show of dominance. More than once he'd been present when one female pinned another to the ground and rode until she orgasmed and covered the lesser female with her scent.

True, occasionally the lesser females offered themselves and were willing participants. But more often it was done as a subjugation, a play for power in a show of who was the stronger.

Once again Severn sent a prayer to The Great Shared Ancestor for gifting him with Sophie. Now if only he could rid himself of both his mother and Audriss he could return to his bedroom and fuck his delectable human mate.

His cock pulsed in warning. Her remembered scent filled his nostrils. For a moment he was forced to take his cloth-covered erection in hand.

He shuddered. His rioting imagination placed Sophie's hand on his organ instead of his own. He saw it move up and down on rigid flesh before it was followed by her mouth.

Severn panted. He wrestled with control and attributed the lack of it to having his runaway mate back in his home and yet not being able to fully sate himself because of his mother's untimely appearance.

For long moments he struggled. His dragon nature insisted he return to the bedroom. It urged him to fight and kill any who dared enter his lair while he was finding pleasure with his mate.

With a final shudder and a low groan Severn forced himself back under control. He promised himself that he would deal with his mother and Audriss quickly and then he would return to the bedroom and take Sophie repeatedly. He would fuck her until he was certain she would obey without question and trust him to keep her safe in both his world and hers.

Severn entered the parlor and took a seat. "Even for the chalice itself I wouldn't mate with Audriss," he said. He had no inclination toward politics, especially in the human world where he'd found the use of wealth or force gained results more quickly.

Anger flashed in Audriss' eyes. Speculation and cunning drifted through his mother's.

"Do not be so hasty, *my son*. You are no weakling. I can't imagine you truly wish to mate yourself permanently to one. I believe you will soon see the advantages of an alliance with Audriss. And perhaps she will allow a human female in her household. I have heard it said that some of the younger females are more tolerant and turn a blind eye to their male's need to indulge and prove himself by rutting on willing humans."

She waved her hand in the air to brush the topic aside. "Time will tell and our kind has plenty of it. Audriss will remain to monitor the activities of the fey. Queen Otthilde is determined to regain the chalice for her petty court orgies. Morgana has already crossed to this realm and I suspect there are others with her. Audriss will attend to them while I maneuver among the dragons." His mother's nostrils flared slightly. "That leaves the humans to you, Severn. You have made yourself at home in this place and no doubt the chalice remains in human hands. I will leave it to you to track it down before the rest of us grow impatient and leave a trail of bodies for the human authorities to ponder."

Severn rose to his feet. His jaw clenched tightly.

Unlike the little-known fairytale Sophie had in her file on the Dragon's Cup, the wizard hadn't so much cursed the dragons to barrenness as crafted a powerful spell and tied the creation magic necessary for young to the chalice. And contrary to Sophie's information, it wasn't a matter of a single dragon drinking from the cup in order to restore fertility, but a pair. So to possess the Chalice of Enos was also to control which pairings and which alliances would be guaranteed offspring.

Severn wanted to reiterate that Sophie was his mate and he would accept no other. But time would indeed tell. Once he'd recovered the Dragon's Cup and impregnated Sophie then his mother would no doubt drop her advocacy of Audriss. No good would come of continuing to argue, nor giving his mother an indication that he had no intention of giving her the chalice when he found it. At the moment the course of action she'd decided on was the very one he'd intended to propose—save Audriss' involvement.

Uneasiness coiled in Severn's chest. Dragons were collectors by nature. They were prone to fixating on the things they couldn't easily gain. The value of an item increased with the difficulty of the challenge in acquiring it. Beneath the flash of anger he'd seen in Audriss' eyes at his refusal of her, there had been a glint of determination. He would have to watch her carefully.

Severn left the two female dragons. He returned to his bedroom and followed the trail of Sophie's discarded clothing to the bathroom. His mother and Audriss and the Dragon's Cup were all forgotten as soon as he found Sophie immersed in bubbles and heated water. Her hair was braided and twisted into a knot. Her eyes were closed.

Satisfaction purred through him. She was no doubt thinking of him. "Perfect," he said and she opened her eyes.

Severn rewarded her by unbuttoning his shirt and dropping it to the floor. His cock jerked in anxious need. It pressed aggressively against the front of his trousers when her tongue peeked out and her gaze roved over his naked chest before lowering to center on his straining erection.

He removed his socks and shoes next, then his belt. Lust twisted inside him like a writhing dragon when Sophie sat up and the hard points of her nipples emerged from the silky bubbles of her bath.

With a groan he removed his trousers. He was glad he'd taken Sophie enough times since recovering her that the magic held and his cock looked human.

"I guess you missed me," she teased.

He joined her in the sunken tub. She wrapped her arms around his neck and pressed her slick flesh against his.

Severn gathered her closer. His lips went unerringly to hers.

His tongue forged into her mouth to rub against hers in a wet greeting. She whimpered into his mouth and his hands slid down her back and around to her hips.

His thighs wedged themselves between hers. He used his upper body strength to lift and position her, then to guide her downward so her tight, feminine channel sheathed his straining cock.

He groaned as his penis was welcomed with a ripple of internal muscles, a clenching and releasing in a thick pool of wet heat that rivaled the water surrounding them.

Sophie arched. She panted as spasm after spasm of sensation pulsed from where his cock filled and stretched her. He was incredible, so huge she wasn't sure she would ever be able to easily accommodate him. Every nerve ending responded to his presence, quivering between pain and pleasure as she ached for the exquisite ecstasy she knew he would give her.

"Please, Severn," she whispered. It was a thread of sound but his hands tightened on her in response. His chest rumbled in a satisfied growl at having her beg him for what they both wanted.

His mouth covered hers again. His hands controlled the depth and rhythm of her movements. They urged her up and down on his shaft. The angle and closeness of their bodies ensured each stroke pressed her clit against his abdomen and sent a burst of heat radiating through her vulva.

When she tried to speed up, to grind herself against him, he tightened his grip and forced her to accept what he was willing to give. He demanded that she surrender herself completely to his control.

Sophie was whimpering and scratching at his back by the time Severn fucked her to the fierce orgasm she craved. His shout of release came seconds later. His buttocks clenched and his body jerked repeatedly. He filled her channel with heated seed while the expression on his face filled her soul with sublime pleasure.

Afterward Severn lifted her from the tub and stretched her out on the steam-wet tiles before covering her body with his. He used his elbows to keep most of the weight off her as they both basked in the afterglow. He brushed his lips against

Sophie's. He nuzzled her cheek, her neck, her ears. She laughed in sated pleasure when he said, "In answer to your comment, yes, I missed you. Did you already explore the chests?"

"Not enough time. I decided on a soak."

Her thoughts went to his mother's comment in the hallway—a not-so-subtle jibe that Sophie smelled of sex and needed to take a shower to *cleanse herself*. A chill swept over her. She shivered despite the sultry heat of the bathroom. The only way she was going to be able to stay was if Severn's mother had a suite of her own on the *far* side of the estate.

"Don't let them draw you into their games," Severn said, guessing at her thoughts.

"Just tell me I won't have to see them very often. And *me* being confined to the bedroom is not an option, Severn." Her gaze met his as she issued the warning. With any other man it wouldn't be necessary to spell out that she didn't intend to be made a prisoner, but she suspected it *was* necessary with him.

Severn laughed and took her wrists. He raised them above her head and pinned them to the smooth tile flooring as he rested more of his weight on her. He allowed her to feel both his strength and his heat. "And here I was imagining tying you to the bed and keeping you there."

Sophie closed her eyes against the image but it didn't do any good. The picture of lying helpless on Severn's bed buried itself into her imagination. It was a dark fantasy waiting to be explored.

"Tell me I won't have to deal with them," she said, trying to regain control of the conversation but knowing she'd failed. The husky sound of her voice revealed how much his words affected her. It was impossible to hide the way her tight nipples pressed against his chest and her erect clit stabbed into his abdomen.

"I will keep you safe, Sophie." He nuzzled her sensitive outer ear. He traced it with his tongue. "And for the most part you will be with me, searching for the Dragon's Cup as we agreed on." He sucked her earlobe into his mouth and she jerked in reaction. Her lower body pumped against his.

Severn freed one wrist long enough to secure both with a single hand. He rolled to his side so he could cup her breast. He rubbed the aroused peak with his palm before taking her nipple between his fingers. He squeezed and tugged in time with his assault on her ear until she was shivering, moaning, begging.

Severn forced his mouth away from Sophie's ear. He cursed himself for once again losing control. He'd meant to make her pliable, relaxed and comfortable so she would be agreeable to what he wanted from her. But instead the need to have her pleading for his touch, straining for the pleasure he could give her had made him forget himself and lose himself in her.

He released her breast and trailed his hand over her belly. He stroked through the pubic hair and settled for a minute to torment her clit. He explored the tiny exposed tip, the soft folds of the hood, the sensitive underside.

Her whimpers filled the air. She arched and thrust the engorged knob against his fingers. Lust roared through him like an eternal flame that could never be doused.

With a groan Severn covered her lips with his. He buried his tongue in her mouth as his fingers moved lower and plunged into her slit. He fucked her in a quick, hard assault that had her crying out into his mouth.

When she settled again, languid and sated with her eyes closed, he removed his passion-slick fingers from her channel and returned to her pubic hair. For long moments he petted her as his tongue slid gently against hers.

"I want you bare down here," he finally said. He cupped her mound. His voice was husky as the fantasies of being able to bury his face in her cunt and encounter nothing but silky skin had his cock throbbing and the tip beading with arousal. "Let me shave you."

Sophie's breath caught at the unexpectedness of the question and the wicked eroticism of both what he wanted and what he was willing to do to achieve it. Heat moved through her along with embarrassment and unwilling arousal.

He kissed her again in a persuasive press of lips and tongue. "Please," he whispered. His sapphire eyes glittered with the intensity of his desire for her to agree.

Sophie shivered. Nerves fluttered in her stomach. Shyness tightened her chest at the thought of allowing him to perform such a personal task.

"Let me do this," he said again, his fingers gliding over her slit and bathing in the moisture gathered there.

Sophie nodded, not trusting her voice.

He returned her to the sunken tub before he padded across the bathroom. Water rolled down his bronzed flesh and over the sculpted muscles of his back and buttocks and legs. The sight of it distracted Sophie from her trepidation and uncertainty.

She watched as he removed a razor and shaving gel from a cabinet drawer. A loofa sponge and tube of moisturizer followed. He pulled a hand towel from a dragon shaped rack before he returned to the side of the tub.

He set the items down then reached over and gathered several thick fluffy bath towels from where they lay folded on a chair. He spread them out on the floor to form a soft, comfortable pallet.

Pain spiked through Sophie's heart at seeing how well prepared he was and how confident he was in his movements. She could easily picture him asking and doing this same thing with countless other women.

She opened her mouth to tell him she'd changed her mind but Severn turned. His eyes met hers and his expression became tender. He picked up on her insecurity and said, "Your unexpected absence gave me time to prepare."

Severn lifted her from the tub and stretched her out on the towels. He covered her body with his and teased her with the feel of his erection pressed against her clit.

"As I have said before, Sophie, do not even contemplate leaving me again. You are mine in every way. You are mine to have as I please and I desire you bare. You are the only woman I have wanted so intimately."

Need curled in her belly at his possessiveness. Thoughts of other women were driven away as he kissed down her body. Any thought of protesting his right to have her any way he pleased left when he suckled at her breast before moving lower to explore her bellybutton. She cried out when his mouth found her clit. She panted and arched when he sucked it.

"Please," she whimpered when his tongue danced over her flushed cunt lips and slid between them.

Severn fucked her with his tongue until all doubt had fled in a burst of explosive warmth.

He groaned and rose to his knees. His cock was a rigid line against his belly.

She thought he might delay but instead he reached for the shaving gel and squeezed some of it onto the tips of his fingers. He massaged and explored every inch of her pussy. He worked the gel into curls already softened by water.

His ministrations were erotic, arousing. They left Sophie flushed with her legs willingly spread and the lips of her sex parted as though anxious for him to bury his face between her thighs when she was completely bared to his touch.

When he was satisfied with his preparations, he dipped his hand in the tub and dried it on the hand towel. He reached for the razor and applied it to her pussy in short strokes. His free hand aided the process. It gently manipulated her, his fingers stretching the skin in difficult spots and making her gasp as they trailed over the pucker of her ass.

Severn's eyes met hers for a brief instant. They glowed with feral intent. His fingers touched her back entrance again in a gesture that told her without words he intended to fuck her there at some point in time.

"Beautiful," Severn whispered when she was completely bare. His voice was thick with arousal.

Sophie shivered. Her labia blossomed like a flower heavy with nectar, like velvet leaves covered with dew.

Severn groaned. He leaned down and covered her mound with his mouth. He kissed her intimately, hungrily. When it came to Sophie his restraint was as nonexistent as a fledgling dragon's.

He feasted. He thrust his tongue into her slit repeatedly. He sucked her cunt lips before attacking her clit. The bathroom echoed with the sound of his sensual assault, with her moans and whimpers and his own growls.

The desire burning through him was hotter than the flame he commanded in his dragon form. His cock throbbed. His balls swung heavily underneath it. His lust was so extreme that he could feel the magic slipping to no longer mask the thick ridges circling beneath the head of his penis.

He took himself in hand. He pumped in time to the fierce stabs and swipes of his tongue in Sophie's channel. The feel of his palm against the ridges sent icy-heat up his spine. It made his buttocks clench against the need to come.

He lost himself in the sweet feminine mystery of his mate. He swallowed the ecstasy of her release. The taste and heat of it filled him with unparalleled satisfaction and destroyed the last of his resistance. Lava-hot semen surged through his cock in an eruption that bordered on pain. It left him lightheaded, his chest and abdomen coated with his own seed.

Severn managed to get them both back into the tub. Sophie was so relaxed she willingly let him care for her. She let him wash her then glide the loofa sponge over her bare pussy. She murmured in pleasure when he eased her out of the water and patted her dry before smoothing the moisturizer on her freshly shaved skin.

A dragon's growl of utter contentment vibrated through Severn's chest as he carried her to the nest of their bed and settled in with her.

Chapter Seven

ഔ

Relieved was too mild a word for what Sophie felt when she and Severn finally made it down to breakfast the next morning and found themselves alone. She didn't think she could deal with his mother or Audriss. The truth was, she was having a hard time being with him.

Her face was still burning from his insistence at not only "inspecting" her newly shaved pussy but in putting moisturizer on it before letting her get dressed—or partially dressed. His hand had grabbed her wrist when she'd reached for her panties. And despite her protests, he'd won the battle over whether she was going to wear them *or not*.

She smoothed her skirt against her thighs and was hyperaware of the warm air flowing under it and across her bare cunt. The intimate alcove where they were sitting across from each other allowed Severn to press his knees against hers and keep her legs closed as though he was guarding a treasure.

"What's the plan for today?" Sophie said, looking up from a table loaded with a variety of foods. His smile made her think of a large, pleasure-lazy dragon basking on an outcropping of rock and soaking in the sun, content with both its surroundings and itself.

"I thought you'd enjoy accompanying me to the VanDenbergh estate today," Severn said. "The family is auctioning off a number of possessions and I've been invited to attend."

Sophie straightened in an instant. Excitement hurled though her. She'd tried to get access to the scene of Carl VanDenbergh's murder and the place where the Dragon's Cup had been stolen but the family had repeatedly refused to let her visit.

Thanks to Storm's unauthorized sharing of information, Sophie had "seen" the treasure room. But photographs weren't the same as actually walking through a room and internalizing the essence of it.

"They'll let me in with you?" she asked, knowing as soon as the words escaped that of course the family would let her in with Severn Damek. He probably had enough money to buy every item they had for sale.

Severn laughed and leaned forward. He cupped her face with his hand. "It's foolish to deny me when I want something." His voice was husky. His eyes shifted from lazy to intent before she could do little more than blink. "Free your breasts, Sophie. I want to enjoy them while we eat breakfast together."

His request sent a shockwave of heat straight to her cunt. She licked her lips nervously and his eyes narrowed. His face became harsh, as if anticipating her denial. A shiver of erotic fear fluttered through her womb.

"Someone might come in," she whispered. Color stained her cheeks even as her labia grew swollen and flushed and wet.

"You are mine and I don't share. Not even an image in your case." He brushed his thumb against her mouth. "Free your breasts. The sooner we're done with breakfast, the sooner we'll be on our way to the auction."

Sophie glanced at the doorway leading to the private alcove. The modern "liberated" woman warred with the primitive one who loved his show of dominance and possessiveness, who thrilled at the idea of being completely conquered by so strong a male.

With an unsteady breath and shaky fingers she undid the buttons on her blouse so it hung free. The line of exposed flesh was broken only by the pale green of her bra, the only undergarment he'd allowed her. Lust moved into his face and she shivered. His gaze was almost a physical caress. Once again she glanced at the doorway to ensure herself they were alone. Then her fingers went to the front clasp of her bra and released it before peeling the cups away from her breasts.

"Beautiful," Severn said. His raspy growl had her already hardened nipples tightening further. He leaned over the table and she couldn't prevent herself from closing the distance so his tongue could swirl over first one rigid areola and then the other.

He suckled for long moments, alternating so neither breast was neglected. Sophie buried her fingers in his hair and held him to her. She gave a small cry of protest when he finally pulled back, leaving her nipples wet and needy, aching for more.

"Eat so we can leave," Severn said. His palm caressed the hard tips of her breasts for an instant before he reached for his coffee cup.

Somehow Sophie managed to eat. But each time his gaze dropped to her chest the ache in her nipples intensified and her cunt wept. His thighs remained on either side of hers and kept them firmly closed, trapping the heat of her pussy against her bare flesh as she grew wetter and wetter.

She thought she was beyond worry about sitting at the table with her breasts exposed until she heard footsteps. In an instant her fork clattered to her plate and her hands started to go to her shirt.

"No," Severn growled. His command stopped her hands in midair.

"Someone's coming," she whispered. The vein at the base of her neck pulsed wildly as the steps grew louder.

"And they will not dare to look at you, Sophie. Everyone in this household knows you belong to me."

She started to cross her arms. This time it was his expression that stopped her. It warned her there would be consequences if she disobeyed him. Sophie lowered her arms and reclaimed her fork as Xanthus stepped into view.

His gaze may have flickered over her bared breasts. She couldn't be sure and even if they had, his attention remained firmly on Severn, his manner giving no indication she was at the table.

"Your mother is not the only one to arrive," Xanthus said.

"Who else is here?" Severn asked, not surprised that word of the chalice surfacing again had brought other ancients to this realm.

"Malik's ancestor is here, as is Hakon's."

"Where are they?"

"At Drake's Lair." A small smile played over Xanthus' lips. "Malik and Hakon maneuvered their elders to the club. Tielo had the foresight to call Pierce and tell him there were wealthy marks waiting to be relieved of some of their treasure. I believe the old ones have been introduced to the game of Texas hold'em."

Severn laughed. Once again he found himself glad he'd supported his cousin's desire to open a club with the Sidhe prince now married to Sophie's cousin. Unlike most of the fey, Pierce had always been a friend to their kind. Even so, few dragons could resist the prospect of gambling against a royal Sidhe—especially one who had made his fortune recovering lost treasures in the human realm. "And my mother?"

"She has not yet left her chambers."

"Audriss?"

A shudder passed through Xanthus. "She demanded one of your cars and took along a servant to drive her."

Since Severn didn't refer to those honoring their liege duty or those he hired as servants, he knew without asking that Audriss had taken someone loyal to either her or to his mother. "The GPS unit in the car has been enabled?"

Xanthus smiled. "Of course."

"Then I'll leave it to you to monitor her movements. She has spent little time here. I doubt she will consider the advances in technology or guess how thoroughly I've embraced them."

Xanthus nodded and left. Severn's attention returned to Sophie.

His cock reminded him of its presence so fiercely that he contemplated clearing the table with a sweep of his arm and fucking her there. His need for her rode so close to the surface he felt raw and vulnerable.

That's the only excuse he could give for insisting she bare herself to him as they ate. That was the only plausible reason for stopping her from putting on her panties when he knew they'd soon be in a room full of other male dragons, most of them unmated and several of them princes as he was.

"You please me," he said. He couldn't resist the urge to lean forward and kiss her as he fondled her breasts.

He wanted to fuck her desperately. He wanted to do nothing more than spend the entire day locked in the bedroom with her. But he couldn't afford to do it. Not with his mother and Audriss in this realm. Not with other dragons and the faeries from Queen Otthilde's court circling and prowling and hunting for the Chalice of Enos.

Reluctantly he pulled away. His hand went to the heartmate stone and closed around it. He felt the fiery burn of recognition against his palm.

"You are mine," he growled before releasing the necklace and closing her bra.

He slowly redid the buttons of her blouse and covered the soft skin that would never know another male's touch again. Only his. *His.* The word was a dragon's flame touching every part of him.

Severn rose to his feet and took Sophie's arm. The urge to maintain physical contact with her was becoming more pronounced the longer she belonged to him. "Do you need to get your purse?"

Sophie nodded. Her thoughts were still scattered from his attention and from the darkly erotic experience of being required to remain partially naked in the presence of a second man.

She shivered when Severn's hand traveled down her back and smoothed over her buttocks before coming to rest on her thigh. She made a small sound. Her cunt spasmed at the look in his eyes. She could see the fight going on inside him—the need to release her so they could leave pitted against the desire to slide his hand under the material of her skirt and play with her pussy.

She licked her lips. He groaned and covered them with his own. He speared his tongue into her mouth. His hand slipped under her skirt. His fingers gathered her wet arousal and painted it over her flushed, swollen folds and bare mound.

Sophie clung to him. She whimpered into his mouth as his palm circled and pressed against her clit.

"A small one now," he said when he lifted his face. His fingers found her engorged knob. He touched it in the way he knew she liked, mimicked the stroke of a tongue along the underside, over the tiny head.

He became more dominant, more possessive as he drove her higher. Even as she gasped and shuddered and crested the message was clear. He commanded her pleasure, her release. Every part of her belonged to him.

As her breathing slowed he fondled her smooth cunt. He cupped it, admired it with his touch. The heat of his palm against her bare flesh made her want to stay in his arms forever. The small orgasm he'd given her mellowed her to the point that even the thought of his mother walking in on them didn't make her want to pull away from him.

Severn gave her another lingering kiss. His fingers raked lightly over her bare buttocks and made her think of a dragon marking its territory.

"We need to leave," he said before releasing her. The tautness of his body and the expression in his eyes filled Sophie with feminine pride. They told her more clearly than words that he'd like nothing more than to spend the day making love.

"Go get your purse, Sophie," he said. "Can you find your way to the garage? Or should I wait for you here?"

"I can find my way."

He leaned in and kissed her again, this time nibbling at her lower lip. "I need to make a phone call. If you get to the garage before I do then choose the car you want us to take."

Sophie laughed. "Is that a male strategy to make sure I don't decide to redo my makeup or change into another outfit?"

"You are beautiful, Sophie. Applying makeup is a waste of time and money." He gave her a warning nip to the side of the neck. "You will feel the sting of my hand on your buttocks if you change clothing or put on panties. Now go get your purse. We're already leaving later than I had planned."

He pressed a kiss to the place he'd bitten then stepped back and put some distance between them. The lack of his body heat made Sophie shiver though the threat of a spanking had her womb fluttering and quivering.

She left the alcove and backtracked to the bedroom so she could retrieve her purse. She was tempted to put her panties on. The thought of being on the receiving end of his carnal punishment was far more arousing than she would have ever admitted or thought possible before Severn came into her life. But then again, every minute she was with him she became more thoroughly convinced that he *was* her heartmate and there was no point in trying to resist him. She grinned, not that she intended to make things *too* easy for him.

Sophie took a minute to look through her notes—or rather Storm's from the crime scene. She knew the information but with the distraction of Severn she wanted to refresh her memory in preparation for the trip to the VanDenbergh estate.

She could easily envision where Carl VanDenbergh's body had been found with a single gunshot wound to the head. She could visualize the pool of blood—something she could deal with in pictures or her imagination even though the sight of fresh blood at a crime scene would make her physically sick.

It embarrassed her that she hadn't been able to work through the reaction. She'd been able to work through the horror of being in small dark places. She'd come to terms with the existence of senseless violence and uncontrollable rage. Her writing had freed her from the gruesome nightmare of her stepfather killing her mother and then barricading himself in the house as he searched for her.

Sophie shivered and closed the door on the memory. The heartmate necklace warmed against her skin and she clasped it in her hand. Her thoughts went to Severn and heat uncurled in her belly with the realization that when she was in his presence, he made her feel absolutely safe.

Her heart shimmered with happiness as the image of Severn's tattoo flared to life in her mind. Dragons were notorious for guarding their treasure and he'd made it very clear she belonged to him. She was finding she liked being claimed.

Sophie was smiling as she left the bedroom and made her way down the hallway. Anticipation and excitement built with each step. If she and Severn could find the Chalice of Enos— She rounded a corner and found his mother instead.

It took effort to keep her smile in place but Sophie managed it, along with a fairly decent sounding, "Good morning." She couldn't imagine ever tacking on *Mom*.

The formidable woman blocked the hall. Her gaze traveled over Sophie with a mix of condescension and pity — though the latter could also be revulsion. Sophie didn't care to speculate.

"You're a phase he's going through," Severn's mother said. "His father went through the same thing before I settled on him as a mate." An unpleasant expression flickered through her eyes. "For the moment I can allow Severn his little amusements. But when the time comes, he is *my* son and he will see the advantages of an alliance with Audriss."

O-kay. Sophie ground her teeth together and refused to react. Doing battle with Severn's mother in the hallway was *not* going to happen unless the woman refused to move out of the way. Then all bets were off.

Whether she read Sophie's willingness to get physical if necessary or whether it was arrogance, Severn's mother's swept Sophie with another desultory glance before she turned her back and walked away.

I am not staying here, Sophie thought, her body shaking slightly in reaction to the encounter. *As soon as we get back from the VanDenbergh estate, I'm leaving. Even for mind-blowing sex I am not going to skulk around the halls trying to avoid Severn's mother and Audriss.* At the moment Sophie wasn't sure which one of them was worse.

Severn was already in the garage when she got there. His eyes roamed her body. They lingered at the apex of her thighs as if trying to determine whether or not she'd dared to put on panties. His heated, possessive expression almost thawed the frozen lump lodged in Sophie's chest.

Tears sprang to her eyes, unexpected and humiliating. She turned away from him quickly and pretended to survey the choice of cars in the garage even though she hadn't gotten there first.

He reached her before she could rid herself of the moisture at the corners of her eyes. "You encountered my mother," he guessed as he pulled her back to his front and allowed her the dignity of not having to face him.

"I can't stay here," she blurted out even though she'd intended to wait until later before battling with him over it. Because given everything that had happened since his arrival at Inner Magick, she knew it *would* be a battle.

"We'll talk about it later." He kissed her neck as his hands roamed over her body.

They went to her breasts then smoothed down her belly and over her mound before slipping under her skirt. One palm curled around her thigh and urged her legs to part. The other settled over her cunt. "My mother will accept you or she will lose her claim to an heir. I won't give you up, Sophie, whatever the cost."

"Severn—" His fingers on her clit sent a jolt of intense need straight to her nipples and derailed her train of thought—for an instant.

"Severn—" She whimpered as he bit down on her neck in the same instant he filled her channel with his fingers.

The hand on her thigh jerked the hem of her skirt up so her bare buttocks were pressed against his trouser-covered erection. "If I bend you over the hood of a car and take you, we will not make it to the VanDenbergh estate," he threatened. "Do you want to continue our argument or would you rather move on to our search for the chalice?" His voice was little more than a masculine growl warning her that he would be happy with either choice.

"We can talk later," Sophie said, echoing his earlier words.

Severn closed his eyes and fought the urge to open his fly and shove his cock deep into Sophie's channel. The dragon part of his nature writhed and twisted almost like a separate entity within him.

Dragons were acquisitive and possessive by nature. They were also very physical.

In the centuries since the wizard's magic had greatly diminished the possibility and number of young a female could have in her fertile years, the wealth and prestige and satisfaction that once came from producing offspring now manifested in claiming a large territory and protecting it with displays of prowess, with battling other females, preferably by fighting and, failing that, then by intimidation and political alliance.

The males were equally fierce. But they preferred smaller territories and larger stores of treasure. Their physical needs were more tactile.

At the moment Severn wanted nothing more than to luxuriate in his mate—a mate who was already swollen and wet, her pussy spasming against his fingers, her buttocks subtly rubbing against his erection, enticing him to mount her even though she'd agreed to stop fighting him over the issue of where she would stay.

He had no intention of letting her stay anywhere but with him. He would ensure Sophie had no further unpleasant encounters with his mother.

Severn growled against her soft skin. He inhaled her. His tongue darted out to taste her. "You are a temptation and a distraction." He bit her again then sucked. He could almost feel the dragon crest of his other form rise in a warning display as he left visible proof of his ownership on Sophie's neck.

The mark wasn't needed. His scent was all over her. But the sight of it gave him immense satisfaction.

"Choose a car," he said. He forced himself to release her and step away, though his fingers immediately encircled her wrist and his thumb stroked across the back of her hand. He needed to touch her when they were in close proximity. His dragon nature insisted on it and Severn had no will to fight the instinct to keep what he valued above everything else well guarded.

In ancient times, before dragons fled this realm, males would steal any human mate left unguarded. The females were a prize beyond value because so few of them survived the shock of being taken away from their families by creatures they saw as terrifying beasts. The ones who did accept a dragon male would—given enough time—usually respond to a new mate. In those days there was no right or claim to ownership except for possession.

Dragon culture had evolved since then. But old instincts, especially surrounding a human mate, remained. If he had his way, Severn would never allow Sophie near any other male, much less those she was likely to encounter at the VanDenbergh estate.

"Let's take this one," Sophie said, distracting Severn from the churn of his emotions.

He opened the door for her. Pleasure rippled over his skin as she slipped into the passenger seat of the small dark blue sports car. She was as sleekly beautiful as the vehicle she'd chosen, and like it, she was his.

Chapter Eight

ഔ

After seeing Severn's home—and even then, only a portion of it—Sophie found it hard to be impressed by the VanDenbergh estate. True, VanDenbergh was a collector like Severn, but he favored display cases that separated him from his valuables while Severn lived with his treasures. And while Severn's home felt welcoming, despite his reputation, VanDenbergh's felt like a museum where visitors weren't expected to linger.

Sophie had expected a crowd and she wasn't disappointed. The rooms cordoned off for viewing the artifacts to be auctioned off were packed with well-dressed society members as well as casually clad news people. She recognized almost none of the former, but quite a few of the latter, though her presence at Severn's side made her a story instead of an honorary colleague.

More than one newspaper reporter approached her and tried to draw her away from Severn. But his hand on her arm served as both anchor and shackle. His fingers tightened on her with each attempt to remove her from his side and when he finally gave a low growl as yet another acquaintance of hers approached, Sophie finally reached a breaking point.

"Enough with the dragon stuff, okay?" she said, placing her hand over his and surreptitiously trying to remove his fingers from her arm.

Severn turned into her. His eyes glittered in warning as his free hand went to her hip. "There are men here I don't trust to be around you. I don't want you to leave my side, Sophie." His fingers glanced over her buttocks and she shivered at the subtle reminder that she wore nothing under her skirt.

"It's going to be a little hard to investigate if we're welded together," she said.

Something wicked passed through his eyes. "I've made the necessary arrangements. In a few minutes we will have a private tour of the rooms relevant to our search for the chalice."

Her aggravation disappeared in a heartbeat, to be replaced by anticipation. Of course they'd be allowed where other people weren't. VanDenbergh's heirs were probably hoping Severn would go on a spending spree.

He released her arm and trailed his fingers upward, stopping when his hand cupped her cheek. Their eyes met, held. His were possessive and unshielded despite the flash of cameras capturing the moment. "Let's look around. I'll buy anything you desire. Just ask."

A blush stained Sophie's cheeks. She was not used to being the center of so much attention. She pulled away. He let her escape though his hand dropped from her hip and his fingers captured hers.

"Do you know if they're auctioning off the sexually explicit figurines?" Sophie asked, remembering her cousin's description of them.

Severn laughed. It was a husky masculine sound that had more than one woman in the room turning toward him. "Looking for new positions already, my heartmate?" he teased.

Sophie grinned and tilted her head so she could look at him through her lashes. "And if I am?"

"Lead and I will follow."

That made her snort. "Somehow I don't see you as the following type."

He brought her hand to his lips and pressed a kiss to it. He smiled against her skin. "Then point in the direction you want to go and I will take you to paradise."

Sophie rolled her eyes. "That line is beyond bad."

He leaned in and whispered, "I have already taken you to paradise more than once. Admit it, Sophie."

She rubbed her cheek against his. "You need a compliment here? Now?"

"Tell me what I want to know." Severn's voice was a low growl, his playfulness gone in an instant.

He placed a hand on her hip again. The fingers stroked lightly over her flank.

Emotion coursed through Sophie in a wild mix that thrilled and humbled her at the same time. She'd never had a man desire her so intensely or be so possessive of her.

Her cunt spasmed and his breath caught as if he could smell the arousal seeping from her slit and coating her inner thighs. She shivered with the need to find release, to touch her clit, or better yet, to have Severn touch it, stroke it with his fingers and then his tongue and cock.

Did he know what his growled demand for an answer would do to her? Did he know it would tighten her body so she'd grow wet and ready for him?

Sophie turned her head slightly and touched his earlobe with her tongue. She decided to fight fire with fire. "What was the question again?"

This time his growl held a hint of amusement. "I'll ask again when you can scream your answer."

Severn straightened and led her to another room. This one contained the less valuable items to be auctioned—though a glance at the catalogue when they found the erotic figurines told Sophie they were still more than she could afford.

The figurines were actually combinations of various figures in amazing sexual positions. Sophie knew immediately why her cousin had wanted one of the groupings.

Two blond faerie men—one with delicate blue-green wings, the other with red-blue wings—were making love to an equally blonde human woman. They had her body trapped between theirs in a way that left no doubt about the pleasure they were all experiencing.

"Wow," Sophie breathed. She was amazed at the uncanny resemblance of the two fey men to Pierce and Tristan. And how, with only a tiny amount of imagination, she could see Storm in the blonde woman held between them.

"Pierce and Tristan have already made arrangements to gift your cousin with this set."

"That'll make her day."

Severn chuckled. "And theirs as well no doubt."

Sophie snickered. "Like those three need an excuse to fuck like bunnies. You could get heat stroke being in the same room with them."

Severn brought her hand to his mouth and nibbled on her knuckles. "Some like it hot." He leaned forward and whispered. "I like it hot. It excites me to know you are completely bare underneath your skirt. I could find a private place and put my hands or mouth on you. I could unzip my trousers and take you at will." He nuzzled her ear. "You would be ready for me, wouldn't you, Sophie? You would be silky and wet, anxious for whatever part of my body I wanted to put in your sweet channel."

Sophie clamped her thighs together and shuddered. His words penetrated her and made her ache.

"Answer me, Sophie," he growled.

"Yes," she said, shivering, knowing she couldn't fight him at the moment. Not when all she wanted to do was pull up her skirt and offer herself to him, beg him to touch her and appease the terrible hunger raging in her cunt.

He sucked her earlobe into his mouth. He teased it with his tongue before slowly releasing it. "Your nipples are hard points against the fabric of your blouse, my heartmate. I am finding I don't like the thought of other men looking at your breasts." His hand slid down her side and maneuvered her so her back was to his front and they were both facing the figurine case, their expressions hidden to the people milling around behind them.

Sophie felt his erection against her buttocks. She couldn't resist tormenting Severn. She leaned over the case and pressed her ass to the rigid line of his penis then wriggled slightly. "Hmmm," she murmured, glad no one was close enough to hear though her face was hot with the knowledge people were probably watching them. "Your cock is hard against the front of your trousers, *my heartmate*. I'm not sure I like the thought of other women fantasizing about what you could do to them with it."

Severn's grip tightened on her hip. "It's dangerous to play with me, Sophie."

She heard amusement in his voice along with the warning. She straightened and leaned back against him, allowed her body to soften into his.

The heartmate necklace was warm where it touched her skin. Its heat was a mirror of her emotions. The attraction to Severn had been immediate and intense, undeniable. The sexual satisfaction unbelievable. But this, the teasing and wicked sense of humor, the mix of tenderness and dominant passion, they were irresistible to Sophie.

"Some like it hot. Some like it dangerous. I'm not afraid to play with you," she said, rubbing against his cock subtly, shivering when his hand moved from her hip to her belly.

His palm burned through her blouse while his thumb lightly stroked her quivering abdomen. He nuzzled the side of her neck. "I would never want you to truly fear me, Sophie. You are mine, the greatest treasure in my possession, the only treasure I would sacrifice all the others for."

Sophie closed her eyes as his words filled her. They made her feel cherished in a way she'd only fantasized about. She knew there were women who would object to being considered a possession, and with any other man, she might have too—but not with Severn. Not when everything about him reminded her of the dragon he seemed to have taken as his personal avatar.

"We're supposed to be investigating," she reminded him. "But I'm finding it very hard to concentrate on the Dragon's Cup."

He laughed. "Choose from among these figurines. I want to give you a gift to remember this outing by. Then we will take our private tour."

Severn kissed the side of her neck before stepping away from her. But like before, he seemed unable to release her completely. His hand recaptured hers in a loose embrace. His thumb distracted her with its light strokes against hers.

Sophie studied the figurines. Some made her blush. Some made her wrinkle her nose. Others had her eyebrows lifting and her mind working to determine whether a depicted scene was even physically possible. One, a figure of a man holding a cock that would rival an elephant's trunk, made her laugh out loud and peek at Severn as she teased, "Don't ask me if that thing looks familiar."

Amusement flashed in his eyes and curled his lips. "I'm glad you noticed the resemblance." He tilted his head. "Still, I believe he pales in comparison to what I have already given you on more than one occasion."

Sophie snickered and moved to the end of the display case. Her breath caught at the last scene, a fantasyscape different from all the rest. Her reaction to the scene was so visceral her cunt clenched violently and she pressed her thighs together.

A woman was lounging on the ground, propped up on her elbows with her knees bent and her legs splayed. Her head was thrown back in ecstasy as a dragon crouched in front of her, his long tongue coiled around one of her thighs before its tip disappeared into her folds.

"You're aroused." Severn's voice told her he was too. "I will arrange to purchase this one as my gift to you. We can place it on the nightstand next to our bed and let it inspire us in our tongue-play."

His words licked through her like a dragon's flame. A whimper escaped before she could stop it.

Severn pulled her into his arms again, this time chest to chest. Sophie buried her face in the crook of his neck and inhaled his scent as she wrestled for control of her rioting body. She'd been in a state of arousal since the moment in his garage when he'd threatened to bend her over the hood of one of his expensive cars and forget this outing altogether. The constant teasing and touching since then, the flashes of dominance, the awareness that she had no panties on, all of it had driven her need to the point where she wanted him here. Now.

"Come," he whispered, turning slightly.

She shuddered at the word. She'd probably scream in orgasm if he slid his hand under her skirt and touched any part of her.

Severn guided her through the crowd with practiced ease. His manner cleared a path in front of them.

Near the entranceway they encountered the same butler who'd greeted them when they arrived. Severn said, "We'd like to see the recreation room first."

The butler led them there without argument. His ready obedience to the command in Severn's voice provided a welcome distraction.

"When we're done here we'll find our way to the room where the chalice was taken," Severn said, closing the door even as the butler was saying, "Very good, sir."

Severn pulled Sophie into his arms and covered her lips with his. He thrust his tongue into her mouth in an aggressive claim of ownership.

The scent of her arousal was driving him crazy. The knowledge that every dragon prowling the sale rooms was inhaling her, growing hard for her, had become intolerable to him. The urge to stake his claim raged like an uncontrollable fire inside him.

He growled and pulled Sophie more tightly against his body. He rubbed against her and wanted to be completely naked so he could cover every inch of her with his scent again.

He'd planned to bring her to this room—VanDenbergh's orgy room—last. But her reaction to the dragon figurine had very nearly snapped his control.

"The room is soundproof," he said when he lifted his head. Satisfaction roared through him at the sight of her well-kissed lips, her dazed, hungry expression.

"I know. Storm told me about this room. The day VanDenbergh was murdered he had six women in here waiting for him to get back with the chalice. All of them were big breasted and wearing negligees."

Severn grinned. Her voice left no doubt as to what she thought of the old goat who'd paid a fortune for the chalice and believed drinking from it would give him the stamina necessary to pleasure six women in a single erotic session.

"Murder will not interrupt our fun." Severn purred the reassurance as he took Sophie's earlobe between his teeth and bit down on it. His hands settled on the back of her thighs and slid upward to palm her bare buttocks.

"Severn," she said, but he knew it was a token protest because her fingers had found the first button of his shirt.

He squeezed her buttocks before releasing them to capture her wrists and prevent her from baring his flesh. All it would take would be the scrape of her fingernails over his back or chest and he'd be lost to the dragon need to take its mate repeatedly.

"Oh no, my heartmate," he whispered against Sophie's lips. "I have something else planned."

He turned them until they were facing the piece of equipment he knew would be found in a mirrored alcove. It was an elaborate sexual jungle gym where wrists and ankles could be secured and bodies held open for pleasure and display.

Severn chuckled at Sophie's gasp. Her eyes widened in shock even as she shook her head in denial. But her reaction didn't stop him from transferring her wrists to a single hand and ruthlessly shoving his freed hand under her skirt and between her thighs. He caressed the slick lips of her cunt before stroking her erect clit. She parted her legs without being told.

He rewarded her by circling her hard nub, by gliding along the underside and over the sensitive head. "Don't stop," she begged when his hand started to retreat.

He slipped two fingers inside her. He curled them and used his thumb so they wouldn't penetrate her as deeply as she wanted. Her cunt spasmed and she whimpered in protest as he fucked her with shallow, unfulfilling thrusts.

"You will allow me to place you on the equipment?"

Sophie shuddered and closed her eyes. She was burning up. She felt flushed and fevered from the inside out.

"Someone might come in," she said. Her cunt tightened around his fingers with the memory of being bare-breasted at the breakfast table when Xanthus arrived to speak to Severn.

"You are mine and I don't share. No one would dare look at your naked body or witness your pleasure. Both belong to me."

He leaned in and kissed her. "All of you belongs to me, Sophie. All of you." His thumb found her clit and stroked over its naked head. "You will allow me to place you on the equipment?"

"Will you let me come?" she whispered.

"I take care of what's mine. Always. Haven't I already demonstrated this today? Didn't I ease you in the kitchen before we left the estate?"

"Yes," she moaned as he touched her clit again.

She allowed him to lead her to the equipment, to place her on a tilted, padded back support that ended at her buttocks. She made only a slight murmur of protest when he secured her wrists above her, then secured her feet in stirrups that left her with her knees bent and her thighs splayed and also tethered.

Severn unfastened the buttons at the front of her blouse and unclasped her bra. He parted them both and freed her breasts before lifting her skirt to expose her bare cunt.

Sophie closed her eyes at the thoroughly wanton display captured in the mirror—her nipples tight, bruised from his earlier suckling, her vulva dark and parted to reveal her hungry slit.

"Open your eyes," Severn growled. "I don't think you want to experience your first true punishment at my hands while we are here."

Her clit pulsed in reaction. She knew he could see the way his words impacted her. How they aroused rather than scared her.

Sophie's eyes flew open when his hand delivered a stinging slap to her bare cunt.

He smoothed over the blow. His eyes darkened and his nostrils flared when she shivered as arousal slid from her channel and coated her back entrance.

"There is always a price for disobedience," he said.

She whimpered when his gaze followed the wet trail of her juices to the tight rosette of her anus.

"Consider yourself warned, my heartmate."

Severn leaned down and kissed her mound. He rubbed his tongue over her clit. "See yourself as I see you."

He sucked her lower lips into his mouth. He pressed his tongue into her slit. She strained against the restraints, bucked against them, begged him to ease her. But instead he retreated from her sheath and sucked her clit until she was moaning, jerking, desperately fucking it past his firmed lips.

Severn straightened from between her thighs. He cupped her breasts in his hands then tormented her nipples with his mouth and fingers until she was shaking.

Sophie cried out when Severn left her. Heat infused her when he stepped back so no part of her was hidden from the mirrored walls.

Her pebbled nipples glistened from where he'd suckled. Her swollen cunt wept with need. She was flushed, her chest heaving from lack of air. Her eyes were dark with lust and her lips parted.

"Is it any wonder I can't keep my hands off you?" Severn said. The possessive hunger in his voice fed her feminine pride. His hands went to her thighs, validating his admission that he couldn't keep himself from touching her. "You are beautiful, Sophie."

Severn burned with the need to mate but once again he'd allowed the lust to build to the point where the dragon ridges were raised and prominent, impossible to conceal, especially in the mirrored alcove. He leaned down and reclaimed his earlier position between Sophie's splayed thighs. He allowed his eyes to close as he pressed his mouth to her woman's folds.

He sucked and kissed, licked and fucked her with his tongue until she screamed her release and went lax. Only then did he straighten and look at her again.

Severn smiled at the way she reminded him of a satisfied dragon, a content beast sunbathing on a ledge, her body sprawled, her eyes closed as if dreaming of treasure.

She was a fitting mate. She was *his* mate.

He freed his cock and entered her. He purred with satisfaction when she moaned in welcome.

His moods were mercurial around her and now he found himself remembering their earlier conversation and feeling playful. "Are you ready to admit that I have taken you to paradise more than once, Sophie?"

Sophie wanted to wrap her arms and legs around him. She wanted to melt into Severn. "Let me loose and I'll tell you."

He settled more of his weight on her and she forced her eyelids opened.

"Tell me what I want to know, Sophie."

For a split second she thought about challenging him, saying, *Make me.* But as soon as she thought it she remembered how desperately he'd made her want him, how she'd reached the point where she wouldn't have been able to keep from orgasming among the crowd gathered for the VanDenbergh auction if he'd decided he wanted that from her.

"Tell me." This time he punctuated the command with a hard thrust.

"You know you have," she whispered. "It's never been like this for me before. I've never come so many times and so easily."

Her words were met with a low growl, with the taking of her mouth in a savage, breath-stealing kiss. His cock drove in and out of her. Its rhythm was matched by the thrust of his tongue and the exquisite nearly painful tugging and tweaking of her nipples.

Severn battled his dragon instincts. He battled the need to completely obliterate any memory of another male touching her.

He was lost in a red haze of possessive fury and passionate dominance. The need to imprint himself thoroughly on his mate consumed him to the point that for an instant the magic was stripped away just enough so his dragon form glittered in a transparent overlay. He breathed his dragon fire into her as the ridges around his penis became more pronounced and Sophie writhed in pleasure beneath him. Only when she climaxed again and became lax, boneless in her submission, did Severn allow himself to come and fill her with his seed.

He collapsed against her. His body was too weak to immediately lever himself away from the equipment though he did free her wrists and ankles and thighs from the restraints.

Happiness filled him, a contentedness that was soul deep. Sophie tormented him, challenged him, teased and amused him, but she also satisfied and pleased him in a way no other would ever be able to do.

Chapter Nine

ॐ

Sophie checked the bathroom mirror one more time. She'd done the best she could, but she still had the look of someone who'd been thoroughly and completely fucked.

She closed her eyes and held the heartmate stone as she tried to force the images of what had happened in the orgy room out of her mind. It was impossible. Not only was her body still humming with pleasure but her imagination was running riot.

She laughed softly. No surprise there.

Besides the detective stories, she *did* write fantasy after all. And not only was Severn a fantasy in his own right, but between the dragon motif throughout his home, the extremely erotic dragon-tongue-fucking-a-woman figurine set he'd said he would buy for her, and the dragon that raged across his chest—was it any wonder that at the height of passion, when she was feeling lightheaded from his kiss, she'd imagined *he* was a dragon? Well, not a flesh and blood dragon exactly. It'd been more like the image of a dragon was superimposed over him, but who could blame her for seeing things?

Maybe she'd share what she'd experienced with him—some other time and some other place, just in case he decided to try for a repeat performance. Her body tightened at the prospect. She wondered if he had a room somewhere in his estate with a sexual jungle gym in it, then forced the question out of her mind when it brought a touch of insecurity with it. "Get a grip here," she muttered. "He's got a past. I've got a past. Just because this is the stuff of fantasies doesn't mean it isn't real." Still, she held the heartmate stone against her palm for several long seconds before slipping it underneath her blouse and leaving the bathroom.

Severn's eyes narrowed and his nostrils grew pinched. Their combined scent reached him before Sophie did but the added smell of soap told him she'd done her best to wash away the evidence of sex.

A low growl escaped in a dragon's protest. Given a choice he would have coated her breasts and buttocks and cunt with his seed. He would have marked her clearly and insisted she remain that way while they were around so many other males.

Severn subdued the primitive part of himself. He reminded himself that in this realm different rules applied. His human mate vibrated with nervousness now, with uncertainty and touches of embarrassment.

He had asked much of her and she had yielded. Submitted. It was enough—for now.

"You are beautiful," he murmured, enfolding her in his arms and rubbing his cheek against hers as soon as she got close.

"I look like I've been thoroughly and repeatedly fucked."

"That too." He made no effort to keep the satisfaction from his voice.

He felt her smile before he heard it in her voice. "You really do see yourself as a dragon, don't you?"

Severn nibbled her earlobe. "Yes, my heartmate. I do."

Sophie's laugh had him pulling back so he could look into her face. He smiled when he saw her uncertainty and nervousness had disappeared.

"We should go look at the room where VanDenbergh was killed," she said. "It's probably almost time for the auction to start."

"We won't remain here much longer unless you desire it. While you were in the bathroom I made arrangements to purchase the figurine set for our bedroom. Perhaps tonight we will do our own reenactment of the dragon pleasuring his mate with the use of his tongue alone."

Sophie shuddered. "Stop," she whispered, immediately making a lie of her words when he pressed his tongue into her mouth and she welcomed the sinuous slide of it against her own.

Severn groaned and deepened the kiss. Blood rushed to fill his cock. He knew better than to tease her, to touch her intimately when he had other business that needed to be attended to.

As much as he'd enjoyed their play on the equipment, the next time he made love to her he wanted it to be in the privacy of their bedroom. He wanted it to last for hours, until they were both so exhausted neither of them could move. Reluctantly, he forced his mouth from hers and stepped back, though his hand slid down her arm and took possession of hers.

"We aren't going to stay for the auction?" Sophie asked.

"No. There are others here who will place my bids." He brought her hand to his mouth and kissed the back of it. "They know better than to fail me. They will not return to the estate without having secured your gift."

Sophie's gaze flew to his. Despite the casualness of his tone she could hear the utter confidence of a man who commanded a private empire.

A tremor of uneasiness rippled through her heart. She wondered what was true about him and what was speculation. She wondered if she really knew him at all.

"You don't have to buy me a gift, Severn," she said as she worried her bottom lip. She didn't want someone in trouble because they'd failed to acquire the figurines.

"It pleases me to do so." His lips curled and his eyes glittered with dark amusement. He leaned forward and nuzzled her neck, then gently nipped it. "Don't let your imagination make you afraid of me, Sophie. Of all those who populate this world, you are the only one who is completely safe from me." He chuckled. "Though perhaps I should punish you for the ways you have depicted me in your books."

Sophie jerked in reaction. "I never wrote a story about you."

He gave her another nip. "But you have used me as a model for more than one of your villains." He caressed the place he'd bitten with his tongue. "Admit it."

She shivered and pressed against him. She stroked the dragon tattoo hidden by his shirt. "And if I did? How much of it did I get right?"

He smiled against her skin. "Am I really as ruthless and possessive as you have penned me?"

Sophie pulled back so she could read his expression. "Yes."

He cupped her face and brushed his thumb over her lips. His smile faded into seriousness. "I live by a code that all I deal with understand. I have never meted out justice where it wasn't deserved, Sophie."

"I believe you," she said.

Sophie turned her head slightly to place a kiss on his palm. "I think maybe you'll serve as a perfect model for a dragon character."

He laughed. "I'll do my best to inspire you, my heartmate, and to ensure you get it right."

They stepped out of VanDenbergh's orgy room and into a hallway free of people. Sophie wriggled the hand Severn was still holding. "I can't get myself into the scene on the day of the murder while you're touching me."

"I'm glad you find my presence as distracting as I find yours." He let her pull free.

Sophie didn't really think they'd gain new information about the current whereabouts of the Dragon's Cup, but visiting the site helped her picture a story and *feel* it—even if it became fictionalized when she wrote about it.

"According to the police report, all the women agree VanDenbergh left this door closed when he went to get the chalice from his treasure room. They also agree that initially only one of them left when he didn't come back." Sophie grinned. "Storm labeled them Dumb, Dumb-squared, Dumb-cubed, all the way up to Dumb-to-the-sixth-power. She said they gave generously endowed women a bad name. D-cubed is the one who found the body."

"And you consider me heartless," Severn teased as they walked down the hallway and halted when they reached a corner containing tall potted plants with thick foliage.

Sophie grinned. "Storm's always been a little sensitive. She'd be richer than you if she had a dollar for every time a man's eyes locked on her chest instead of her face."

Severn chuckled and closed in on Sophie. He pulled her back to his front. His hands reached around to cup her breasts. "Should I risk mentioning how grateful I am that lushness appears to run in your family?"

Sophie closed her eyes. She should remind him she couldn't think when he was touching her, but at the moment having him massage her tight nipples seemed more important than re-creating a murder scene.

"You are a constant temptation," he whispered, the hard ridge of his penis serving as an exclamation point.

"What are you going to do about it?"

He explored her ear with his tongue. He fucked into the shallow canal and made her moan. "I could lift your skirt and take you against the wall."

She shivered and bit her lip to keep from telling him to do it.

One of his hands left her breast to travel downward over her belly, then lower, over her thigh. He stopped at the hem of her skirt.

"Admit you'd let me take you now," he said. "Tell me that if I lift your skirt I'll find you wet and ready for me."

She whimpered. She already knew where this particular game led.

"Yes," she whispered.

"Say the words, Sophie." His fingers stroked the skin beneath her skirt.

"I'm wet for you."

His hand slid upward and found the arousal on her inner thigh.

"I'd let you take me here. Now."

He nuzzled her neck. "If I did I wouldn't be able to stop until we were too spent to move. That's the only reason I'm letting you go."

Her body screamed in protest even as her mind sighed in relief when he set her aside.

They lingered for a moment near the plants. Both of them silent until Sophie said, "I don't understand why he didn't have cameras, at least in the hallways outside his treasure rooms." She glanced at Severn and wondered at her initial escape from his estate. There was the barest hint of a question when she added, "I assume you have them."

Severn nodded. His lips pulled upward as if he guessed the direction of her thoughts.

"You benefited from the confusion generated by my mother's unexpected arrival as well as from the fact that you are the only woman I've brought to the estate and taken to my bedroom. Those who owe their allegiance to me could only guess at your status." His nostrils flared. "Now they know your importance."

Sophie heard his implied warning—she wouldn't escape again. She decided against confronting him. The issue of staying at his estate while his mother and Audriss were there was far from settled in her mind but she had learned one

111

lesson thoroughly today. Severn would use her body against her if that's what it took to make his point or get his way.

A small smile played over her lips as she noticed he was once again holding her hand. She didn't intend to prove her theory at the moment but she suspected she could turn the tables on him. She believed she could get him to see *her* point of view with a few well-placed touches and kisses.

"What are you thinking?" he said, leaning in and rubbing the tip of her nose with his.

"How irresistible you are." Sophie grinned as she imagined Severn as a dragon, his chest puffing out with her compliment, his spine straightening.

The man growled and slid his tongue along the seam of her lips. "I suspect you're not telling the complete truth, my heartmate, but in the interest of time, I will not pursue the matter."

Sophie only barely managed to contain a snicker. His casual arrogance was going to be his undoing.

If she weren't afraid of some reporter sneaking around the corner and capturing Severn being brought to his knees—literally—with his cock in her hands or mouth, then she'd drive home a certain truth. Namely that Severn might *think* he controlled her, but it was only because she *let* him.

He growled again, most likely guessing the direction of her thoughts as he seemed able to do. She laughed out loud when he crowded her and nearly forced her into the potted trees.

"Enough of the dragon stuff," she said, not for the first time and probably not for the last.

Severn gave her a hard kiss. He relented only when she was boneless and clinging to him. "Shall we continue?" His voice purred with satisfaction.

"I assume you mean to the crime scene."

He chuckled and stepped back so she could escape the foliage that had tried to claim her. Sophie hesitated for a moment as the muse struck her. A scene unfolded in her imagination—one of the women leaving the orgy room to find out what was delaying VanDenbergh, hearing voices, maybe even a gunshot, and taking cover behind the heavily leaved potted trees at the corner.

Sophie glanced back to the room she and Severn had just left. Then forward to the room she guessed was the treasure vault where VanDenbergh was murdered.

What if one of the women saw someone leaving with the chalice? It would make an interesting twist to her story. What if the woman decided to blackmail the killer rather than tell the police what she had witnessed?

Sophie startled when Severn's knuckles brushed across her cheek. "What is it?" he asked, concern etched on his face.

She laughed and turned her head slightly to lick over his knuckles. "Nothing. Just something that comes with being an author. Sudden flights of unexpected fantasy."

His eyebrows lifted and amusement replaced the concern. "Should your fantasies become carnal, I had better be the only man who appears in them."

She nipped his knuckles though her smile widened. He was impossible to resist, especially when he teased. "Ready to see the treasure room?" she asked.

They moved out of the corner. Sophie shook her head as her hand remained clasped in his. She was probably going to have to learn how to work around the distracting effect he had on her since he seemed driven to touch her constantly.

When they stepped into the room where VanDenbergh had been killed, Sophie found it easy to picture the scene in her mind. It wasn't surprising. She'd looked at the photos Storm supplied repeatedly. A single bullet to the head and VanDenbergh's life had ended.

Since the night of the murder the room had been cleaned. And now, with the artifacts it contained up for auction, it had also been stripped of most of the display cases. Sophie looked around but felt nothing other than a kind of melancholy at how quickly life could not only end but how easily a life's work could be destroyed.

VanDenbergh had inherited the bulk of his money. He'd devoted most of his time to collecting art, antique automobiles and eventually relics from the past. Now his heirs were racing to dispose of everything—including the buildings that housed his material goods. As far as she'd been able to determine, VanDenbergh's possessions were the only thing marking his existence, their accumulation the only thing he'd accomplished during his lifetime.

She glanced at Severn and felt a tightness in her chest. She wondered what he truly wanted out of life. His reputation was one of ruthlessness and acquisition, but she had seen a softer side to him. She had to believe he wanted more than material possessions.

"Do you want children?" she asked, the question escaping before she could second guess whether or not she really wanted to ask it.

Severn's reaction was immediate. Intense. His attention shifted from a casual survey of the room to a complete focus on her. "Yes. And you will be their mother."

Heat burned in Sophie's womb. A tiny part of her, the modern feminist whispered, *Whoa*. But the woman who'd spent time in Severn's arms said, *Of course*.

Sophie took a deep breath. "Not right away."

Something flickered in his eyes. He leaned in and pressed a kiss to her forehead. "Not until we find the Dragon's Cup."

She didn't know whether to be reassured or worried. She decided to let the matter drop. "I've seen enough of this room."

They returned to the area cordoned off for those viewing the auction items. It took only a few minutes for Sophie to decide she should excuse herself and find a bathroom. She felt normal but the glances some of the men were giving her made her think she was still sporting an *I've been fucked look*—or worse—an *I'm available to be fucked* look.

She tried to extricate her hand from Severn's only to have him once again position her in front of him with her back to his chest. The fingers of one hand settled around her arm while the fingers of the other gripped her hip in a possessive display. The reason became instantly clear when two of the men she'd noticed staring at her walked over.

"Yours?" the first one of them to get within speaking distance asked Severn.

"In every sense," Severn said. His grip tightened. It kept Sophie quiet long enough for her to notice the red and green dragon embroidered on the man's tie. Irritation gave way to intrigue, especially when the second man arrived. The sleeves of his shirt were rolled up to reveal a green and gold dragon on one forearm.

"I'm envious," he said. His eyes roamed over her briefly but it was enough to have Severn's body stiffening aggressively. "Do you plan on introducing us?"

Sophie's curiosity was completely peaked. Her imagination was going wild in contemplation of writing a book entitled *Cult of the Dragon*.

"I'm Sophie," she said, extending her hand to the gorgeous blond with the flashing green eyes and rolled-up sleeves.

He grinned in response to Severn's low growl. "I am Hakon."

Sophie recognized the name immediately. "Oh, one of your relatives is playing poker with Pierce at Drake's Lair."

"So Severn has spoken of me. I'm surprised. Hopefully he said only good things." Hakon laughed. It was a low sensual sound that curled in places it shouldn't and had Sophie stiffening against Severn and trying not to wonder what Hakon looked like without the shirt…or the pants.

The hand on her hip moved to her belly. It burned through her blouse and trapped her in Severn's heat. The hard ridge of his cock against her buttocks served as a reminder and a warning.

"I am Malik," the more elegant of the two men said. His eyes were so dark the irises seemed black. He took her hand from Hakon's and brought it to his lips. Her skin was pale against his. "Perhaps Severn has mentioned me as well? The three of us have always been drawn to the same priceless and beautiful treasures. It is unfortunate Severn discovered you first." He smiled but the look in his eyes as he glanced at Severn was assessing.

Severn's hand left her belly and settled on her arm in a not-so-subtle demand for Malik to release her fingers. Malik laughed in response. It was a low rumble that affected her the same way Hakon's laugh had. He relinquished his grip and Sophie breathed a small sigh of relief when some of the tension left Severn.

"Your ancestors are still at Drake's Lair?" Severn asked.

Both Malik and Hakon nodded. Hakon's gaze flickered to Sophie then returned to Severn. His eyebrows rose. "And your mother? I heard she descended on your estate with Audriss in tow."

"My mother remains there for the moment. My men are monitoring Audriss. No doubt along with your own." There was a hint of amusement and camaraderie in Severn's voice.

Hakon shuddered. "Do you blame me? Even if we weren't all chasing the chalice I would know where Audriss is at all times in order to avoid drawing her attention again."

"Speaking of the chalice," Malik said, "Hakon and I came here in the hopes of discussing its ultimate disposition with you. The situation has changed now that our ancestors are on the scene."

Malik's gaze flickered to Sophie before returning to Severn. "I suspect it would not serve your interests to have the cup surface, only to come under your mother's control."

"True," Severn said. His fingers left Sophie's arm to tug the heartmate necklace free from where it was hidden from view.

Hakon gave a low whistle. Malik studied the stone for a long moment. "So it was not a boast. She does belong to you in every sense of the word."

"Yes." This time there was no mistaking the purr of complete satisfaction in Severn's voice.

Sophie's face heated and she started to pull away. She felt a sudden need to excuse herself and retreat to the bathroom to escape from Malik and Hakon's knowing eyes. The way their nostrils flared had her nearly cringing as she imagined a couple of huge dragons scenting the air and getting a very clear message about what she and Severn had been doing in VanDenbergh's orgy room.

Severn tightened his grip to prevent Sophie from escaping. Though he would never completely trust a dragon from another lair around Sophie, the moment he'd displayed the heartstone he'd realized it would serve as a deterrent. And though it galled him to admit it, it would probably be more effective than any threat he could issue to other males.

The elves were haughty and snobbish, but when it came to working the magic of the heartstone, they were incomparable. Malik and Hakon would realize the impossibility of claiming Sophie's love for their own.

"I am open to discussing matters with you before things get out of hand," Severn said as he retrieved his cell phone. "Do you wish to deal with this matter now?"

At Malik's nod, Severn called Xanthus. It took only a few sentences to arrange for others to watch Audriss while Xanthus came to collect Sophie.

ory Strong

Severn caught the gleam in both Hakon and Malik's eyes when he closed the phone and pocketed it. He knew they'd heard how carefully he'd worded his conversation—all so his human mate wouldn't realize that not only was Xanthus to take her wherever she wanted to go but he was to remain with her until Severn reclaimed her.

No doubt he'd serve as a target for their humor. It couldn't be avoided. Separating from Sophie was nearly intolerable, it would be impossible if he didn't know she was well guarded and easily retrieved.

Chapter Ten

ཀྵ

By habit and custom and unspoken accord most used Drake's Lair as a neutral meeting place. Technically it belonged to Severn's lair, but in the human realm, technicalities were often abandoned in favor of practicality. With Malik and Hakon's ancestors at Drake's Lair, Severn assumed they would find a quiet café in which to discuss the disposition of the chalice. It surprised him when they went to Malik's estate instead.

"Dragon's Flame?" Malik asked as he waved them to seats positioned around a small table in his office. When both Hakon and Severn nodded he reached for a crystal flask full of the fiery brew their kind preferred.

Malik filled the glasses and distributed them. As he took his seat he said, "Perhaps we should drink to Severn's good fortune and hope we are so lucky." He lifted his glass. "Congratulations on gaining a human mate, and an exquisitely beautiful one at that."

Severn touched his glasses to theirs. The heat in his cock equaled that of the Dragon's Flame. All it took was the mention of Sophie to fill him with satisfaction and desire. "May you be so lucky," he said before swallowing the potent drink.

He found humor in the realization that while Sophie fanned certain flames into an uncontrollable roar, she dampened other fires. His toast was no empty mouthing of words. He felt mellow enough to actually hope Malik and Hakon *did* find human mates.

There was a perfunctory knock on the door before it opened to reveal a human. The man carried a text so ancient he shuffled across the room as though he feared the jar of footsteps would cause the pages to crumble. Severn noticed the amused roll of Malik's eyes, but the other dragon said nothing until the book was placed reverently on the table between them.

"I'll spare you the history of this particular text and how I came by it," Malik said. "It will no doubt ease your minds to know I had Tristan Lisalli offer an opinion on its authenticity."

Hakon startled at the mention of the Sidhe lord. Severn offered a small nod in acknowledgement of Malik's coup. Tristan was an honorable man for whom knowledge held the same value as treasure did for a dragon—but now his opinion would also carry the weight of gold. How could it not? He was a husband to Sophie's cousin. "What opinion did Tristan offer?" Severn asked.

"He believes it is as old as it appears and is probably not too many generations removed from the original histories— though of course there is always the possibility exact meanings have been lost in translating from old languages to new ones, and from word of mouth to the written word. There is no way to verify the information, but he saw no reason why the passages of interest to us would have been altered by those preserving the stories."

Both Severn and Hakon leaned forward as the human twitched and hovered nervously over the old book. The text was written in Latin and many of the letters were faded. Even so, they recognized the wizard's name.

"Read for us," Malik instructed the human.

The book's guardian read.

Even though the wizard had been dead for centuries, Severn wanted to engulf the tome in fiery breath as he listened to the tale of how Enos had come to the aid of some ancient noble house and was proclaimed a hero. He was not alone in his irritation. The temperature in the room rose with Hakon and Malik's added heat.

The human was aware of the undercurrents swirling around him. He hunched over the table, practically lying on the book as if he felt the need to shield it with his body to protect it. Only when he got to the end of the passage where there was a mention of the wizard's daughter did the air cool and the anger recede.

Without being instructed the human carefully turned to where another passage had been marked. This one was a recounting of a gathering to celebrate a battle victory. He read only a small section where the wizard Enos and his daughter were noted to be in attendance then moved to a third marked passage in which a son-in-law had been added.

The human hesitantly straightened and stepped back when he finished reading. His eyes darted nervously between Severn and Hakon as the book was left unprotected on the table. When neither man made a move to lean forward and study the text, Malik nodded and the book was gently retrieved and removed from the room in a slow shuffle.

Malik reached for the flask of Dragon's Flame and replenished the glasses. "I have acquired other texts since that one, but unless you insist, I will summarize what I know and spare us all from the professor who serves as my librarian. He is, as you witnessed, somewhat nervous when the books are actually put to use."

Hakon shuddered and picked up his glass. "The next time I visit the dragon's realm, I'll make an offering to The Great Shared Ancestor for sparing me from dealing with those who dedicate their lives to books."

Severn hid his smile before taking a sip of Dragon's Flame. Apparently Hakon had yet to explore the human realm thoroughly enough to gain an appreciation of the wide range of reading material the mortals created. Severn freely admitted that some of the scenes in Sophie's books had invaded his dreams and filled his cock with blood, even as others, the ones where he saw himself in the villain, had left him vacillating between anger and amusement.

Now, of course, amusement would prevail and he would enjoy correcting Sophie's errors of perception. In fact, he would relish the role of model for the heroes in her books. And she would feel the heat of dragon fire if he thought for a moment any other male ventured into her fantasies as inspiration.

His cock pulsed and burned. His chest tightened at being separated from his mate.

Severn glanced at his watch and contemplated calling Xanthus to find out what Sophie was doing. The amused chuckles of the two males in the room kept him from reaching for his cell phone.

"After witnessing the effect Severn's human mate seems to have on him," Hakon said, "perhaps I will not be so quick to fall under a female's spell. What about you Malik?"

"It is a sight to behold." Malik picked up his glass and took a sip. "Most of us who prefer this realm and are unmated fantasize about finding a human female who will be submissive and content with what we have to offer her. But from the looks of our friend here, it would seem that what he has found between his woman's thighs has left him little room or will to concentrate on other matters." Malik grinned. "He does seem happy though. And perhaps it is too soon to tell who will rule his household."

"With the specter of his mother and Audriss hanging over him, my gold is on Severn," Hakon said, raising his glass. "May he control his estate and his mate with equal success."

Malik touched his glass to Hakon's. "To Severn, may his mate keep him busy in bed while the rest of us are out hunting treasure."

Severn tipped his glass into theirs and laughed at their rough jibes. Mated less than forty-eight hours and Sophie had already tamed some of the competitive fire that burned in him.

Hakon finished his drink and waved off a refilling of his glass. "So what's the significance of the wizard's daughter and son-in-law? None of our stories mention him having children, but what does it matter?"

Malik leaned forward. "I believe the spell could be undone completely if we have the chalice in our possession as well as someone of the wizard's line. For the last year I have searched genealogy records. I am close to having a name. Then it will be only a matter of locating the person. What I fear is that the chalice will be taken by one of our ancestors, or worse, fall into the hands of the fey court again. If either of those things happens then we will lose the opportunity to be free forever from the spell tying our fertility to the Dragon's Cup."

"You're sure the wizard's spell can be undone?" Severn asked. "Have you spoken to Tristan about it?"

"He agreed to take the matter up with some of his university colleagues who are familiar with the realms outside of the mortal one. There was enough of an agreement among them to give me reason to think we could undo the spell," Malik said. "But it must be done in this realm because this is where the chalice was fashioned in the first place."

Hakon sat back in his chair. "What do you suggest? None of us is free of obligation with respect to our ancestors."

"I suggest the three of us join forces and swear an oath that we will work together and keep the chalice in a neutral place when it is located. Those who wish to drink from it will be allowed to do so, without discrimination or price, until we are ready to attempt the magic necessary to break the spell. Once the cup is secured then our ancestors will have no choice but to accept what we've done. They cannot order us to foreswear ourselves, nor would they have a chance of wresting it away from us in a realm where we have human technology to aid us and our own resources to ensure the chalice remains in our possession." Malik settled in his chair with a smile of satisfaction.

Severn took a sip of Dragon's Flame. He savored its burn as he contemplated Malik's daring proposition. Sharing a treasure, especially one like the cup, went against every instinct. A dragon's nature was to hoard and guard its treasure, to keep it for its own pleasure and use.

Until he met Sophie, Severn had given little thought to what he would do with the chalice beyond securing it in his home. Even after gaining a mate, he hadn't gotten past the vision of enticing Sophie to drink from it with him, then tumbling her to the bed and keeping her there until she became pregnant.

Severn shifted in his chair to ease the pressure on his cock and balls. He took another sip of Dragon's Flame in an effort to distract himself from the ache of a heavy erection trapped against unyielding material instead of inside Sophie's slick cunt. "What neutral place did you have in mind for the chalice?"

Malik grinned. "Drake's Lair. It might belong in part to someone of your lair, but it has served as a gathering place for us all from the very start."

Hakon laughed. "Knowing Pierce and Tielo, they'll convert whatever space they can into bedrooms and find any number of reasons to parade human women through the club."

"Given Pierce's Sidhe glamour," Malik said, "that shouldn't be too difficult."

Severn chuckled. "You forget that Drake's Lair is constantly under surveillance by one branch of human law enforcement or another. No doubt if a steady stream of women were seen to come and go, the club would be raided yet again, this time for suspicion of prostitution instead of the usual charge of gambling."

"The idea does have merit though," Malik said.

Severn wasn't sure whether Malik was arguing for keeping the cup at Drake's Lair or for inviting human females to the club in the hopes they would become dragon mates. Either way, he was anxious to get back to Sophie.

"I will swear an oath of cooperation. I will agree to keeping the Dragon's Cup in a place where all can benefit from it until such time as the spell can be broken," Severn said, finding it surprisingly easy to accept Malik's proposal.

"As will I," Hakon said, "though I would modify our agreement so only males have the right to access the chalice."

Malik steepled his fingers in front of him. "Your point is well taken. Perhaps a change can be wrought by doing as you suggest. The females have always been fierce but if our historians are to be believed, they became more dominant and power-hungry after the creation of the chalice." He glanced at Severn. "Do you accept Hakon's suggestion?"

"Yes."

Malik rose from his chair and moved to his desk. "Having anticipated we could reach an agreement, I took the liberty of drawing up a simple document. We can easily modify it to make the chalice accessible to all males instead of to all members of our race." He returned with three copies of the agreement, each written on traditional parchment. He also carried a small sharp dagger in which to seal their alliance in blood.

* * * * *

Sophie sighed in utter contentment when she walked into Inner Magick. Even before she'd met Aislinn and they'd become friends, she'd always loved coming to the shop.

"You look like you're getting along well with Severn," Aislinn said as she came around the counter and gave Sophie a hug.

"You mean I look like I've been well and truly fucked."

Aislinn laughed. "That too. Now come see the rune sets Marika's friend crafted. I just got finished putting them in the case."

Sophie grimaced. "I'm sorry about not getting that done after I promised to do it. But when Severn came into the shop..."

Aislinn grinned. "At best I thought you might actually get them unpacked. I knew they'd never make it to the display case because it would take you most of the evening to decide which ones you could live without."

"I was about ready to start agonizing over the fourth set when Severn walked in," Sophie admitted as she followed Aislinn to the display.

Out of the corner of her eye she saw Xanthus lean against the counter near Aislinn's assistant Marika. Sophie hadn't been surprised when he came into Inner Magick with her. From the very start the heat between Marika and Xanthus had been unmistakable—though for some reason Marika was looking everywhere but at Xanthus today.

"What do you think?" Aislinn asked.

"I'm wondering if they had a fight."

Aislinn's laugh brought Sophie's attention back to the display. Thoughts of Xanthus and Marika faded.

"I want them all," Sophie said on a sigh.

Aislinn snickered. "You and Severn are well matched. I wasn't sure whether you'd put the three sets aside for yourself or not so I mixed them among these to see how much of an impression they'd made on you. I remembered thinking the last time I was at your apartment that it was probably a good thing you'd begun limiting yourself in what you collected."

"Oh, that's evil, especially when you consider how many of the things I've carried home came from *your* shop."

"You do have a point," Aislinn admitted with mischief dancing in her eyes. "Of course, little did I know that you'd eventually fill your apartment to the point where I'd have to offer you a place to sleep above Inner Magick."

Sophie grinned. "You know that's only because I've got the battle of the evil neighbors going on at my apartment complex. Speaking of which, since I'm here, I'm going to force myself away from this display case and pop up to the apartment so I can take a quick shower and change clothes. You want to grab a frappachino and take a walk on the beach? Or do you have to stay here?"

"Marika has already been to Starbucks and I've finished putting the new items out on display, so I'm free to go." Aislinn glanced over at her assistant and shook her head slightly. "If we leave them to themselves they might resolve whatever they're fighting about."

Sophie laughed softly. "Yeah, I noticed how quickly you ducked out of your kitchen and left me alone with Severn. I couldn't believe it when all of a sudden you had to take a broken coffee mug to the *outside* trashcan."

"It worked out for the best and I suspect you didn't mind being left to his mercy."

"You have no idea." Sophie snickered and cut a look at Aislinn then amended her statement. "I take that back. Trace gives off the same kind of uber-possessive, uber-dominant vibes whenever the two of you are together. If you show up at my apartment and he comes looking for you, I think I'll suddenly have to be elsewhere too." She glanced at the beaded curtain separating the customer area from the back room and the inside stairway that led to the apartment. "Speaking of elsewhere, I'll hit the shower and then we can head out."

By the time Sophie got to the inside staircase leading to the apartment Xanthus was in the back room with her. "Wait," he said.

Sophie stopped with a foot on the first stair. She expected Xanthus to say something to the effect that he had to leave but Severn would pick her up when he'd finished meeting with Hakon and Malik. Instead he said, "Let me go up first to make sure it's empty."

A hit of adrenaline struck Sophie. "Why wouldn't it be empty?" For a wild instant she had a vision of Severn's mother or the nasty Audriss lying in wait for her.

Xanthus smile was easy and relaxed. "There's no reason to expect someone is up there but it's my job to check anyway."

Sophie frowned as a sudden suspicion formed. She'd *known* Xanthus picked her up at the VanDenbergh estate and brought her to Inner Magick because he worked for Severn and Severn asked him to. She'd *assumed* Xanthus stayed at the shop because of Marika. But now she had a bad feeling her assumption had done what many of them did—it had turned around to bite her on the ass. "Are you guarding me?"

He'd been Aislinn's bodyguard for a time recently when Trace was involved in a high-profile murder case. That's how he'd met Marika in the first place.

Xanthus' blink of surprise gave him away. Then he actually chuckled and shook his head slightly. "Severn didn't tell you?"

"So you *are* guarding me?" Sophie wanted the confession nailed down. At the moment she wasn't sure whether to be flattered, frustrated—or quite possibly, angry.

When she'd agreed to stay with Severn while they hunted for the chalice, her one condition had been that she could come and go as she pleased. As soon as the words left her mouth, she'd known he didn't like the condition. But he'd agreed. For Sophie, *come and go as I please* was naturally connected to *in total freedom.* She was starting to suspect Severn's interpretation was different from her own. "Well?"

Xanthus shrugged. "Severn is a powerful man and you are his mate. He'd be a fool to leave you unprotected." Something like amusement flickered in his eyes. "I believe you have researched him thoroughly enough to know that no one considers him a fool."

Sophie groaned in defeat. Was it obvious to everyone that some of the villains in her novels were based on the mysterious and reclusive man who lived behind dragon-emblazoned gates? Or was Xanthus simply using knowledge he'd gained from Marika or Aislinn or even Storm?

Sophie capitulated and let him go into the apartment first. Within minutes he'd ensured it was free of danger and the door leading to the external stairs was securely locked.

"Don't leave except through the store," Xanthus warned. He waited for a nod indicating her acceptance of his terms before he left the apartment.

Sophie stripped and stepped into the shower. She'd hoped the hot water would calm her emotions and ease some of the panic starting to churn in her chest.

When she was with Severn, everything seemed so right. She felt powerful and weak at the same time. She felt utterly feminine and completely desired.

It was too early to call what they had love, but she felt adored, cherished, and she didn't doubt it would deepen into something to last a lifetime. She believed he was her heartmate and they were meant to be together.

But at the same time a spike of fear stabbed through her and the nightmare from her childhood threatened to encroach on her present. Intellectually Sophie knew there was a difference between a wealthy man protecting his lover and an obsessed man who was willing to kill the object of his affection rather than let her disappear from his life. Intellectually she knew it, but faced with the unexpected revelation that she had suddenly lost the very freedom she'd used as a tool for ridding herself of fear, she felt shaky, uncertain, like a giant mental stop sign had been placed in front of her.

When she actually visualized Severn standing on the other side of a big red stop sign some of Sophie's natural humor reasserted itself. The red faded to yellow and *stop* transformed to *yield*. Her cunt clenched and she shivered just thinking of how fond he was of making her yield and how much she enjoyed doing it.

The modern, *I've fought my way out of hell and made a place for myself,* part of her was appalled by how much she liked knowing Severn would take care of her and protect her. But it *did* make her feel safe to know that on every level he believed she belonged to him.

There it was and she wasn't going to lie to herself about it. She'd longed for what Aislinn had with Trace and now she had the same thing—with a few complications.

Sophie got out of the shower and toweled off. She'd tossed the blouse and skirt she'd been wearing in the dirty clothes hamper without thinking about it. Now she opened the hamper and looked inside. Severn's earlier warning about changing her clothes made a shiver of erotic fear flow along her spine. But there was no way she was going to fish the clothing out and put it back on.

Blood pooled in her labia. Her gaze moved to her bare cunt. Her hand followed.

"He's made me constantly horny," she joked even as she ran her fingers over the smooth skin. A moan escaped when she grazed the tiny erect clit and stroked her fingers through the arousal seeping from her slit.

She wanted his mouth on her. She wanted him to tie her down again like he'd done at VanDenbergh's estate. She wanted him to bury his face between her thighs. She wanted… With a groan Sophie forced her fingers away from her mound and her thoughts away from Severn.

What she wanted was to get her life and herself under control and go back to researching and looking for the Dragon's Cup. That's what she wanted *and* needed to do. But when she glanced into the bathroom mirror, the image she found there mocked her. The tight nipples and swollen cunt, the erect clit and glistening slit all belonged to a woman who looked like she needed to find her man because she wanted to fuck.

Sophie escaped to the bedroom. She chose a light green tank top with a built-in bra. Erotic fear shimmered through her once again when she slipped on barely there panties that matched.

She bit her lip and closed her eyes for an instant. She was practically begging for the punishment Severn had threatened her with. It hadn't started out as intentional, at least not in her conscious thoughts, but now she was starting to wonder…

Sophie shook her head to clear her mind. *Think Dragon's Cup*, she reminded herself as she pulled on a pair of shorts and found her sandals. Aislinn was waiting and a walk on the beach would serve as therapy as well as a chance to contemplate what might have happened the day VanDenbergh was murdered and the chalice stolen.

The back room was empty when Sophie got to the bottom of the stairs. Xanthus' absence actually made her feel a lot better about having him assigned to her. It made her feel like someone to be protected rather than a prisoner to be guarded.

She walked into the shop. Goose bumps rose on Sophie's skin. It was colder than usual, like someone had opened the door and let a blast of Arctic winter inside.

Xanthus was leaning in his usual spot near the cash register but there was nothing casual in his pose. His focus was on Aislinn and a customer she was talking to—not on Marika the way it usually was. He glanced at Sophie and frowned slightly. She had the distinct impression he wanted her to return to the back room.

A suspicion formed. A longer glance at the woman with Aislinn and Sophie was pretty sure she was looking at one of Severn's former lovers. She shrugged off an attack of insecurity with a mental reminder that she and Severn both had pasts but those pasts didn't matter now.

Sophie joined Marika behind the counter. As soon as she did the goose bumps crawled from her arms to her back. She shivered and contemplated waiting for Aislinn outside where the sun would warm her. But before the idea of leaving the store could settle, her stomach tensed. She didn't want to force Xanthus to choose between guarding her and guarding Aislinn.

Sophie's eyebrows drew together at the thought. It'd be easy to blow it off and say her imagination was running away with her even more than usual, but she didn't. Instinct had saved her life when she was a kid. She trusted it—especially when it warned her about people and situations that should be feared.

For the first time Sophie noticed Aislinn's body language. It was wary instead of welcoming.

She shifted her attention to the woman she'd assumed was a customer. The woman turned slightly. Their eyes met. Sophie felt as though her lungs were suddenly frozen. A small smile formed on the woman's lips but her features remained glacial. In a heartbeat Sophie knew Severn would never have been attracted to this woman. He was a creature of fire and this woman was ice cold.

Chapter Eleven

ဢ

Xanthus shifted position, effectively blocking Sophie's view of the woman, though more likely his intention was to block the woman's view of Sophie. Either way, Sophie was content to have his well-muscled body between the two of them until the bells above the front door gave a soft tinkling sound as the woman left.

"Who was that?" Sophie asked as she moved around the counter so she could see Aislinn.

Instead of answering her directly, Aislinn looked at Xanthus. "She called herself Neryssa. Do you know of her?"

Xanthus gave a small shake of his head. "I haven't seen her before but I'll speak to Severn about her and tell him she came here." He hesitated slightly then glanced briefly at Sophie before adding, "Tristan and Pierce could tell you who she is. It would probably be wise to speak with them."

"Why did she come to Inner Magick?" Sophie asked with a frown. There were undercurrents between Xanthus and Aislinn she didn't understand, but she decided to tackle them when she and Aislinn were alone.

"Neryssa said she was curious about what she'd find here," Aislinn said.

Sophie rubbed her arms and realized the goose bumps were gone. She wasn't cold anymore. "Weird," she mumbled.

Xanthus snorted. "Deadly is a better word. Her kind might be beautiful to look upon, but their glamour masks their poison."

"Her kind?" Sophie asked.

Xanthus shrugged. "You and Aislinn are going to the beach?"

"By way of Starbucks," Aislinn said, looping her arm through Sophie's. "Do you want to drive to your favorite spot or walk to the beach from here?"

Sophie felt the warmth of the heartstone hidden under her tank top. Aislinn had presented it to her at her favorite stretch of beach, but going there would entail driving and Sophie suspected that would mean Xanthus in the car with them.

"We can walk," she said, wanting to talk to Aislinn privately but not sure how much time they had before Severn was finished with his meeting.

Xanthus moved to the front door and opened it. He followed a short distance behind them as they made their way to the coffee shop and to the beach. Sophie glanced back at him. He was probably far enough away he couldn't hear their conversation but she was finding it hard to ignore his presence. "I'm not sure I'm going to be able to stand this."

Aislinn wrinkled her nose. "You'll get used to it, Sophie, and no doubt there'll be times when you find it useful to have help close by." She took Sophie's hand and gave it a quick squeeze before releasing it. "I'd worry for you if you weren't under Severn's protection." She shook her head. "If only the VanDenbergh family hadn't leaked the theft of the chalice to the press...but then they had no way of knowing how desperate some would be to get their hands on it."

"Like Hakon and Malik?"

Aislinn's eyebrows lifted in surprise. "How do you know them?"

"They were at VanDenbergh's estate."

"You were there too?"

"Severn and I both were. The family is holding an auction today."

"So you visited the orgy room Storm told us about? Is that why you looked like you'd been well and truly fucked?"

Sophie felt heat creep up her neck and then deepen. "I'm taking the Fifth."

Aislinn snickered. "It's probably just as well. I'll assume the answer to both my questions is yes and I'll carry on with my questioning of the witness. Did you learn anything new while you were at the VanDenbergh estate?"

Sophie grinned. "I can tell you're married to a cop now. You used to hate it when I'd make you watch *CSI* and *Law & Order: Criminal Intent* and you've always told me to write more fantasy stories and fewer crime stories. Now you're curious about what I learned at the scene of a murder."

"Guilty as charged. But in my defense I have a feeling this story might turn out to be more about fantasy and less about crime."

Sophie's thoughts flashed immediately to the alcove with its sexual jungle gym and mirrors—oh yeah, definitely fantasy. But she answered, "I can't say I actually learned anything new, except that Malik and Hakon wanted to meet with Severn and reach some agreement about the chalice."

She frowned as she remembered how important it seemed to each of the men, especially now that they had ancestors in town who were searching for the chalice too. The memory coupled with the dragon tattoo on Hakon's forearm and the embroidered dragon on Malik's tie made her feel suddenly uneasy. She'd joked to herself about one day writing a book entitled *Cult of the Dragon*, but at the moment she couldn't help but think of the tongs whose members sported elaborate tattoos. "Do you think Severn's involved in organized crime?"

"No." Aislinn motioned toward an unoccupied bench on the boardwalk and they claimed it. "Did he say something to make you think he is? Or are you thinking of the rumors you collected when you were researching him?"

Sophie tugged the heartmate necklace out and wrapped her hand around the stone. "When I'm with him I'm so sure about everything. But when I'm away from him the doubts start creeping in." She tilted her head toward Xanthus who'd taken up a position a short distance away. "Take him for example. I agreed to stay with Severn as long as I could come and go as I please. He agreed even though I could tell he didn't want to. And now here I am with a bodyguard. I know, technically I can still come and go as I please, but this isn't what I meant. What I meant was that I could come and go without Severn knowing where I was and what I was doing every second." She sighed in frustration. "That sounds pathetic, doesn't it? A million women would happily change places with me, and the truth is, I would die if suddenly I wasn't his heartmate."

Aislinn leaned over and touched her fingers to the hand Sophie had wrapped around the heartmate stone. "You believe in the magic, Sophie, but you're still human. It's natural to have doubts." A teasing smile played over her lips. "And besides, I don't think even a heartmate could be expected to tame a dragon like Severn in only a couple of days."

Sophie laughed and felt her earlier worry and panic flow away. Aislinn always had that effect on her. "Dragon is right. I'm going to stop modeling my villains after Severn's mysterious persona. From now on I'm going to use what I actually know about him when I write my fantasies. And before you say anything, I'm not talking erotic fantasies. I'm talking mythical beasts, wizards and dragons."

Aislinn laughed. "He's a worthy role model."

"You don't know the half of it." Sophie slipped the necklace back under her top and grimaced. "You also may be seeing a lot of us. My neighbors haven't been evicted yet and Severn's mother is at his estate. You could say we've taken an extreme dislike to each other. She's got her own idea of who Severn should end up with." Sophie shuddered. "Audriss could *definitely* serve as a role model for one of my villains."

"You know the apartment is yours for as long as you need it."

They settled into a companionable silence. Sophie glanced at Xanthus and found him in a casual pose, alert but not focused on anything in particular. He was gorgeous with his long mane of blond hair and dark, dark eyes, and though she hadn't seen it for herself, or given it much thought when Marika had mentioned it, she knew he also had a dragon tattoo.

She wondered again about the tension between him and Marika. She couldn't help it. Curiosity fueled her imagination. Without it she didn't think she would be an author. Not that she could turn it off either.

Her thoughts veered to Severn and his meeting with Hakon and Malik. Given that Hakon and Malik also sported dragon images and apparently collected valuable artifacts, it made sense they'd be after the chalice too. But why were they so worried about one of their ancestors getting the Dragon's Cup before they did?

Even before actually meeting Severn, Sophie had assumed he wanted the cup because it was both extremely beautiful and extremely valuable. Not only was it gold with jewels embedded in it, but there were scenes etched into it, most of which contained dragons.

Despite the worry that had crept in earlier about Severn being involved in organized crime, in her gut, Sophie didn't believe it. She couldn't believe it. But she also wasn't going to deny the evidence when it came to the tattoos. She knew for sure Severn, Hakon and Xanthus each had one. She'd bet money Malik also had a dragon tattoo.

It was no coincidence. So maybe her private joke about writing *Cult of the Dragon* wasn't just her sense of humor kicking in, but was the same intuition and insight she used when she was creating mystery stories.

She'd first gotten interested in the chalice when Storm landed the VanDenbergh murder as her first homicide case. It wasn't only that the artifact was insured for five million and still missing that had attracted Sophie's attention and fired her imagination. It was the fact VanDenbergh had actually believed drinking from a cup said to have been created to induce orgies would have a Viagra-type effect on him. The six women waiting for him in his orgy room were a testament to how thoroughly he believed in the magic of the cup.

Sex and murder were great bedfellows when it came to writing a story. Then add a second legend over the first—namely that the Chalice of Eros was really the Chalice of Enos and had been created by a wizard who used it to bring the dragons to their knees—and it got even better.

Sophie's mind hummed with possibilities. She wondered if Severn would tell her about the dragon societies, because that's what he had to be a member of. That's what they all had to be members of. Secret societies though she couldn't imagine what they were after except maybe who could collect the most dragon artwork.

It was probably something they were all born into. That would explain why Severn and Hakon and Malik had been more like friendly adversaries instead of deadly rivals. It would also explain how Hakon and Malik's ancestors could be playing poker together at Drake's Lair even though Severn's cousin co-owned it with Storm's husband Pierce.

So instead of secret societies maybe they were organized along family lines, which fell in with the talk of ancestors and her earlier thought about tongs. Sophie grinned. Maybe they even referred to themselves as being members of a certain *lair*.

The buzz in her veins told her she was on the right track. It explained so much, including why Severn's family had been after the Dragon's Cup for hundreds of years. Maybe the cup was kind of like the Holy Grail, the supreme prize in their competition.

Why they all stayed with it and seemed to take it seriously was a bit beyond her at the moment, but still... She frowned as she suddenly remembered the conversation she'd had with Severn as they were leaving the room where the chalice had been stolen.

Do you want children?

Yes. And you will be their mother.

Not right away.

Not until we find the Dragon's Cup.

A tendril of uneasiness began threading its way through Sophie's excitement at having unraveled the mystery of the dragon tattoos. She'd been happy to let the subject of children drop. She'd ultimately translated "not until we find the Dragon's Cup" to "after we've gotten to know each other better and had plenty of time to ourselves." But Xanthus' presence proved it was a mistake to make those kinds of assumptions when it came to Severn.

He couldn't mean it literally, could he? He couldn't believe the cup was important when it came to having children in the same way VanDenbergh had thought it would give him a hard-on that would allow him to satisfy six women all by himself.

Sophie grimaced. As much as she hated to think of Severn's mother, he had one and obviously she hadn't had a sip from the cup since it went missing hundreds of years ago.

But it would explain why all three men wanted to keep the chalice from falling into their ancestors' hands. What if they actually believed that if their ancestors possessed the cup, then the only way they could father children was by pairing up with the women their relatives chose for them? That'd certainly explain the specter of Audriss and why both she and Severn's mother appeared confident that in the end he'd see the advantages of an alliance.

Sophie wanted to ignore the voice in her head. Maybe having the chalice fall into their ancestors' hands meant *game over*. Grown men, even if they had been indoctrinated since birth, couldn't really believe drinking from a centuries-old cup would have any impact at all on either getting a woman pregnant or on what the children would turn out to be like. Could they?

Sophie shook her head to clear it. She knew her imagination had gone too far when suddenly she was wondering if Severn and the others thought that by drinking from the cup, their children would actually be able to *turn into* dragons.

"I think I've got the beginnings of a new fantasy story," she mumbled, more to herself than to Aislinn though Aislinn picked up on it.

"Want to share? Or are you going to torture me as usual by making me wait until it's completely done?"

"You can't be my test reader if you already know what the story is about."

"What about a hint?"

Sophie laughed. "How about a question? Then you can wonder whether it has anything to do with the fantasy story that seems to be percolating in my subconscious despite the fact I've been planning on writing a mystery."

"What's the question?"

Sophie turned to Aislinn and mentally kicked herself. Why hadn't she thought of asking Aislinn this earlier? Aislinn so often seemed otherworldly and magical herself. It's why Sophie had been drawn to her in the first place, though now they were true friends. And the things Sophie had seen Aislinn do…

"Do you believe the Chalice of Enos is something more than a valuable artifact?" Sophie asked.

"Yes." Aislinn reached out and touched the back of Sophie's hand. "But if you want to know what it means to Severn then you'll have to talk to him about it. It's not my place to tell his secrets."

Sophie's mind pounced on the implication that Aislinn knew what the significance of the cup was even though she'd only just met Severn. A cascade of additional questions flowed through Sophie but respect for Aislinn kept her from pushing when she knew Aislinn didn't want to say more. She remembered her intention to question Aislinn further about the woman who'd come to Inner Magick and asked, "Why would Pierce and Tristan know Neryssa?"

Aislinn laughed as though she was expecting the question, but she answered by asking, "What have you guessed about Severn, Malik, Hakon and Xanthus?"

Sophie told her what she'd guessed about "dragon" families chasing treasure and competing against each other.

"You're close to the truth," Aislinn said. "The dragon lairs, as you've come to think of them, have been after the chalice for a long time. They form alliances and battle against each other. But for the most part they respect one another and play by rules they are all aware of. Unfortunately, they aren't the only ones trying to recover the Dragon's Cup. Between the dragons and the others, the competition is deadly serious."

Sophie frowned. "Are you telling me Pierce and Tristan's family is also after the chalice, and that Neryssa is related to them?"

"Probably only distantly, if that. Even so, if Pierce and Tristan involve themselves at all in this, they will side with the dragon lairs because the cup rightfully belongs to dragons."

Sophie laughed. "This is going to make a great story, isn't it? Dragons, a magic cup created by a wizard." She grinned as she remembered the figurine set Pierce and Tristan were buying Storm. "And faeries. I think we'll throw in a couple of those too. What do you think?"

Aislinn's eyes sparkled with suppressed mirth. "Definitely more of a fantasy story than a crime story."

They rose from the bench and began walking in the direction of Inner Magick. Sophie's thoughts went to the rune sets waiting for her and the difficulty of trying to pick out only one, or two, or three, or maybe as many as four sets to take with her. But her attention didn't stay on that mental task for long. She'd been unpacking the runes when Severn came to the shop looking for Aislinn. It hadn't occurred to her to ask why at the time. But now that she'd been in his home and seen his collection ran to both ancient and priceless, she had to wonder.

Inner Magick catered to tourists and locals alike. Nothing sold there was in the same league as even the cheapest items being auctioned off at the VanDenbergh estate. Sophie's hand lifted and her fingers curled around the hidden heartmate necklace. Even the pieces Aislinn created were only priceless to the people who owned them.

"Why do you think Severn was coming to see you? As much as I'd love to believe it was fate and the necklace leading him to me, it doesn't seem very likely. It seems a lot more likely he thought you'd be able to help him find the chalice."

Aislinn's footsteps slowed until finally she stopped and leaned against the railing separating the boardwalk from the drop to the beach. Sophie mimicked the pose.

"My only true talent is with stones and even then only the least precious of them, and only in this...place," Aislinn said.

Sophie wondered at the hesitation but she also heard the pain in Aislinn's voice. She knew it had to do with Aislinn's mother and her mother's family, though Aislinn rarely mentioned either—or their rejection of her.

"That's not true," Sophie said, fiercely proud and royally pissed off on behalf of her friend. "You've found missing people before. You've helped the police solve more than one murder case. You've saved lives with your abilities and your contacts."

She put her arm around Aislinn's shoulder and gave her a quick hug. "Forget I asked. I didn't mean to make you sad. Severn will probably come to the shop to get me. If I'm not completely lost in the task of picking out rune sets, I'll ask him why he was looking for you." She shrugged. "Whatever it was, it must not have been too serious. He didn't say anything when he was at your house yesterday."

Aislinn laughed. "No, he was completely focused on you."

"Well, when you've got it, you've got it. What can I say?"

They eased into another comfortable silence.

Sophie let her mind go quiet. She loved the beach and couldn't imagine not living near it, though she wasn't as crazy about actually going into the water.

There was something about sand and surf and the timeless noise of the ocean that soothed her like nothing else could. Some of her favorite stories had been created while she walked along the beach.

Heat curled in her belly as she imagined walking hand-in-hand with Severn as the sun set. It was hopelessly romantic but she knew he'd be more than willing to indulge her.

The warmth moved into her breasts as she imagined spreading a blanket on the sand and making love. A grin formed. Hell, she might as well add a bottle of wine and something to eat to her fantasy.

In fact, maybe she should turn it into a reality. She could take Severn to her favorite spot, which also happened to be the very spot where Aislinn had given her the heartmate necklace. They could celebrate finding each other by —

Sophie startled at the sound of Aislinn's voice. Her cheeks reddened. She'd been so lost in her thoughts she'd actually forgotten where she was.

"When I went to live with my mother, there was a woman, a very distant relative who also had an affinity for stone," Aislinn said. "She was like a...I think they're called witchers here, only instead of finding water, she'd walk over the land with a staff and locate a certain type of stone."

Sophie was immediately captivated by the imagery. "And you think a staff like that might help find the Dragon's Cup since it's got jewels along the rim?"

Aislinn's eyebrows drew together in concentration. "She was ancient and found it hard to get around. I'm not sure it was the staff itself that was important but the symbols carved onto it and the crystal set at the top of it."

Sophie felt like every nerve in her body was vibrating. "Is there a way for you to see the staff? Can you duplicate the symbols on it? Can you find a crystal that would resonate with the stones on the Dragon's Cup?"

A sudden thought made Sophie's hopes plummet. "How would you know if you had the right combination of symbols and crystal? Without having the chalice in the first place, you can't do a test."

Rather than look defeated or overwhelmed by the barrage of questions or the doubt Sophie had expressed, Aislinn's face grew more thoughtful. "Give me some time to think about this. I may be able to come up with a way to help you find the chalice."

Chapter Twelve

ഗ

Sophie was relieved Xanthus didn't insist on following her into the police station—not that it mattered. As soon as she stepped into the homicide bullpen, her cousin Storm said, "I take the day off and you hook up with the *one* person I've been telling you to watch out for."

They hugged though Sophie felt a small knot of worry form. Storm might not have started out wanting to be a homicide cop, but Sophie knew her cousin was hooked on the job and really liked Brady Sinclair, the partner she'd drawn. "Is my being with Severn going to be a problem for you?"

Storm shrugged. "Eventually some bored newspaper person will catch on and parade a conspiracy theory out."

Sophie grimaced as she thought of the reporters who'd seen her at the VanDenbergh estate with Severn. "You might want to warn your captain." She started to tell Storm about being at the auction but stopped when she remembered the figurine surprise Storm's husbands were planning for her.

"I'll tell him," Storm said. She gave Sophie another quick hug. "It is what it is. Severn's not going to give you up. And I suspect you're not going to give him up. Congratulations."

"Thanks. It's going to turn out okay, I think. It's just complicated."

"You don't know the half of it yet."

Sophie caught the laughter dancing in Storm's eye. It was the same amusement she'd seen in Aislinn's. She guessed Storm was alluding to what the future held for a woman who ended up with a sexually dominant man in her life. Trace made no secret about the fact Aislinn was his and he was alpha. Storm's guys were subtler, but Pierce, who ironically enough—or not—co-owned Drake's Lair with Severn's cousin, was like a fire out of control when he was with Storm.

Heat pooled in Sophie's belly. She bit her lip to keep from opening her mouth and confessing what she *already* did know about dominant men. She felt like a hormonal time bomb. She could almost hear the clock ticking down as the need for physical contact with Severn ratcheted up.

Not for the first time—and she ruefully admitted to herself, it probably wouldn't be the last—she forced her thoughts away from Severn and onto the matter that had brought her to the police station to begin with, the Dragon's Cup. "I have this idea that won't go away," Sophie said as she snagged a chair from a vacant workstation and positioned it next to Storm's desk.

Storm laughed. "A hunch?"

"Could be writer's imagination." Sophie glanced at the empty chair across from where Storm sat. Like a lot of the partnered detectives in the homicide bullpen, Storm and Brady had pushed their desks back to back. "Where's Brady?"

"Taking another vacation day." Storm's voice oozed satisfaction. "The maiden voyage on the boat went so well yesterday that Pierce lent the *Treasure Hunter* to Brady so he and Ilsa could do some deep sea fishing today." Storm's eyebrows went up and down. "Not that I want to envision Brady actually doing the deed, but I'm hoping some of the action takes place below decks."

Sophie grinned as she thought of the fortune-teller and the cop hooking up. "You called that one right."

"I'm not without my own instincts. So what's the idea that won't leave you alone? Let me guess. It has something to do with the missing Chalice of Enos."

"You don't get credit for that one, but you're right. Severn got me into the estate."

"So you saw the treasure vault and the orgy room."

146

It was a statement of fact but a guilty flush worked its way into Sophie's face with memories of how up close and personal she'd seen the orgy room.

"You didn't!" Storm said. "Tell me you're turning red *only* because you're embarrassed and shocked by the thought of some rich old geezer using the sex-gym with bimbos who are the same age as his granddaughters."

Sophie managed to say, "Can we stay focused here? I do not ask you about your sex life."

Storm laughed. "That's only because we haven't had a girls' night out since I acquired a sex life worth talking about. I can loan you some handcuffs. They can be an effective tool when dealing with a man like Severn."

Sophie's cunt clenched. Arousal soaked into her panties. Her womb fluttered with the image of handcuffing Severn to his massive bed and rendering him as helpless and desperate as he'd so often done to her. "I'll get back to you on that," she managed, knowing that if her voice didn't give her away, the way her nipples pressed against the thin tank top would. "Let's talk about potted plants instead."

Storm blinked but quickly segued to the search for the Dragon's Cup. "Are we talking about the potted plants located in the hallway between VanDenbergh's orgy room and his treasure vault?"

"Those are the ones. I know there's already been an arrest and the case is closed as far as you're concerned, but do you think it's possible the woman who discovered the body could have seen something from the corner?"

Storm frowned. "It's possible. But why hold the information back?"

Sophie leaned forward. "Maybe she intended to blackmail whoever she saw leaving with the chalice. Is your guy still claiming he didn't murder VanDenbergh in the act of committing a burglary?"

"That's what our guy is saying." Storm glanced around the bullpen then lowered her voice. "I'm trusting you with this but it doesn't go any further. His lawyer has started hinting that part of his defense is going to be an assertion his client was framed for the murder. Since the athame was stolen at the same time and we have an evidence trail following it somewhere else, and a couple more dead bodies who can't confirm or deny anything, it's possible the D.A. is going to let him plead down to accessory to murder."

"He's going to get off?"

"It's possible he'll cut a deal and admit he was there when VanDenbergh was killed but claim the other guy pulled the trigger." Storm shrugged. "We've still got him cold on embezzlement. He's still going to be an old and extremely poor man by the time he gets out of prison."

"Unless he's got the Chalice of Enos."

"True," Storm said. "But I don't think he does. I like the theory of two guys being at VanDenbergh's that day. One to kill, one to steal."

"Which brings us full circle to the scenario I can't get out of my head," Sophie said. "Let's go with there being two people and assume the woman who discovered the body, whom you refer to as D-cubed I believe, but whose legal name is Honey Mercante, saw the chalice leave with someone she recognized. It was insured for five million. Even if she didn't know exactly how much it was insured for she probably had a good idea of its worth. She could calculate a reasonable price for her silence."

Storm shook her head. "For blackmail to work she'd have to retract the statement she made to us. That'd give the thief plenty of time to cover himself, but the bigger problem is believability. First thing we'd ask her is why she lied in the first place."

Sophie bit her lip in consternation. She hadn't gotten that far in her thinking. It was one of the reasons she liked to plot her mysteries, so inspiration didn't lead to a dead end a hundred wasted pages later. "She could say he threatened her and she was terrified."

"Not credible. She wasn't hysterical at discovering the dead body of a man she was getting ready to have sex with. Hard to imagine her being terrified of the thief. Plus we would have offered protective custody until we brought in the perp and she might still have been able to collect from the insurance company for leading us to him."

"You're right. The only way my scenario works is if she had proof of what she saw. That would mean Honey had a cell phone with a camera and she just happened to have it out and ready as she went to see what was keeping VanDenbergh from getting the orgy started. That's a big stretch."

Sophie slouched in her chair. She felt deflated. By the time she'd gotten to the police station she'd been sure she was on to something. The hunch had felt so strong.

Storm reached over and opened a file cabinet drawer. "Let's play with this some more. Your hunches have always been closer to right than wrong."

"That's because I've got cop blood running through my veins even if the sight of real blood makes me puke."

Storm pulled out a file and opened it on her desk. "It's always bothered me that we found the chalice case but not the chalice itself. We assume the guy who sold it to VanDenbergh in the first place intended to steal it and resell it. He had his computer locked down tight but the e-tech guys managed to crack it open. There's no indication the chalice went anywhere else. My gut read is he intended to sell it to Severn next and retire from the business." Storm lifted a questioning eyebrow.

Sophie laughed as her cheeks grew uncomfortably flushed. "Severn and I are working together on this, but so far we haven't exactly spent a lot of time talking about the Dragon's Cup."

Storm snickered. "I'm guessing your conversation has been limited to one- or two-word sentences like *please* and *fuck me*."

"Is that the voice of experience talking?"

"Taking the Fifth."

Sophie grinned. "I think we should schedule a girls' night out."

"Anytime. Now back to VanDenbergh's missing chalice. The day Pierce took me to Severn's estate, Severn said he hadn't been contacted again about the cup. I believe him. I also believe he should have been contacted because I can't imagine the thief wanting to spend the rest of his life looking over his shoulder. Severn is not someone a sane person would want to con, cheat or play games with. The only reason I'm not freaking out at having you hook up with him is because Pierce and Tristan have told me more about him, so I know you're completely safe."

Sophie smiled. She'd come to that conclusion herself, but she still felt relieved to hear Storm say it and to know her cousin accepted Severn.

Storm said, "We know the thief's house was searched. Brady and I assumed someone was looking for the murder weapon. But what if we circle back to your hunch and apply it differently. What if Honey saw our thief leave with the chalice and knew who he was. Maybe instead of blackmail she decided to steal the cup from him."

A shiver of excitement slid down Sophie's spine. "I like that theory. It's plausible and it's not complicated."

Storm nodded. "Since the D.A. might think her chances for getting a murder conviction are taking a dive, I've got to run this scenario by the captain. He may tell me to pull Honey Mercante in and requestion her or he may tell me to let it go. Your reputation as an author who researches her projects gives you a legitimate reason to approach her, but the Severn connection and our relationship complicate the situation. Can you hold off doing anything, including telling Severn, until I talk to the captain?"

Sophie felt torn between loyalties. She didn't want a murderer to get off. She understood where Storm was coming from and she owed an allegiance to her cousin. But there was Severn to consider. They'd managed to get past a less than honest beginning. They'd agreed to work together. He was her heartmate and she owed him an allegiance too. But she also knew the Dragon's Cup was more important to him than seeing VanDenbergh's murderer get convicted of the crime— especially when the man was already looking at a long prison term for embezzlement. "When do you think you'll know something?"

"Hopefully within twenty-four hours. I'll hunt down the captain as soon as you leave. I'll call your cell when I know something."

"Okay." Sophie gave her cousin a hug and left. She found Severn waiting for her outside the police station.

Every nerve in Sophie's body came to life in quivering excitement at the sight of him. She bit down on her bottom lip to keep from whimpering under the onslaught of need that assailed her.

She wanted to run to him. She wanted to press every inch of herself against him but she was acutely aware of where they were.

Sophie forced herself to close the distance between them at a walk. Severn's heated glance and taut features told her he was fighting some impulses of his own.

He opened the passenger door of the sports car. When she was seated he leaned down and purred, "Why did you come here, my heartmate? Is there trouble? Beyond what you're already in with me?"

Sophie's nipples beaded further. Erotic fear fluttered through her belly.

His fingers trailed over the inside of her thigh. "You've changed your clothes though I warned you against it this morning. The punishment will be harsher if I peel these shorts down and find you're wearing panties."

Sophie managed to hold back the moan until he'd shut the door. She clamped her legs together and closed her eyes. Only the thought of being hauled back into the police station for lewd conduct kept her from slipping her fingers into her panties and giving herself some relief.

She glanced at Severn when he got in the car. His jaw was clenched and his cock was a prominent ridge against his expensive trousers. She licked her lips and saw his penis jerk. Her gaze flew to Severn's. "Where to?" she managed.

"Home."

The single word, accompanied by the possessive, predatory way his eyes swept over her, made Sophie shiver in anticipation. She knew it was a bad sign when the trip to his estate seemed to take forever.

She should be defending her right to change clothes and wear panties. Instead she grew wet thinking about his threatened punishment and her own need to offer at least a token resistance.

It's dangerous to play with me, Sophie.

Her heart rate sped up as she remembered his words at the auction. Her cunt lips grew more flushed. She'd seen little of his estate but she knew she didn't want to be racing through the antique-filled hallways and rooms. The gardens at the back were extensive and she thought he might even have an English maze—or maybe she'd simply imagined it. She was the first to admit her imagination went wild around Severn. A laugh escaped. Who was she kidding? *She* went wild around Severn.

The gates to his estate swung open. Even though she'd seen it before, her breath still caught at the fantasyscape in front of her. "It's beyond beautiful."

Severn carried her hand to his mouth and kissed the back of it. "I'm glad it pleases you."

The garage door opened as the car approached. Sophie managed to extricate her hand from Severn's on the pretense of leaning forward to adjust the strap of her sandal. She wrinkled her nose as she studied the delicate shoes and waited for the right moment to escape. Sandals weren't exactly sprinting shoes. Then again, the outcome of this particular race wasn't really in question.

A sense of fairness made her ask, "Am I still in trouble with you?"

"Yes."

Her breath caught at the rough-edged masculine satisfaction contained in his voice. Her pussy clenched so hard it was almost painful.

The sleek sports car glided into the garage and slowed to a stop. She was out and running before he'd cut the engine.

Dragon instinct roared to the forefront of Severn's being. For an instant the magic shimmered as if it would fade so he could pursue her in his true form. He longed to take flight, to trumpet a song of victory as he snatched Sophie and carried her off to an isolated rocky lair.

By The Great Shared Ancestor, with no effort at all, his mate was able to strip away the mortal trappings he'd worked so hard to acquire in this realm. She chased every thought out of his head except for those centered on claiming and fucking her.

Severn ducked under the closing garage door and followed her to the back of the house. He checked his pace, allowing her the illusion of escape as she slipped into the maze of statues and plants.

He hadn't lied when he told Sophie he'd never brought a woman to his estate. This was his lair now, his private place. But other males, both dragon and human, had lived in it before he came to this realm. They'd created a landscape suitable for seduction and conquest.

Severn took his shirt off as he entered the maze. He let it fall to the ground, heedless of whether it landed among rose thorns or on dirt. He needed the feel of Sophie's flesh against his.

Her scent filled his nostrils and made his cock leak. She was aroused, playing with him, delaying her punishment even as the thought of it made her wet and slick and ready for him.

There was no fear in her scent, no trepidation. She longed for his touch as much as he longed for hers.

"You are making it worse for yourself, Sophie."

His ears told him she'd stopped running. She moved through the maze silently now, no doubt straining to hear him in order to determine where he was. He needed only the lush perfume of her arousal to find her.

Severn paused long enough to take his shoes and socks off. He'd be lucky if he managed more than a few spanks to her smooth buttocks before he freed his cock and impaled her with it.

He shuddered as the image of her bare cunt filled his thoughts. He cupped himself through the trousers. The need to taste her trapped the breath in his chest until he burned with dragon fire.

"Come to me, Sophie." The command was a growl. His dragon nature was starting to dominate.

Sophie shivered. She knew she was in trouble. She'd be lucky if she had any voice left after Severn was finished making her scream and beg.

He really was the human embodiment of a dragon, one moment playful, the next dominant, but always possessive. She shivered again, remembering his mercurial shifts at the VanDenbergh estate and how he'd put her on the edge of orgasm while surrounded by a crowd of people.

She slipped her sandals off and left them hanging from an elaborately trimmed shrub. The act gave her an idea of how she might catapult Severn past the need to punish her and right into the frenzy of fucking her.

Sophie moved deeper into the maze before removing her tank top and draping it over a slender tree branch. It left her bare-chested and blushing and praying she and Severn were the only two people in the maze.

A little further she slid out of her shorts. She snickered as she imagined herself starring in a private version of *Girl Gone Wild*.

"I've warned you that it's dangerous to play with me, my heartmate," Severn said.

Sophie's cunt clenched at the sound of his voice. It was deeper, a growl that licked along her slit and over her clit.

He was gaining on her. She guessed he'd found the tank top.

Sophie bit her lip. She'd intended to lose the panties too. She'd thought they might be like a red flag to a bull and he'd charge. Now she wasn't so sure about leaving them for him to find. Erotic fear shivered through her at the thought of Severn punishing her.

She rounded a corner and saw a wide padded bench. Her womb spasmed. Fire streaked to her nipples. The urge to strip and wait for Severn with her legs spread and her cunt lips flushed and open had her nearly panting. She ached for him. She burned for him.

Scorching heat raced along her spine, warning her that he'd caught up to her. Instinct kicked in before she could stop it and she bolted. He captured her close to the bench, but took her to the ground. Despite the hardness of his body and the fierceness of his expression he ensured she landed gently.

Severn pinned Sophie's wrists to the grass. He didn't spare her his weight as he lay on top of her. His mate was far too cunning to be trusted. He'd guessed at her plan to distract him from punishing her as soon as he found the first article of her clothing.

He captured her lips with his. His tongue plunged into her mouth.

He wanted to rip the tiny scrap of material she considered panties away from her body. He wanted to sheath his cock in the wet heat of her. He wanted to thrust and thrust and thrust—to never stop thrusting, to never leave his mate's perfect channel.

She inflamed him. She made him crazed with lust. She'd ensnared him.

He kissed her as she writhed and whimpered beneath him. He took her breath and gave her his own. He filled her lungs with fire and dragon magic as he fought against the overwhelming need to fill her slick channel with his cock and seed.

Only when she was close to passing out did he lift his mouth from hers. And even then his fiery mate tried to escape her punishment by saying, "Please fuck me."

Primal, nearly uncontrollable lust swamped Severn. His hips jerked. He pumped against her despite the barrier of their remaining clothing. He growled because no human words would form. If he'd been close to the mystical doorway leading to the dragon realm then he would have abandoned everything and taken Sophie there. He was barely hanging on to the magic that kept him in human form.

That didn't stop his sensual assault. He repositioned her hands so he could claim her breasts. He bit and sucked at nipples that were hard and tight.

He slid lower and punished her by finding her clit, by letting her feel his mouth through the panties she'd dared to put on—the material that now separated her from the pleasure she was begging for. She was drenched in arousal. Its scent was a heady drug Severn knew he was hopelessly addicted to. He kissed and licked and sucked the juices off her inner thighs.

He ran his tongue over her cloth-covered slit until her pleading had turned into the whimpered sounds of complete submission.

He levered himself above her. She was shaking with her need, her eyes dark with lust.

"Do you accept your punishment?"

She pressed her mouth to his. She licked and nipped and had him grinding his cock against her protected mound. "Haven't I already been punished enough? I need you so much that I'll do anything if you'll just fuck me."

Severn's penis pulsed in warning. Emotion writhed inside him.

He'd thought she was conquered and yet he was pleased she could hold her own against him. He wanted to pound into her and demonstrate that his will would prevail but at the same time he wanted to purr with satisfaction that she needed him as desperately as he needed her.

He kissed her again. He moaned as she welcomed his tongue. He nearly spilled his seed when she sucked at his tongue hungrily and images of having her take his cock into the wet heated depths of her mouth filled his thoughts.

Severn lifted his face away from Sophie, then his body. He pulled her to her feet and found immense satisfaction in the way she clung to him. Only his need to reinforce his right to rule her gave him the strength to make her stand on her own feet before he moved to the bench several steps away.

"Come and accept your punishment, Sophie," he said as he sat.

Sophie shivered. The modern woman, the one who longed to bring Severn to his knees, was tempted to bury her face against his cloth-covered erection and do to him what he'd done to her. But the woman who thrilled at having such a dominant lover wanted nothing more than to let him administer the spanking he seemed determined to give her.

She closed the distance between them and found a way to balance the two. She brushed her lips across his as her fingers explored the bulge in the front of his trousers. "If I let you punish me, will you put this inside me?"

She draped herself over his lap before he could answer. She wriggled and hoped he felt the heat of her through his pants. His cock responded. She could feel it throbbing against her side.

"Enough, Sophie," he growled in warning.

She stilled, glad her position hid the smile of feminine satisfaction she couldn't suppress.

His palm settled on her barely there panties. She shivered despite her pride in holding her own against him. Her ass lifted and quivered.

The blow came without warning. It was followed by a second and then a third.

He smoothed his hand over her burning flesh. She bit her lip to keep from moaning.

Severn's fingers slipped underneath the elastic of Sophie's panties. He pulled them to her thighs despite the fact they did little to protect her from either his view or his blows.

He wasn't sure who was being punished more, his mate or himself. By The Great Shared Ancestor, Sophie was perfect for him.

He leaned down and kissed one supple buttock and then the other. His fingers slid between her thighs. She was wet and hot and his, only his.

She whimpered and he spanked her again. He had to suppress a groan when her ass lifted in a silent plea for more.

"You will not disobey me again," he said, more than ready to shove his cock inside her.

"I'll think twice about the panties," his fiery mate dared to say.

He rewarded her boldness with harder spanks followed by kisses to her heated flesh. She softened against him. The scent of her arousal engulfed him in a flame of lust.

"Please, Severn, I need you so much."

He bit down on her buttock hard enough to mark it. She whimpered but accepted the loving chastisement. It was enough to appease the dragon instinct to dominate and possess.

He'd thought to stretch her out on the bench and make love to her, to watch her beautiful face as he impaled her with his cock. He'd thought to capture her screams of release as she orgasmed, and to witness her pleasure as he filled her with the hot wash of his seed. But now images of covering her as a dragon covers its mate, of draping himself over her back as he mounted her, filled his mind to the exclusion of everything else — including the presence of others in the maze.

Audriss' disdain broke over him. Her voice was as venomous as it was unwelcome. "You debase and degrade yourself," she hissed.

Chapter Thirteen

ɛɔ

Sophie felt as though she'd been doused in a bucket of ice water. The shift from burning, nearly unbearable lust to the cold, unwelcome presence of Severn's unpleasant house guest left her head spinning and her stomach churning.

Or maybe I've been upside down too long, she thought, making a weak joke in an effort to steady her emotions. She didn't lift her head or struggle to get off Severn's lap. None of her clothes were nearby and he'd appeared without a shirt. She didn't intend to give Audriss more of a show than she was already getting. Sophie's heart filled with warmth when Severn pulled her barely there panties up then left his hand on her buttocks to expand her privacy.

Fury pulsed through Severn. He wanted to shift form and attack. If they'd been in the dragon realm he would have. Not only had Audriss dared to interrupt him with his mate but she'd dared to bring two of her male servants into the maze with her.

They were in human form but the magic couldn't alter their reptilian nature. When their tongues flicked out to catch Sophie's scent, Severn growled and they stepped back. He could kill them easily enough in either of their forms but their bite was toxic to humans. He would never risk Sophie's life by attacking them in her presence unless the situation was dire. When it came to human victims, there wasn't an antidote for their poison. An "accidental" bite was just as effective as an intentional one.

"No doubt you have accomplished what you set out to do when you entered the maze," Severn said. "Now leave."

Audriss glanced at Sophie. Her features contorted with revulsion and fury. "I won't allow these playthings once we're mated."

"I suffer your presence in my home because treaty and law demand it. Don't mistake my tolerance for acceptance or encouragement. The plans you and my mother have agreed upon will never come to pass. I have a mate."

"You have an amusement that distracts you when you should be searching for the Dragon's Cup. This female is not your true mate."

"You will not win a challenge against me, Audriss."

A gloating triumph blazed for an instant in Audriss' eyes before she turned and disappeared into the maze. The sight of it only served to reinforce Severn's belief that he would need to guard Sophie at all times. In a direct challenge, dragon against dragon, Audriss could not win. But Sophie's "accidental" death would serve Audriss and his mother just as well. Until he took Sophie to the dragon realm and completed the bond with her, she was fully mortal and very vulnerable.

"Well, that was fun—up to a point," his priceless mate said as she repositioned herself on his lap and buried her face in the crook of his neck.

Severn hugged her tightly and savored the feel of her breasts against his chest. Love and pride filled him. He would not let anything happen to her. She was bold and brave and incredibly beautiful. She was his.

He was tempted to abandon the search for the Dragon's Cup and take her to the rocky lair he claimed in the realm of his birth. She *would* survive the shock of it. After all, didn't she write fantasy? Didn't she already recognize much of his dragon nature?

He rubbed his cheek against Sophie's luxurious hair. Now was not the time to abandon the quest for the chalice. He was convinced they were close to recovering it. To find it and have Sophie drink from it…

Severn nuzzled her until she turned her face and their lips met. "What took you to the police station?" he asked.

"A scenario I couldn't get out of my mind."

"Involving the Dragon's Cup?"

Sophie smiled against his mouth. It'd taken him longer than she thought it would to get around to asking. Then again, they'd been a little distracted by the possibility of sex. She wriggled on his lap and watched as his nostrils flared and his eyes narrowed—a possibility that was still very much alive despite the unpleasant interruption.

She kissed him in apology before she said, "I promised Storm I wouldn't say anything to you until she had a chance to talk to her captain. My original idea was unworkable but when the two of us brainstormed we came up with a viable alternative." She kissed Severn again, this time sliding her tongue into his mouth and tangling it with his. She found the idea of hurting him or having him angry with her completely unbearable.

His growl sent a shiver down her spine and straight to her clit. When he took charge of the kiss she softened and yielded.

"How long?" he asked when he lifted his mouth from hers.

"Twenty-four hours, maybe less. She was going to talk to her captain as soon as I left." Sophie rubbed her nose along Severn's. "I'm sure we could find a way to occupy ourselves."

Her enthusiasm for sex in the great outdoors of Severn's estate had *definitely* waned. In fact, her earlier reservations about staying there at all had resurfaced. She played with strands of his hair. "We could get away from here. We could go to the apartment above Inner Magick. Aislinn's okay with us staying there. Or you could do your dragon imitation and terrify my neighbors into silence."

She shivered at just how scary he could be when he set his mind to it. There'd been a lethal promise in Severn's voice when he talked to Audriss, a clear message that tangling with him could be deadly. "I don't think I'm up for too many more encounters with either your mother or Audriss."

Severn tightened his grip on Sophie. Dragon instinct flared to life with fiery intensity. She would not leave him nor would he abandon the estate and the treasures it housed. "We will remain here."

He felt her tense and knew she intended to fight his dictate. He took her mouth in a kiss that rivaled the one he'd given her when he'd caught her in the maze. Fire flashed between them, lust rose and pushed everything else to the side.

Severn stripped her panties off before tumbling her onto the padded bench and following her down. His mouth left hers only long enough to say, "You are mine and you will stay with me." His hands left her only long enough to free his cock and guide it to the wet, welcome channel of the only female who would ever satisfy him.

He swallowed her moan as he impaled her with one hard thrust. He groaned at the ecstasy of being completely sheathed in Sophie's heated depths. He fought to stay still and failed the instant Sophie's legs wrapped around his waist.

He pistoned in and out of her. He thrilled at the way she met his thrusts. He reveled in the savagery of her kisses.

The dragon instinct to mate overwhelmed him and when her fingernails scratched down his back, he could think of nothing else but filling her with his seed as she screamed in orgasm. The hollow spurs at his wrists extended. He couldn't keep himself from raking her back with them. Serum pumped into her as she thrashed in ecstasy and milked him of every drop of semen.

For long moments afterward Severn lay on his mate in utter contentment. Satisfaction purred through him. He envisioned them together in the dragon realm, lying stretched out on a sun-baked rock after making love. His cock stirred and filled with blood as he imagined his human shape slowly giving way to his true form. He leaned in and ran his tongue along Sophie's shoulder as he thought about the figurine set he'd gifted her with. Contrary to human legend, dragons weren't huge building-sized beasts. In his true form he was larger and stronger than he was in his human one, but he could still pleasure a human mate.

Once again he was tempted to abandon the search for the chalice in favor of taking Sophie to the dragon realm. She would sleep for hours now. If he acted quickly he could get her to his lair and seal his bond with her.

Instinct warred with intellect. His cock protested when the latter won.

He couldn't afford to leave. He'd agreed to join forces with Malik and Hakon because the thought of the chalice being found by one of the old dragons was as unacceptable as the idea of undoing the spell altogether was exhilarating.

Severn forced himself to stand and restore his trousers. He laughed as he did so. In the short time he'd known his mate she'd reduced him to behaving like a randy human teenager who couldn't be bothered to shed his clothing before fucking.

He scooped her into his arms and smiled when she curled into him. In his other form the crest along his neck would have risen as he preened with the knowledge that she craved the feel of his skin against hers as much as he did.

With great satisfaction he left her panties where he'd tossed them on the ground. He'd send someone out for the rest of her clothing and her shoes, but the panties would remain. He suspected she'd be driven to retrieve them, and he wouldn't waste his breath forbidding it, but he also thought it would serve as a lesson. Next time his fiery mate would think twice before she disobeyed him—Severn laughed softly and rubbed his cheek against Sophie's—or not.

By The Great Shared Ancestor he adored her. She freed him from burdens he hadn't been aware of carrying. He'd never let a female see his playful side before. He'd never experienced such a wide rage of emotion. She made him both more human and more dragon.

As Severn moved through the estate his thoughts shifted to Audriss and his mother. The sooner the Dragon's Cup was found and secured at Drake's Lair, the sooner they would be gone. His mother hated taking a human form. She wouldn't linger in this realm and he wouldn't tolerate Audriss' presence a moment longer than he had to.

He placed Sophie on their bed. Contentment filled him at the sight of her there. He could stare at her for hours. She was lush and alluring and completely mesmerizing to him. She was long-limbed and beautiful, a perfect dragon's mate.

He couldn't resist the urge to settle next to her and run his hands over her smooth curves. Her scent made him purr. He wanted to stretch out on top of her and wallow in the pleasure she gave him.

Severn grinned. No doubt the image of him lying in his other form on the thousands of smoothed and polished gemstones that served as bedding in his dragon lair would make its way into one of her stories. He wondered if she would guess at the intensity of his desire to luxuriate in, on and with her. She was his most priceless treasure.

He slid his leg over hers and pressed closer. He brushed a light kiss over her mouth.

New treasure was always fondled and admired. But a dragon's eye quickly turned to the next item to acquire. Not so with a mate. With a mate the need to touch—especially for the males of his kind—became more intense, not less.

There was a brief knock on the door. Severn rubbed his cheek against Sophie's and growled at the interruption. He hated leaving her but knew he must. The knock meant Xanthus had returned with a report.

Severn buried his face in Sophie's hair and inhaled deeply. The need to stay with her, to be there when she woke was almost unbearable.

Dragon heat filled him. Once the chalice was found and she was bound to him then they would go away for a while. He would marry her in the human way. He would even allow her to choose the location of their honeymoon. As long as she understood she would remain naked for most of their trip, he didn't care where they went.

The rap on the door sounded again. Severn left the bed and the room. No one would dare enter his quarters without permission.

Over the centuries Dragon law had become very precise and detailed, especially when they were in this realm. With so few of their kind and the possibility of extinction if they diminished their numbers further by killing one another, he knew neither his mother nor Audriss would harm Sophie openly, at least not in this realm and not without some provocation to vindicate their actions.

"Shall I summon someone to guard the door?" Xanthus asked.

"The cameras monitoring this hallway are activated?"

"Yes. I assumed you'd want it done before leaving her unattended. If anyone approaches the room, we will be summoned."

"Good."

They went to Severn's office and closed the door.

"What have you learned?" Severn asked.

"Your mother went no further than Drake's Lair. She visited briefly with Malik's and Hakon's ancestors, but those within hearing range say it was not a friendly conversation. They are old rivals."

"And Audriss?"

"Before we speak about her, I talked to both Pierce and Tristan and asked them about the fey who appeared at Inner Magick while Sophie was there. Neryssa is Morgana's cousin. Morgana once had a claim on Tristan. It's one of the reasons he settled in this realm. He had no wish to bed her by order of the queen. When the chalice resurfaced she was sent here and learned of Storm and her importance to Tristan and Pierce. Before they could fully claim Storm as their mate, Morgana attempted to kill her. Tristan and Pierce send an offer to help in any way they can. Morgana is capable of taking vengeance by using Sophie as a surrogate for Storm. Queen Otthilde will look the other way and claim ignorance even as she celebrates the death of a dragon's mate."

Severn nodded. He'd assumed as much. There was no love lost between dragon and faerie. Storm was now beyond the reach of Morgana and her cousin, but Sophie wasn't. "Neryssa's element is water?"

"More air than water but she can wield and become both."

Severn made a guess as to why Xanthus had brought up the topic of Morgana and Neryssa. "Audriss was seen with one of them?"

"Morgana." Xanthus frowned. "It occurred while I was guarding Sophie so I didn't witness it with my own eyes. The one who reported it said it could have been a chance meeting or an arranged one. From outward appearances the exchange appeared to be unfriendly and yet it lasted longer than one would expect."

"Where was it?"

"At the beach. Close to the surf. Morgana walked out of the water as though she'd been swimming. There was no way to hear what was said without revealing to Audriss that she was being followed."

"And afterward?"

"Audriss went by Drake's Lair, which is where I found her with your mother when you claimed Sophie at the police station. From Drake's Lair she came here. Unfortunately I didn't know you and Sophie were on the grounds until it was too late to prevent an encounter with Audriss." Amusement lurked for a moment in Xanthus' eyes. "But I gather you were able to salvage the situation."

No doubt word of his carrying Sophie naked from the maze had spread through his estate. The nerve endings along the back of his neck tingled in a phantom rippling of his dragon crest. Severn couldn't suppress a smile of masculine satisfaction. "Yes, all is well with my mate."

Severn contemplated Xanthus for a moment. Given the presence of Morgana and Neryssa as well as that of his mother and Audriss, he couldn't afford to free Xanthus from his liege duties, but he now appreciated how much worry accompanied the claiming of a human mate. "You have been spending a lot of time at Inner Magick. Is Marika a passing fancy or a serious interest?"

The flash of deadly possessiveness in Xanthus' eyes was answer enough for Severn. He said, "If you wish to bring the female here so she can be protected, you are welcome to do so. As soon as the chalice is recovered, I will seal the bond with Sophie and then take her away for a while. I will consider that your service to me has been completed until the next tithe period begins. As far as I am concerned, you will be free to stay among the mortals with my protection or return to the dragon realm as you choose."

Xanthus tilted his head in acknowledgement. One corner of his mouth curled in self-directed amusement. "I would love nothing more than to bring Marika here and tie her to my bed. Unfortunately we are engaged in a slight…battle at the moment. She'll be safe enough at Inner Magick. There is no reason to think the fey or dragon females will take an interest in her."

"Assign some of the others to guard her when you can't be there if you feel the need to do so."

Xanthus nodded. Severn took a moment to fill him in on the agreement he'd reached with Hakon and Malik. The phone rang as Xanthus was leaving the office. It was Malik.

Malik said, "Other than you and Hakon, I had another interesting visitor today. Do I have you to thank? Or your beautiful mate?"

Severn straightened in his chair. "What are you talking about?"

"Your mate didn't tell you about the visit with Aislinn Dilessio? I can only assume it was the visit to Inner Magick that brought the half-elf to my estate with the confidence to ask to use my library." When Severn growled, Malik laughed and said, "I will spare your reputation by not spreading tales of your *blissful* ignorance. You are new to mated life and your female's beauty would blind even an ancient."

Severn growled again. His mate was out of reach until the serum was fully metabolized and she woke up. In frustration he directed his fire at Malik. "You have your men watching Sophie?"

There was a second of silence on the other end, a dragon temper brought swiftly under control. "Not since we reached an agreement earlier today. My men watch Inner Magick. I thought it would be only a matter of time before the fey showed up there."

Irritation flowed through Severn. He should have come to the same conclusion and assigned one of his men to monitor Inner Magick. Instead he'd relied on Xanthus' personal visits. He had no excuse for the lapse other than the fact that since meeting Sophie his thoughts had swirled in a continual maelstrom of lust—one he wasn't sure he'd want to escape even if he could.

Severn exhaled and the air shimmered orange-gold and full of heat. If he wasn't careful he'd torch his desk and fill the room with smoke like a fledgling that had no business being in the mortal realm.

"Your men saw Neryssa visit Inner Magick?" Severn asked.

"Yes, and followed her afterward. She met briefly with Morgana then summoned a driver and appeared to take a tour of the city. At some point she became air and slipped through an open window."

Severn picked up one of the dragon statues on his desk. The exquisite emeralds set in its eyes made him think of Sophie's eyes. He shifted position to ease the pressure of a rigid cock constrained by fabric. Naked images of Sophie filled his mind but he forced them away in order to contemplate Neryssa's actions. "What was her purpose?"

"I have studied her route. If we assume her travels were related to finding the Dragon's Cup or monitoring our activities, the only point of interest on her tour is the prison where VanDenbergh's murderer is housed."

"He has no idea where the cup is. I have assured myself of it."

"As have I."

Feeling calmer, though he still intended to have a conversation with his mate about her earlier activities, Severn circled back to Malik's conversational opener. "What was Aislinn looking for in your library?"

"She studied several texts containing information about gems, their lesser known properties, the histories of their use. Some of the manuscripts are Elven. I hesitated to acknowledge owning them for fear the information they contained could be used against us. She is half-human and can tap into magics in this realm that a pure elf could not. But given what might be gained along with her reputation and her friendship with your mate, I allowed her unrestricted access to my library. For the most part I left her to her own devices though I required my librarian to note everything she took an interest in." There was a brief pause. "Your mate said nothing?"

"No. But you can be sure my mate will soon be begging to tell me everything she knows and everything she did since leaving the VanDenbergh estate."

Malik chuckled. "I can hear her screams now and envy you the sweet torture of extracting information from her."

Chapter Fourteen

ഔ

Sophie woke to shades of déjà vu. Only this time she recognized the bedroom furniture. This time she knew the masculine body pressed so intimately against her back belonged to Severn Damek. She was also reasonably certain she hadn't been drugged and relocated, though she suspected she was going to have to deal with a great deal of male ego over sex that had been so good she'd passed out because of it.

"You're awake, my heartmate?" Severn's voice purred next to her ear.

She smiled at the feel of his erection trapped against her buttocks. She couldn't resist the urge to wriggle and tease. "And if I am? Let me guess, you've got something for me."

His leg shifted to trap hers. His arm became a vise. "I assumed our time together in the maze would have taught you a lesson about the dangers of playing with me. Apparently I'm mistaken."

Sophie snickered. "I might be a slow learner when it comes to you."

Severn leaned down and nipped her shoulder. By The Great Shared Ancestor it was impossible to maintain a decent rage when it came to her.

"What did you talk to Aislinn about?" he asked.

Sophie turned in his arms.

He couldn't prevent a groan from escaping as her smooth, bare pussy rubbed against his cock. Fire tightened his testicles and his penis wept in greeting. His mate's knowing expression only made him more determined to lay down the law—

foremost of which was that she would have no secrets from him.

"What did you talk to Aislinn about?" he repeated.

"You. Me. The Dragon's Cup. Why?" Sophie's lips found his. Her tongue danced along the seam of his mouth and he didn't rebuff her. She'd answered his question quickly and he saw no reason not to reward her.

Severn opened his mouth and sucked her tongue into it. His arms loosened and his hand found her lush breast. She moaned and pressed closer. Her nipple was a dusky bud begging for his attention.

He rolled so he lay on top of her. Her bare cunt tortured him. The scent of her arousal filled his mind and very nearly cleared it of thought. Lust roared through him and almost distracted him from his need to question her.

"I passed out again," his seductive mate said when the need for air forced his mouth from hers. "That's never happened to me with any other man."

Severn's hips jerked in reaction. Dragon instinct had him recapturing her lips and breathing his fire into her. She was his and she would never know another male's touch, much less any cock but his own. No other would fill her with seed or make her scream and shudder in orgasm.

He shivered as her fingers found his shoulders. If he didn't gain control now he'd soon be raking his spurs down her back and sending her into unconsciousness again.

"Enough," he growled as he pinned Sophie's wrists to the bed. "You will not distract me!"

Her eyes widened. She softened underneath him though there was a tension in her that hadn't been there before. Severn found he couldn't stand its presence.

He leaned in and his hair formed a curtain on either side of their faces. He laughed because he could find no other response. She'd removed the expensive hair-tie without him being aware she'd done so. "We are supposed to be looking for the Dragon's Cup together," he said. It didn't come out nearly as fierce as he'd intended, but the intimacy of their contact had him struggling to remain focused on the task of laying down *his* law to her.

Sophie blinked in confusion. Her forehead wrinkled. "I know that."

"Twice today you've taken action related to the search but failed to inform me of the details."

Her forehead wrinkled further before suddenly clearing, only to wrinkle again. "How do you know Aislinn volunteered to help?" Sophie's eyes narrowed. "You're not listening in on my conversations are you? It was bad enough to find out you'd assigned Xanthus to guard me, but I'll be totally pissed if you've got listening devices and cameras recording my every move."

Severn groaned and rolled to his back. She was impossible!

His breath caught when Sophie slid on top of him. She pinned his wrists to the mattress in a perfect imitation of the position he'd placed her in. Lust assaulted him.

"I have ways of making you talk," Sophie said. "I answered your question, now you owe me an answer. How do you know Aislinn volunteered to help us find the Dragon's Cup?"

Severn raised his hips and rubbed his erection against the silky wetness between her thighs. He was tempted to resist just so she'd torture him with a sensual onslaught.

Sophie's sultry laugh made his cock pulse in response. "You're only making it harder on yourself," she said, riding his length and coating his penis with her arousal. "It's going to go badly for you if you don't answer my question." She abruptly lifted her lower body from his. The movement deprived him of the feel of her slick, heated flesh.

He grunted. His hips bucked. For a split second he was tempted to use his superior strength to overpower her and take control of the situation. But he found he was enjoying Sophie's mock dominance too much to end it.

"Talk," Sophie ordered.

Severn laughed. Hadn't that been his goal to begin with?

"Malik called me. Aislinn visited his estate and spent a number of hours in his extensive library."

Sophie lowered her hips so once again her hot folds were caressing his cock. "See how much better it is when you cooperate?"

She leaned down and nuzzled a tight male nipple. Her wet tongue sent a bolt of sensual agony rushing to his penis. Her mouth latched onto the tiny knob and had him lifting his hips in the same rhythm as her sucking.

It took concentration for Severn to string enough words together to form a sentence. "What is your friend looking for?"

Sophie didn't answer right away. She couldn't bring herself to free his nipple, not when he was panting and straining, reacting so strongly to each swipe of her tongue, to each pull of her lips. He made her feel like a goddess, a siren. She bit down on his nipple and thrilled at the sharp intake of Severn's breath before he freed his hands and buried his fingers in her hair to hold her to him.

"Sophie," he growled.

"Aislinn is looking for a way to help us. There was a woman when she was growing up, a distant relative of hers, who could find gems like a water-diviner finds water. Aislinn's not even sure something like that would work with the Dragon's Cup, but she's exploring the possibility."

Sophie reached down and guided him into her. She hummed in pleasure against his chest as he filled her. It didn't seem to matter how many times they fucked, each time felt as though she could barely accommodate his size. He was hot, hard, velvety softness surrounding sheer masculinity.

Her fingers replaced her mouth on his nipple. She grasped and tugged on one of them while she covered the other with her palm. She shifted her weight and lodged him more deeply inside her. "You've turned me into a sex addict," she admitted as her inner muscles rippled and spasmed, tightened on Severn in hungry welcome.

His hands cupped her breasts. His hips lifted. "I could say the same about you. You're a constant distraction."

Sophie closed her eyes and rose above him. She lifted along his length until only the tip of him was inside her. For a heartbeat she hovered, held him as flushed cunt lips quivered and arousal slid over him like a hot summer storm.

He tightened his fingers on her nipples in a silent command to engulf him in liquid heat again. The painful pleasure of his demand radiated through her clit.

She settled. She sheathed him in her depths. She savored the feel of him before repeating it again and again, until it became a torture neither of them could endure.

They writhed together in shared release. The sounds and scent of it filled the room.

Sophie pressed a kiss to the dragon on Severn's chest afterward. Her stomach grumbled a reminder that it had been a long time since the frappachino. "What time do you think it is?" she asked.

"Close to sunrise."

Sophie startled. She'd slept for a long time after playing in the maze with him.

"Hungry?" Severn asked.

"Starving."

"My cook will already be at work in the kitchen. There are apartments at the other end of the estate where those like Xanthus live. We can go downstairs to eat or I can have something brought up."

Sophie levered herself up onto her elbows. A flutter of nervousness marred her contentment. She knew he was rich, beyond rich, but sometimes the unexpected reminder of how different his life was from hers made her feel unsettled.

Severn's hands glided up her spine. His fingers tangled in her hair. "What's wrong?"

What could she say? She couldn't realistically change any of it. But at the moment she wanted…something simpler.

Sophie remembered her earlier fantasy about a picnic at sunset. Sunrise could be just as wonderful. "How about breakfast on the beach?"

Severn guided her mouth down to his. "By the time we shower a basket will be waiting for us. Any preferences for what we'll find in it?"

"Beyond coffee? No. Surprise me."

He nibbled on her lower lip. "I'd be content to make a meal of you but I'll let my cook surprise us both."

Sophie's heart turned over. How could she resist him?

She settled more heavily on his chest. The heartmate necklace burned with their combined heat as if to remind her she wasn't supposed to be able to resist Severn.

Her nipples tightened when he sucked on the lip he'd been nibbling. She moaned when he released it to caress the seam of her mouth with his tongue. She opened readily and shivered as he kissed her deeply, hungrily.

"We'd better shower separately or we'll never get out of here in time to watch the sunrise," she warned several minutes later.

She thought it might already be too late. She was finding it difficult to move, to peel herself away from Severn. And the longer they lay naked against each other, the more she hated the idea of being separated not only by physical distance but by clothing.

It wasn't only his magnificent body — it was his heat, his scent. It was everything about him.

177

She laughed as the sudden image of a dragon lying on a mound of treasure came to mind. He was starting to rub off on her.

"What's so funny?" he asked, his hands cupping her hips briefly before gliding over her buttocks.

Once again Sophie rose to her elbows so she could look down on his gorgeous face and meet his sapphire-colored eyes. She grinned. "My imagination has gone into overdrive since I met you. I had this image of a dragon lying on treasure." She leaned down and gave him a quick kiss. "And since you're on the bottom, that makes you the treasure and me the dragon."

He laughed an instant before he rolled and took her with him, reversing their positions. "Or maybe it makes you the dragon's mate."

* * * * *

They made it to the beach and spread a blanket over the sand with only a few minutes to spare. Severn pulled Sophie onto his lap and wrapped his arms around her waist as a breathtaking sunrise spilled across the sky.

"I'm glad we made it," Sophie said, snuggling into him and weaving her fingers through his. "This is perfect."

"You're perfect." His arms tightened. "Don't ever think to leave me, Sophie."

It was said with such ruthless possessiveness that Sophie's heart stuttered in her chest for an instant as old fears and memories tried to overwhelm her. She forced them away, just as she forced herself to remain relaxed and calm in his arms. "Don't ever give me cause."

He stilled completely. The sound of the waves and the sea birds were the only ones present besides the beating of their hearts—his steady while hers became more rapid. She didn't feel threatened so much as she felt his attention, like that of a dragon who would know every facet of a treasure, who would allow no secrets.

Severn eased her from his lap and reached for the picnic basket. Sophie felt bereft, lost. She wanted to take back her words even though she'd meant them. Even if the two of them were made for each other, they were both going to have to adjust and adapt to make their relationship work. There were things she could be flexible about, but there were also things she *couldn't* be flexible about, not if she was going to maintain her self-respect.

"Severn—"

He leaned in and stopped her with the press of his mouth against hers. "I would never knowingly hurt you, Sophie."

Relief and heated emotion poured into Sophie. "I'd never hurt you on purpose either."

Their tongues met and twined in a gentle restoration of the harmony between them. When the kiss ended they explored the contents of the picnic basket together. They savored the food and the coffee. Afterward they repacked the basket and stretched out on the blanket facing each other.

Sophie couldn't resist the urge to unbutton Severn's shirt so she could trace the dragon on his chest as the sun warmed her back. "Getting this done had to have been really painful. But it's beautiful, and unique."

Severn's hand moved to her thigh. She shivered when he reached the hem of her skirt. Her stomach fluttered with nerves. She didn't trust him to stop. She didn't trust herself to stop him. Not when she'd lost the battle over panties again.

Sophie's face reddened as she thought about the last pair of them she'd worn. She prayed no one would go into the maze until she could retrieve the barely there panties.

Severn's masculine chuckle told her he knew exactly what she was thinking. "I believe the punishment fit the crime. But no doubt, you'll test me again." His fingers danced upward until they encountered the first traces of her arousal.

"Probably," Sophie said, unable to do anything about the breathless quality of her voice.

His fingers inched higher. They gathered the moisture from her slit then swirled over her clit like a wet tongue.

"Severn," she gasped.

He closed the distance between them. His sheer masculine presence forced her onto her back.

She whimpered when his fingers slid into her. "Tell me something important, something I should know if I'm going to avoid giving you cause to try to leave me."

Instinct told her to clamp her legs shut while she was on a public beach—even a nearly deserted one—but the feel of him curling his fingers deep inside her, brushing over the spot that would soon have her keening in pleasure, made her lift her hips instead. "I bet you have an army of private investigators. You could know my life story in a day, maybe less."

Severn leaned down and kissed his mate. He liked that she dared to tease him, to resist him, to question and even command him. "True," he said. "But some treasures are so valuable they deserve to be explored personally, intimately and very, very thoroughly."

He removed his fingers from her hot folds and zeroed in on her erect clit. Its exposed head was a temptation beckoning him to slide down her body so he could suck the tiny knob into his mouth. Only the knowledge that he'd lose all control of the situation if he got near her bare cunt kept him from doing it.

His tongue wrestled with Sophie's as his fingers stroked the underside of her clit, swirled over it, teased it mercilessly. He took pleasure in the way she clung to him as she shuddered and finally cried out in release.

"What do you want to know?" she said. Her hand went unerringly to the dragon raging across his chest. He smiled slightly and wondered if she had a preference for where she'd soon wear a smaller version of his avatar. He stroked her flushed folds then reluctantly left the heated place between her thighs.

"Something you believe, Sophie, something that has made you the person you are, something you think is important for me to know about you."

Sophie eyes met his. She didn't answer immediately, but when she did she said, "My father was a cop. He saved my mother from being raped. He was off-duty at the time. She was walking home from work. I think that's why I write mysteries, because of him. He was killed when I was eight. Wrong place, wrong time. A convenience store robbery gone bad. My mother fell apart. She'd always been needy, but when he died it got worse. She went from man to man. I think she was trying to find someone to rescue her. Ultimately she found my stepfather. He was a control freak. He'd unplug the telephone and take it with him when he left the house. He'd count out the grocery money and watch the clock the few times he'd let my mother do the grocery shopping by herself. For the most part he didn't care about me. I wasn't his—until I started developing."

Severn hissed. Rage burned deep in his chest at what he guessed was coming. "He had better be dead." *Or I will ensure that he soon will be.*

Sophie startled. Her hand cupped Severn's cheek. Her mouth touched his in a brief kiss. "He is. He didn't molest me. He would have. I think he was working up to it. I think he had been for a while but I'd always been uncomfortable around him. It was worse after I developed breasts. On some level maybe my mother knew it. I'd like to believe she finally decided to leave him because she was protecting me instead of because she was afraid she'd lose him once he crossed the line and crept into my bedroom one night.

"He killed her in the kitchen. There was no way to escape, not without him hearing a window breaking. He had deadbolts, inside and outside. He'd painted the window jambs and let the paint dry in the cracks so you couldn't open them.

While he was searching the house for me I ran into the one room I didn't think he'd come back to for a while, the kitchen. I hid under the sink. The police eventually came. They tried to get him to surrender. When he got back to the kitchen, he was completely out of control. He started ripping the cabinet doors open and screaming at the top of his lungs that we were a family and we were all going to die together. A police sniper shot him. He died lying in my mother's blood."

Severn hugged her tightly and for a long moment she clung to him. Finally she kissed the tattoo on his chest. "And that's why I write fantasy and collect crystals and am completely enamored with a certain man who seems to think he's a dragon a lot of the time. I still *need* to believe in magic. Otherwise it's too easy to see only the ugliness and the horrible things people are capable of doing to each other." She nipped his chest. "But it's also why sometimes old fears surface even though I believe you and I are meant to be together."

Her lips found his and Severn opened for her. He allowed her to control the kiss, to be the aggressor, the supplicant, to be his equal, his mate, and when she moaned and softened completely, her body willing him to take command, his kiss became a promise to cherish her, to protect her, to honor her.

The ringing of a phone finally penetrated the haze of passion. Severn groaned in protest but yielded to Sophie's hands pushing against his chest.

Sophie smoothed her skirt down as she reached for her cell phone. Her heart pounded, not only from kissing Severn, but with the realization of how close they'd been to a very public fuck. Despite the relative seclusion of the private beach there were a lot more people walking along the surf than there had been.

She recognized Storm's cell number and mouthed the name to Severn as she answered. "Good news or bad news?"

"It depends," Storm said. "Are you with Severn?"

"Yes. Did you talk to your captain?"

"I did, but it's a moot point now. The D.A. returned the captain's call a few minutes ago. They're not interested in anything Honey Mercante has to say or anything she might have seen. VanDenbergh's killer, or at least the guy we've put in jail for it, was found dead in his cell. He drowned in the toilet."

"What!"

"They've got an autopsy scheduled for tomorrow. He was in a minimum security facility. Those guys have a toilet with standing water. His cellmate was working his prison job at the time. No reason to think murder. No reason to think suicide either. My guess is they'll rule it a freak accident—guy's feeling nauseous and worshiping the porcelain goddess when he has a heart attack or something, loses consciousness and slumps into the bowl."

Sophie shook her head. Truth could be so much stranger than fiction. "So there's no problem with me talking to VanDenbergh's orgy guest?"

"No. I assume you've got enough background information to find her."

Sophie laughed. Her copy of Storm's personal case notes was in her purse and locked in Severn's sports car, not that she needed the subtle reminder of where to look. "I take it you're surrounded by homicide cops."

"Yes, including one who acts like he spent the night with his hand instead of his wife. Is Aislinn involved in this?"

"She thinks she might be able to help."

"Be careful, Sophie. The Chalice of Enos is priceless. Not everyone who wants it will stop at offering money in order to acquire it." There was the slightest hesitation. "Don't go swimming, okay?"

Sophie's eyebrows drew together in confusion at her cousin's abrupt change of topic and even stranger request. "You know I'm not a big swimmer, but what does that have to do with anything?"

"You could say I'm spooked by a guy drowning in his toilet."

Sophie might have laughed and called Storm superstitious. It'd be a well-deserved payback for all the times Storm had rolled her eyes when Sophie had invited her to a psychic fair. But her cousin's serious tone and the worry Sophie heard in Storm's voice kept her from teasing. "I'll be careful," Sophie promised before saying goodbye.

Severn waited only long enough for Sophie to put her phone aside before he took her to the blanket and pinned her there with his body. His hearing was excellent, better than a human's, so he had caught Storm's side of the conversation as well as Sophie's.

The death of VanDenbergh's killer didn't concern him but the manner of his death did. While some of the fey had once enjoyed taking the form of a kelpie, a horse that lured humans to their death, others liked to appear as the reflection of a beautiful woman and then drown those who grew enchanted by the image and got too close to the water's surface. He didn't doubt this death was the work of Morgana or Neryssa. He could only assume they were frustrated by their lack of success in getting close to the chalice, or perhaps they were merely eliminating any possible leads to it. Regardless, he would instruct Xanthus to keep Sophie from swimming. Storm's concern was justified.

Severn turned his attention to his lush mate. Even knowing they might be closer to finding the Dragon's Cup, she was a heady distraction. His cock ached. His heart raced. He wanted to pull her skirt up and join with her.

"You will tell me everything," he said. "And then we will go question VanDenbergh's playmate."

Chapter Fifteen

ᔕᗇ

VanDenbergh's playmate, Honey Rose Mercante, lived well, better than well in Sophie's opinion. Honey's house was a sprawling peach-colored home with a landscaped yard and a winding pathway leading down to a dock.

"Nice," Sophie murmured as Severn cut the sports car's engine. "Maybe I missed my calling. Apparently being a rich man's escort and party girl pays better than being an author."

Severn's response was entirely predictable. Sophie laughed as he growled and very nearly hauled her into his lap. "You seem to have a short memory, my heartmate. Have you already forgotten your last punishment?"

"As if I could! I should punish *you* for leaving my panties in the maze. I can't believe you did that!"

Severn chuckled. His hand slid under the hem of her skirt. His fingers teased upward. "It would appear that at least some of my methods are very effective though, wouldn't it."

A shiver went through Sophie. She clamped her legs together more tightly. "No fair," she whispered as heat radiated from her swollen vulva.

Severn's nostrils flared. Desire burned in his eyes. "I believe you started this."

He took her lips in a dominant, possessive kiss that left her breathing fast and desperately wanting him to fondle her breasts. "Now behave," he said before sliding from the car and going around to open her door.

It took every minute of the long walk to the front door for Sophie to get her rioting libido under control. Part of her was horrified at how easily she kept getting distracted. Up until she met Severn, finding the Chalice of Enos had been constantly on her mind. Then again, she hadn't been expecting to find her heartmate either. And in reality, the Dragon's Cup and Severn were so entwined with one another it seemed perfectly natural to alternate periods of looking for the chalice with periods of making love with him.

A young maid showed them into an elegant room at the front of the house. If she recognized either of their names, it didn't show. She left them, saying only that she would see if Ms. Mercante was receiving visitors.

Apparently Ms. Mercante was, though the Victoria's Secret dressing gown she wore as she joined them suggested the visitor she was most interested in receiving was Severn. "I'm not a morning person, so I hope you'll excuse me for not getting dressed when I plan on returning to bed shortly." Honey licked her lips in a manner guaranteed to have a man fantasizing about joining her between the sheets.

Sophie glanced at Severn. She wouldn't blame him if he played along. Not that she'd like to witness him flirting, and not that she'd stand for him disappearing into the bedroom with the very voluptuous and very available Honey, but despite the sultry glances and flash of long, tanned legs, Sophie didn't feel threatened or jealous.

The realization gave her pause—and confidence. She settled more comfortably against the couch cushion and tried to be inconspicuous. Their best bet at learning anything would be if Severn did the talking and she tried to make herself as invisible as possible.

"Is this about Carl's missing chalice?" Honey asked, her complete attention on Severn as a delicate shudder widened the opening of her gown to reveal more of her deep cleavage. "I know you're a collector too, just like Carl was. I was with him at Sotheby's once when your agents outbid him."

"You were the one to discover the murder?" Severn asked.

"Yes. It was horrible." She placed her hand on her chest. A perfectly manicured fingertip touched the bold outline of a hard nipple. "There are nights I find it difficult to sleep alone. When I close my eyes I see it all over again."

The entire act was so blatant and over-the-top that Sophie had a difficult time processing it mentally at first. But then her creative abilities kicked in and she imagined herself in Honey's position—suddenly given that one, completely unexpected chance to make an impression on the very rich and very elusive Severn Damek.

Severn leaned forward. Consciously or unconsciously, Honey did the same. The angle made it possible to see all the way down to her bellybutton.

"I'm hoping you saw more that night than you shared with the police," Severn said.

Honey's eyes widened. Surprise, fear, speculation were all present before she blinked them away.

Pride at his mate's cleverness filled Severn. He wanted to pull Sophie into his arms and kiss her soundly for the hunch that had led them here but whatever advantage he'd gained with VanDenbergh's former playmate would be lost if he did so.

"You saw something?" he asked, deliberately speaking in the rough purr that by rights should only be heard by his mate.

Honey licked her lips in a gesture undoubtedly meant to stir his cock and muddy his thinking. It did nothing for him other than make him want to get this visit over with more quickly—before Sophie's tolerance and understanding reached their limit.

"It's difficult for me to think about that day," Honey said. Her hand slid upward to linger at the base of her neck.

With a great deal of cynicism Severn calculated how much it would take to make her remember. If he'd known the details of Storm and Sophie's discussion yesterday, then he would have had a complete dossier on Honey Mercante *before* visiting her home. Unfortunately his law-abiding mate had correctly guessed at his unwillingness to wait until VanDenbergh's playmate had been re-interviewed by the police.

Had he known about Sophie's theory, he would have visited immediately. He would have arranged for Honey's home to be thoroughly searched.

Any delay was dangerous. What the police knew, the other dragons and the fey of Otthilde's court would soon know as well.

The untimely death of VanDenbergh's murderer had unwittingly worked in his favor. It had most likely slowed the flow of information to the others seeking the cup. Still, he didn't intend to waste time.

Hoping his fiery mate wouldn't lose her temper and scorch him with her anger, Severn said, "Perhaps fresh air and sunshine would make it easier to talk. We could go for espresso. There's a small shop right next to Renaldo's. Do you know it?"

At the mention of the exclusive jewelry store and the implied promise that perhaps she'd see the inside of it, his quarry's tongue darted out to gloss over her plump bottom lip. "Yes, I know it."

Her eyes darted quickly to Sophie, who Severn hadn't dared look at. "Perhaps we can meet later?" Honey stretched slightly, cat-like, so the cloth of her thin grown rubbed over her nipples. "I need time to get dressed."

"Would an hour and a half be long enough?" Severn tilted his head slightly in Sophie's direction. "I need to run back to my office."

"Perfect," Honey said. "You'll pick me up?"

"Of course."

Severn started to rise from the couch but hesitated. "Besides the police, have you shared what you saw at VanDenbergh's estate with anyone else?"

The briefest flicker gave her away. She recovered quickly with an impressive show of wet, tear-laden eyes. "I...I'm sorry. Let me get dressed and gather my thoughts. Remembering that day is so difficult. We'll talk over coffee." She rose. "I'll have Maria show you out," she said before hurrying from the room.

Severn's eyes met Sophie's but neither of them spoke until they returned to the car. He used his cell phone to order some of his unseen bodyguards to remain behind to watch Honey Mercante's house. As soon as he set the phone down, Sophie placed her hand on his swollen cock and very nearly caused him to swerve off the road.

"This belongs to me," his fiery mate said. "My logical, crime-writing side understands what happened back there and knows you played it exactly right. But my emotional, fantasy-creating side is having very violent, very dragon-like thoughts. It's screaming mine, mine, mine and it does not like even the appearance of sharing."

Severn grinned despite the pulsing, hot agony centered in his cock and balls. By The Great Shared Ancestor she pleased him.

His hand covered hers. He wanted to open his trousers and wrap her fingers around his erection, to urge her to lean forward and take him in her mouth and claim him completely. He longed for the day when he could let the magic fade and would feel her tongue exploring the ridges underneath the head of his penis.

A moan escaped. His cock spasmed then jerked when her thumb grazed over the pulsing, cloth-covered tip. "Sophie," he growled, torn between pleading for more and warning her against tormenting him further.

"This is mine," she said. "All mine."

"There will never be anyone for me but you."

She squeezed him through the material then mercifully allowed her palm to settle on his erection like a heated blanket. "Good. Now that we're clear on what's important, it looks like Honey saw something and shared it with at least one other person."

"True, my beautiful and very clever heartmate." He stroked his thumb over the back of Sophie's hand. "I believe I will be successful in gaining both pieces of information. It will be easier to extract if you aren't there." He decided against telling Sophie that while Honey Mercante was drinking espresso and choosing a fitting piece of jewelry, her house would be thoroughly searched by his men.

"I know," Sophie grumbled.

"Xanthus will remain at the estate. You are free to come and go as you please, Sophie, but he needs to remain with you. You are priceless to me. Even if the Dragon's Cup were found and the danger to you minimal, I'd ask you to accept his presence and see it as a need to ensure your safety rather than a need to control you."

Warmth blossomed in Sophie's heart at the underlying fear in his voice. She leaned in and rubbed her lips against his cheek. "There are probably going to be times when I chafe at always having someone watching me, but what we have together is completely different from the relationship my mother had with my stepfather."

He brought her hand to his lips and kissed the back of it. "I would never knowingly hurt you, Sophie," he said, repeating the promise he'd made at the beach.

"I believe you. And it's not like I'm the only one being watched. I didn't know you had bodyguards until you told some of them to stay behind. Do you always have them with you?"

"Yes. Not usually so many of them. But you're with me at present."

Sophie frowned. "Are you saying I have more people watching me than just Xanthus?"

Severn spared a glance at her as if trying to gauge her mood. "Yes. Xanthus serves as a warning to anyone who might become interested in you. His presence is an announcement you are under my protection, though at this point, it's probably well known you are my mate."

The word *mate* made Sophie smile. She imagined thousands of little bubbles of happiness floating from her heart upward. He really was a dragon in human form. She couldn't envision him calling her his girlfriend, yet if another man had ever called her his mate she'd have wrinkled her nose at the oddity of it—even after gaining the necklace from Aislinn and growing accustomed to the thought of having a heartmate.

Another thought surfaced. This one had the bubbles sinking and the first threads of mortification rising to Sophie's face. "Were your men watching us when we were at the beach?"

His chuckle did *not* make her feel better. "They couldn't see anything. My body shielded yours."

Sophie shivered. That may be true, but what they were doing—more specifically, where his hands were—would have been obvious. "I think we're going to need to set some ground rules."

Severn's hand went to her thigh. His fingers traced the hem of her skirt. "Where there are rules, there are punishments for breaking them."

Sophie's closed her eyes. He was impossible. Incorrigible.

Arousal seeped from her slit. He was pure temptation.

Severn inhaled deeply and cursed silently. He knew better than to touch Sophie, to goad her into a reaction.

The scent of her had his testicles pulled tight against his body. The desire to plunge into her silky folds had him very nearly panting. But he knew as soon as he pulled to a stop in front of his estate that there wasn't enough time to mount her.

"You will stay here?" he asked as he opened the passenger door and took her hand.

"For a while. I thought I'd work on my computer." He led her to his office. She laughed as soon as she saw the jewel-encrusted dragons lining his shelves and resting on antique tables and pedestals. "Storm told me about this room." Her breath caught when she saw the figurine set from the VanDenbergh estate at the edge of his desk.

Lust seared through Severn. He'd known his gift to Sophie would be delivered today but he'd left others to deal with the details. Now the sight of the dragon pleasuring its human mate stirred his fantasies. He didn't have time to fuck his mate, but he could satisfy them both in another, exquisitely carnal way.

Sophie stifled a shriek when Severn picked her up without warning and spilled her across his elegant desk. His quick hands pinned her wrists to the polished surface of the wood while his thighs wedged between hers, opening her and sending the skirt riding up toward her waist.

She knew what he intended. His words at the auction came back with a heated rush of wetness.

I will arrange to purchase this one as my gift to you. We can place it on the nightstand next to our bed and let it inspire us in our tongue-play.

She whimpered as his tongue plundered her mouth. His kisses were so hungry and distracting that she didn't notice he'd freed her wrists until her blouse and bra parted and she felt the silk of his shirt against her bared flesh.

"If I had time, I'd fuck you," he said, pulling her skirt upward as his lips traveled downward.

Sophie arched when he captured a nipple. She cried out as he laved and bit and suckled with hard, firm pulls. She moaned when he licked down to her bellybutton. Her skirt was a narrow band of bunched material separating her abdomen from the place she wanted him most.

"Severn," she said, shivering, using her grip on his shoulders to push herself further onto his desk. She rose to her elbows, her position mimicking the human figurine. The wet heat of his mouth had her cunt lips parting in anticipation of his kiss.

The dark red of Severn's braid was draped over her thigh just as the dragon figurine's long tongue was wrapped around the woman's thigh before its tip disappeared into her folds. Sophie closed her eyes but the figurine images were burned into her mind. They blurred with the feel of Severn licking over her clit, sucking it into his mouth, tormenting her as his carnal assault blended with dragon fantasies.

"Please," she whispered, pumping into his mouth as though her clit was a small, sensitive penis.

He ate hungrily. He took her to the edge then left her there as his mouth found her cunt lips and his tongue pressed into her slick depths in a kiss that had her shuddering and begging.

He suckled on flushed lower lips. He thrust his tongue into her again and again.

His growls joined her moans. His hands gripped her buttocks and held her to him as he feasted like a man starved for what she had to offer.

Her keen of release only made his assault on her more aggressive, more possessive. In her imagination she heard a dragon's roar. *Mine!*

Sophie felt sated, decadent, amused. All around her glittering, jewel-encrusted dragons stared at her. Between her thighs, a human dragon lapped and nuzzled, kissed and sucked the bare flesh of her mound. She shivered when his tongue found her clit, her slit. He seemed determined to consume every drop of her arousal but each one of his touches only created more.

"You're going to be late," Sophie said, not caring. She trusted Severn but she still hated the thought of him meeting Honey for coffee and a trip to the jewelry store.

With one last open-mouthed kiss Severn lifted his mouth from Sophie's cunt. His eyes were shimmering sapphires. "Only the Dragon's Cup could draw me away from you at this moment."

She shivered in reaction. Her womb fluttered and her channel spasmed. Severn's nostrils flared as though he could smell just how arousing she found his words. She wanted to say, *Don't leave.* She wanted to sit up and draw him to her at the edge of the desk. She wanted to feel his cock sliding into her as she wrapped her arms and legs around him.

"You'd better go," Sophie said. "Honey's the only lead we've got at the moment."

Her breath caught when Severn's hand covered her mound possessively. Her clit stabbed his palm.

"I trust you'll remember what happened the last time we parted because of the Dragon's Cup. The punishment will be worse if I return to find you wearing panties."

Heat flooded Sophie's face in a combination of anticipation and embarrassed resolve. As soon as he left she'd be making a trip out to the maze.

She sat up on the desk and draped her arms over his shoulders. With Severn it was better to fight fire with fire. "I'm not afraid of you."

His smile was a predatory flash though humor flickered in his eyes. "Perhaps I'll see what I can do to remedy that when I return."

He pulled her to him and covered her mouth with his. His kiss was deeply carnal, the taste of her arousal on his lips and tongue darkly erotic.

"You are a distraction, my heartmate," Severn said, releasing her and stepping back. He stroked her cheek. "Use my office as your own. Explore the house and grounds as you wish but should you encounter my mother or Audriss, make your excuses and escape. I don't really believe any harm will come to you here, but I need to know you're protected. Xanthus will watch over you until I return."

Sophie grimaced but didn't protest. She had no desire to go one-on-one with either of Severn's houseguests. Only the unpleasantness of her first encounter with Audriss enabled Sophie to suppress—for the most part—the memory of having Audriss interrupt the spanking in the maze.

With a final kiss, Severn left. Sophie retrieved her panties though not without blushing at the knowing look in Xanthus' eyes. As soon as she deposited them in the bedroom, she returned to Severn's office.

Sophie shook her head as she placed her laptop on his desk. If almost every moment with Severn hadn't been an adventure of one type or another, she'd have been anxious about how easily she'd abandoned her computer. She grinned. Then again, Severn could be placed under the category of necessary *research* and she could claim she was *suffering* for her art.

She took a minute to check e-mail. She snickered at all the spam for products to enlarge a man's penis and give him staying power. She thought about ordering some of it and leaving the bottles on the nightstand next to Severn's side of the bed. If that didn't get him to breathe fire, nothing would.

She laughed. Better yet, next time she talked to Storm she'd see what her cousin could scrounge up in the way of bogus product. Cops were notorious practical jokers.

Sophie's thoughts flicked to Severn as she typed Honey Mercante's name into a search engine. She wondered how much it would cost him to pry information out of VanDenbergh's playmate and whether the information would be useful.

There were a lot of hits on the name, more than Sophie expected. A frown formed as she followed link after link.

Honey liked to have her name in the society column of the paper, especially when a photograph showing her with a wealthy man accompanied it. A knot formed in Sophie's stomach. She reached for her cell phone only to realize she still didn't know Severn's number. Xanthus was lounging in an office chair. He wouldn't leave her unattended and she hadn't seen any point in making him stand in the hallway while she worked in the office.

"What's Severn's cell number? Honey's probably arranged for a society page photographer to catch her with him."

"I'll give it to you but there's no need to contact him." Xanthus smiled with predatory intensity. "Haven't you ever wondered why there are no pictures of Severn?"

Sophie blinked. She should have wondered but somehow Severn's being labeled elusive and reclusive had made the lack of newspaper photographs seem perfectly natural. Then again, given his reputation, she'd assumed he was an old man until Storm told her what Severn looked like. "No."

"There are no photographs because it is part of our job to ensure there are none."

O-kay. It was shades of *The Godfather*, or maybe her future creation, *Cult of the Dragon*. Sophie decided this was definitely a case where *Don't Ask, Don't Tell* applied.

She was saved from thinking about it further by the ring tone of her cell phone. Excitement flashed through her when she saw the call was from Aislinn.

Chapter Sixteen

ဆ

Severn was finding it tedious to deal with VanDenbergh's playmate. Even in the days before he'd met Sophie, he'd never been drawn to women who traded on their good looks in order to live an idle lifestyle.

They'd been through a first cup of espresso and were on a second. His companion's gaze strayed far less than her hands and feet. He'd lost count of how many times she'd brushed her fingers across his hand as she imparted some tidbit about a priceless artifact she'd seen in someone's home. He'd endured several sly rubs of her toes against his ankles before positioning them out of her reach.

He was finding that despite his tactile nature, he abhorred her touch. The only female he wanted touching him was Sophie.

Amusement struck with the realization that a mate's hold on a dragon male was far more potent than the lure of any treasure, and far more enslaving. A laugh escaped, a sultry sound that came at the wrong moment and encouraged the woman across from him. She leaned forward far enough to make him wonder if her breasts would escape the dress completely or if he was supposed to begin salivating at the sight of her exposed nipple.

He pinned her hands to the table when they started to stray toward his. He'd had enough. "Tell me what you saw the day VanDenbergh was murdered." This time he didn't cloak his impatience. It'd been a mistake to play it this way. She was too used to men who liked a beautiful arm piece and easy bed companion.

She pouted but he saw the flash in her eyes. Irritation, speculation, a hint of triumph. He could guess the source of each emotion. She was destined for disappointment if she thought his name would be linked with hers. Even the piece of jewelry he'd no doubt have to provide at the end of this exchange wouldn't be traced back to him, nor would the images captured on the security camera be recoverable. He smiled slightly. Only the youngest of dragons kept every gem they acquired. As he'd aged and grown more powerful his tastes had become more refined. Renaldo's was just one of many jewelry stores that were part of his holdings in this realm.

"Tell me what you saw the day VanDenbergh was murdered," Severn repeated.

* * * * *

Sophie stared at the piece of jewelry in her hands. She was having a hard time looking away from the shimmering crystal held in place by a fine net of gold. Either her imagination was working overtime or the strange stone was humming against her palms. The sensation wasn't unpleasant, but it wasn't pleasant either.

Aislinn's hands cupped Sophie's. Slowly they forced Sophie's to fold, enclosing the glittering crystal inside the locket that contained it.

"Weird," Sophie said, blinking, free of the humming and the odd feeling of being trapped. "That was like having an out-of-body experience. I saw your hands on mine but I couldn't react. I didn't even think of reacting." She blinked again and met Aislinn's gaze as the back room of Inner Magick came into focus.

"This is a fascination stone," Aislinn said. Her expression was serious, her tone somber. "With so many dangerous...people after the chalice, I wanted you to have some measure of protection."

Sophie's eyebrows drew together. "I can see how this might work to distract someone but it also seems to paralyze me."

"That's because the charm is still raw." Aislinn pulled her hands from Sophie's. Sophie turned the oyster-shaped locket over and noted the symbols etched into the gold on the back. When her thumb grazed over the tiny clasp keeping the locket closed, Aislinn said, "Open it only three more times. The first two times will be today. You need to submerge it in saltwater and speak the word that will bring the stone into its full power. It will be keyed to your voice and command so if you are in danger you can trigger the stone. Open the locket again when you're alone and rinse the salt away. Then leave it closed until you need it for protection. The third time you open it, give it to whoever is threatening you. They won't be able to look away from it until long after you've made your escape."

Sophie studied the symbols. "This almost seems more like a spell."

"The magic is in the stone. The fascination will build the longer you wear it and the longer you keep the locket closed. But without the words the gem isn't usable for the purpose of defense. Its power isn't focused."

"So I say the trigger word, open the locket and whoever's threatening me will become instantly fascinated by the stone?"

Aislinn laughed. "It's a little more complicated than that. You're the one freeing and directing the stone. The full force of your will should be on the person you want to affect. It's also important their attention be on the locket as you open it. Now do you want to key it to you here? Or are you going to take it to the beach?"

Sophie grinned. "Beach. Look what happened when I took the heartmate necklace to my favorite spot and dunked it in the ocean."

Aislinn smiled but shook her head. "With or without the heartmate stone, you and Severn would have found each other. The stone only helped you see the truth and accept it sooner."

Sophie pulled the pendant out from underneath her blouse. It was warm, almost hot. The deep blue coloring and sparks of red seemed to pulse with a life of their own. She blinked in surprise as she realized for the first time how closely the colors matched those of the dragon tattooed on Severn's chest. She couldn't believe she'd missed it before. It was so obvious.

She glanced at Aislinn. "Did you know he was the one?"

"No. When you became fascinated with the Dragon's Cup, I wondered. But until Severn came to collect you at my house I'd never seen him before."

The tinkling of chimes signaled that someone had come through the main entrance of Inner Magick. Sophie stiffened when she heard Severn's mother say, "I see you are cursed with the same weakness my son is. In your case it is understandable. You come from a long line of deviant males and the weak females who allow themselves to be shared."

Sophie's eyes widened. She wondered if forming a threesome was what Xanthus and Marika were fighting about, then firmly pushed the idea aside as she considered its venomous source. "That's Severn's mother. I'd better head out, if for no other reason than to spare Xanthus from her abuse." She slipped the heartmate necklace under her blouse then put the locket in her pocket.

Aislinn grimaced. She gave Sophie a quick hug. "You're going to the beach next?"

"Yes."

"Good. I'll feel better knowing you've got the fascination stone."

They stepped through the beaded curtain and into the customer area. Intense hostility slammed into Sophie and sent her heart racing.

Xanthus had positioned himself next to Marika. He was rigid with the desire to attack but instead of being focused on Severn's mother, his attention was on the two men with her.

Sophie shivered at the sight of them. They were lean and thin-faced, dark-eyed and reptilian.

Aislinn gasped softly then stiffened her spine before moving deeper into the store. The movement caused Severn's mother to glance away from Xanthus and Marika. Her face tightened in distaste as soon as she saw Sophie.

"I don't believe you'll find what you seek here," Aislinn said. "Perhaps I can direct you to a more suitable place?"

Hell would work perfectly, Sophie thought. *She'd fit right in there.*

Fire flashed in Severn's mother's eyes but she didn't retreat from Inner Magick. She turned away from Aislinn and began examining a display of tarot cards.

Sophie headed toward the door, happy to make her escape. She stopped when she saw Xanthus take a reluctant step away from Marika.

He was still coiled with tension, still focused on the two men with Severn's mother. He'd be forced to leave if she did. The realization was a blast of fresh air clearing away a tangle of emotions. Sophie stiffened her spine and her resolve. She wasn't going to spend the rest of her life running away from Severn's mother—avoiding the woman whenever possible, most definitely, but not running or hiding. She was stronger than that, she'd faced something much more terrifying and had not only survived but had overcome.

Sophie walked to the case containing the rune sets. As she studied them her tension eased. They were all exquisite works of art.

A smile formed on her lips as she picked out the set she'd unwrapped just before Severn arrived and irrevocably changed her life. Those she definitely had to have.

There were decorative boxes and satin drawstring bags on the bottom shelf of the display case. Sophie mentally chose a dark blue bag to house the runes. She grinned when a red bag caught her eye and the familiar voice of temptation prompted her to choose a second set.

I'm as bad as Severn is.

As soon as Sophie thought it she saw herself tumbled across Severn's desk with hundreds of jewel-encrusted dragons looking on as he made love to her with his mouth and tongue. Her cunt clenched in painful need. She bit her bottom lip to keep from moaning.

Severn's mother chose that moment to arrive at the case housing the runes. Sophie almost welcomed the cooling effect it had on her libido.

"My son believes he can keep you safe but he is mistaken. If you are smart, you will run and hide while you still can."

Ice slid down Sophie's spine. Her heart rate trebled but she forced herself to turn so she was facing Severn's mother. "Are you threatening me?"

Severn's mother leaned in. "I am warning you and speaking a truth. Look how far away your guard is. If I intended to harm you he would not be able to stop me."

Sophie mimicked Severn's mother's actions. She leaned in so their shoulders were very nearly touching. The fascination stone was a heavy weight in her pocket. She was almost glad it wasn't yet ready to use, otherwise she'd have been tempted to try it out right then.

"Severn and I are together. You can accept the fact or not. Personally I don't care which you do because so far nothing I've seen makes me want you as either a mother-in-law for myself or a grandmother for my future children." Something prompted her to pull the heartmate necklace from beneath her blouse.

Severn's mother flinched at the sight of it. Loathing filled her face before she turned and left Inner Magick, her two guards in tow.

Sophie felt a surge of triumph. She'd stood up to the old dragon and won!

* * * * *

Impatience slithered along Severn's spine as he leaned against a glass display case housing a collection of sapphires and rubies. The gems winked as if trying to gain his attention, but he was impervious to them. He had thousands of stones with even greater value left as unattended bedding in the rocky lair he claimed as his own in the dragon realm.

VanDenbergh's playmate was several cases away looking at diamond necklaces. Severn smiled with thoughts of his mate and how clever she was. Sophie's hunch had been correct.

The female companion who'd discovered VanDenbergh's body had witnessed the thief leaving with the Dragon's Cup. She'd intended to profit from the information, either through blackmail or theft. That much she'd admitted over coffee though she claimed the thief had been killed before she could set her plan into motion.

Severn's cell phone rang. His impatience faded when he checked the coded text message. His men had finished searching Honey Mercante's home. They hadn't found the chalice but at least he'd soon be free of her company.

He pocketed the phone and joined VanDenbergh's playmate. "I need to leave. Have you made your choice?"

She tapped a long, manicured fingernail against the glass. "This necklace."

Severn gave a slight nod. The clerk who'd been hovering discreetly in the background removed the necklace from the case.

"Who else knows what you saw?" Severn asked.

VanDenbergh's playmate licked her lips. He moved into her but her look of anticipation quickly fled when he said, "Before you answer, consider carefully what you might have heard about me and what it will cost you if I find you've cheated me."

A hint of fear perfumed the air. "Carl's grandson, Carl VanDenbergh the Third. He's the only one I told."

Severn held her gaze long enough in assure himself she was telling the truth. Her answer didn't please him.

* * * * *

Sophie waded into the ocean. She couldn't see it, but she could feel Xanthus' frowning disapproval. It burned her back and made her ultra-self-conscious about what she was doing.

He hadn't wanted her to wade into the surf. Yet he wouldn't give her a reason except that Severn had specifically said she should stay away from water. It made no sense at all. There'd been no shark sightings and no beach closures because of hazardous waste.

Sophie took another step, this one putting the water at mid-thigh. She stopped.

Be careful, Sophie. The Chalice of Enos is priceless. Not everyone who wants it will stop at offering money in order to acquire it. Don't go swimming, okay?

Storm's strange comment when she'd called to say VanDenbergh's alleged murderer had drowned in his toilet sounded in Sophie's mind. Sophie's eyebrows drew together. What in the world was going on?

A shiver of nervousness danced along her spine and had goose bumps rising on her arms in premonition. It was enough of a warning for Sophie to pull the locket out of her pocket.

She closed her eyes to concentrate on what she was doing. It was hard, given Xanthus' intense focus and her own tingling sense of danger, now magnified by lack of sight.

Sophie sighed and opened her eyes. No sharks. No crazed boogie boarders or radical surfers. In fact, the ocean was fairly calm.

None of those observations reduced her feelings of uneasiness. It was possible Storm's odd warning and Xanthus' trying to keep her out of the water had agitated her subconscious imagination, but Sophie didn't discount her fight-or-flight instincts. They'd kept her alive before.

She took a deep breath and willed herself calm. She didn't close her eyes again.

When she felt centered she opened the oyster-shaped locket and immediately felt the pull of the fascination stone. Sophie blinked in an effort to free herself from it. She blinked again and hurriedly dipped it into the saltwater as she said, "Look."

For a word of magic, *look* wasn't too impressive. Readers would roll their eyes if she used it in one of her stories. But it was perfect for a weapon like the one Aislinn had given her. What better way to draw an enemy's attention to the fascination stone than to say *look*?

Sophie closed the locket while it was under water then pulled it up. As she clasped it around her neck she thought she heard a woman's voice call, "Help me."

"Sophie!" Xanthus yelled.

"Help me." The female voice came again. It was low, just barely above the sound of the surf.

Sophie thought she saw movement out of the corner of her eye. She took a step, anticipating sand and calm water only to be gripped by a fierce cold undercurrent that made her lose her balance and go under.

Her heart thundered. It felt like she was caught in an undertow. Panic made her kick and scramble and fight to her feet. She emerged from the water coughing and sputtering.

"Sophie!" Xanthus' voice demanded her attention.

She turned. Xanthus was hurrying toward her.

Despite the warmth of the water, Sophie was cold and covered in goose bumps. "I'm okay but I think someone's in trouble. Did you hear a woman calling for help?"

"It's a trick of the wind and water."

"I'm pretty sure—" A hint of cold reached her ankles. She retreated as Xanthus increased his pace, sending water splashing even higher onto his jeans and shirt. Behind him Sophie saw several men on the beach. Their alert stances told her they were Severn's men, the hidden bodyguards she'd only just learned about.

"What's going on?"

"Severn's on his way back to the estate. Let's go."

The terse command added to the shakiness Sophie was already feeling at the strange current that made her lose her balance and go under. She felt disoriented, like she'd taken a step into *The Twilight Zone*.

"You're sure you didn't hear anyone calling for help?" Sophie asked, turning away from Xanthus and scanning the water.

His hand closed around her arm in a firm grip. "There is no one out here in need of rescue except for you."

Sophie gave in a moment later and turned back toward the shore. "You can let go of my arm. I'm not going under again." She grimaced when she looked at his wet clothing. "You didn't need to wade in."

Xanthus snorted. "Severn might well kill me if I allowed anything to happen to you. Wet clothing is a small price to pay to ensure my continued good health." His grip tightened before he released her. "My thanks for not leaving Inner Magick before Severn's mother and her servants did."

"No problem." Sophie glanced at him as she reached back to squeeze water from her hair. A multitude of questions raced through her mind, most of which weren't her business, so she limited herself to asking, "Are Aislinn and Marika safe?"

"Yes. Both Severn and Malik have men protecting Aislinn. Some of Severn's men also watch Marika when I'm not free to do so."

"Because of the Dragon's Cup?"

"Yes."

They reached the shore and paused to coax as much water out of their clothing as they could before going to the cherry red sports car she'd chosen from Severn's collection. Sophie grimaced. "I hope we beat Severn home. I doubt he'd like to see us emerge from one of his toys like this."

"I'll drive fast," Xanthus said, holding his hand out for the key.

Sophie figured he deserved a reward for wading in after her, even if she didn't need rescuing. She unlocked the passenger door then dropped the key into his palm. As she slid into the car, Sophie saw a woman walking along the surf, her long black hair snapping behind her in the wind. There was something familiar about the woman. It took Sophie a moment to make the connection. The woman who'd been at Inner Magick, Neryssa, looked a lot like this woman.

Xanthus' entry into the water suddenly made a little more sense to Sophie. She still thought he'd overreacted, but maybe the combination of seeing her go under and having an enemy nearby had tipped the scales in favor of action.

Sophie shivered. Then again, in all the times she'd come to the beach, she'd never experienced anything like what had happened to her out in the water.

"Do you know her?" Sophie asked, pointing, testing her theory.

"Morgana."

The name rang a bell. Sophie searched her memory and found an interrupted — because of her arrival — conversation between Storm and Aislinn.

"Is she the same woman who tried to kill Storm over Tristan?"

Sophie frowned as she remembered how frustrated she'd gotten when Storm backpedaled and refused to elaborate. Though maybe there hadn't been anything more to the story, otherwise Morgana would be in jail.

"Yes," Xanthus said. "What else do you know about Morgana?"

"Nothing, but I'm guessing she's related to Neryssa."

Xanthus gave her a quick look. "They're cousins and both dangerous. There's no love lost between them and Severn. The one they owe their allegiance to possessed the Chalice of Enos for a time. They will stop at nothing to reclaim it."

Sophie read between the lines and said, "So they're not dragons."

Xanthus jerked in reaction. He cut a surprised look in her direction. She laughed and answered his unspoken questions. "I'm a writer. I observe people for a living and put things together with the help of a very active imagination. I haven't figured it all out, I'm sure, but the dragon tattoo you guys all wear and the way you're competing for treasure practically screams *secret society*."

Xanthus chuckled. "It's a good thing Severn found and claimed you. He's going to be the envy of many a dragon."

Sophie rolled her eyes. "You guys take the dragon thing to an extreme but somehow, at least in the men I've met so far, it's kind of fun. In the women on the other hand..." She gave a dramatic shudder. "I hope I'm not supposed to use Severn's mother and Audriss as role models."

Xanthus gave a shudder of his own. "I think you'll find yourself imprisoned in a rocky lair high in the mountains if you do."

They pulled into the garage. He cut the engine and looked around. "We're in luck. Severn isn't back. I'll see you to the bedroom then make sure the sand and salt water is removed from this car."

Moments later, as she felt the first hot blast of water against her skin, Sophie decided to drag out the shower and let Severn find her in it.

Chapter Seventeen

ဢ

Severn stepped into the bathroom. Lust roared through him at the sight of water cascading over Sophie's naked back and buttocks as her fingers worked conditioner through her long tresses. Some of the rage burning in his chest cooled, though not all of it. If the covenants didn't prevent it, he would find Morgana and incinerate her where she stood. That she'd dared to attack his mate— Severn's nostrils flared, his rant cut off when he saw the oyster-shaped locket resting on the counter next to the sink.

Elven. He recognized the stylish script engraved in the gold. He could sense the magic Aislinn was able to imbue it with in a realm that had lost much of it when the dragons, fey and elves left.

From Xanthus' account, Severn knew this was the reason his mate had been in the ocean despite his orders to keep her out of it. Severn growled. It was a good thing for Aislinn that he trusted her and knew she sought only to protect and help Sophie.

Still, his mate had once again defied him, not directly since he hadn't told her to stay out of the water. But Xanthus had conveyed the message and she'd chosen to ignore it.

He stripped out of his clothing. Perhaps his mate needed a more thorough demonstration of his dominance.

Severn's hand went to his cock. His gaze followed. He longed to feel her mouth on his penis. But every time he was near her she threatened his control of the magic. One hot, wet lave of her tongue and the ridges would be exposed. One sweet, heated pull of her lips as she suckled his cock head and she'd see him in his most natural state while in human form.

His hand slid up and down his shaft. His balls pulled tight. His mate chose that moment to turn around and sear him with a leisurely perusal of his body.

By The Great Shared Ancestor, he barely had a thought when he was in her presence.

Severn closed the distance between them. He got into the shower with her and immediately held her to the wall with his body.

His lips captured hers. Her hands joined his in caressing his cock, his balls.

Thoughts of punishment and dominance fled as their tongues met and tangled in greeting, as she cupped his testicles in one hand while the thumb of the other danced across the tip of his penis. When the need for breath forced his mouth away from hers, his mate pushed at his control further by rubbing at the leaking slit in his cock head and saying, "You don't have to take care of this yourself, I'll do it for you."

His hips jerked in reaction. A lance of fire stabbed through him when she started to slide downward. He wanted nothing more than to step back and let her pleasure him with her mouth.

Severn groaned in frustration. He could feel the first hint of the dragon ridges against his palm. Once her lips and tongue were on him, he'd be lost.

He leaned more of his weight against her. He forced his mind back to thoughts of discipline. "You went into the ocean even though Xanthus told you I didn't want you to."

She responded by fondling his testicles, by measuring their weight and stroking them. He quivered under her touch like a fledgling about to make its first leap from a high rocky lair.

"Aislinn gave me a necklace for protection. I just went in long enough to activate it." She nibbled at his neck. Her thumb stroked over his slit and gathered a bead of arousal, then sought out his nipple, smearing the silky moisture over his hard nub. "Let's not fight. I need you."

His hips bucked as she slid down far enough to put her mouth on the nipple. Her tongue rubbed against it and sent ice-hot pleasure through his cock. The thought of her tasting his essence had his balls pulling tighter, burning as lava-hot semen threatened to rush through his shaft and spew across shower-slick flesh.

"Sophie," he moaned as she began suckling. His hand stroked up and down his penis in the same rhythm.

The magic holding him to human form began to fail. The steam of the shower took on hues of dark blue and red.

With a deep growl Severn wrenched himself away from Sophie. He turned her toward the wall before he lost all control. His mouth found his mark on her shoulder. His teeth clamped down on it in a hold guaranteed to telegraph his dominance and demand her submission.

She sobbed and pressed her buttocks against his groin. "Please, Severn."

He rubbed his cock through the cleft of her ass. Moisture beaded on the tip of his penis, a thick, heavy lubricant meant to go along with primitive urges he'd never given in to before.

Severn altered their positions. He squeezed her wrists in a silent command that she was to leave her hands where he'd placed them against the shower wall.

She whimpered in acknowledgement then arched in pleasure when he cupped her breasts. "Mine," he said, molding and stroking. The feel of her hardened nipples against his palms fed the dragon desire to mate, to fill her with seed, to protect her as her belly grew swollen with his young.

The need to thrust into her slit and seek her womb nearly overrode the darker, more carnal urge to claim her in a way that reinforced his dominance. Severn growled as he forced his hands downward, over her flat abdomen and to her cunt.

One hand cupped her mound while the other gathered her arousal and rimmed her back entrance with it. When she startled and moved, he sank his teeth into her shoulder again.

She moaned as he prepared her with his fingers. She quivered under his touch and whimpered as he opened her, stretched her, made her ready for him.

The shower trapped them in a world of wet, sultry heat made more intense by the bond they shared, by the need they had for one another. "Mine," Severn said again as he placed the tip of his penis against her anus. "Say it, Sophie."

"I'm yours," Sophie said, feeling it in every cell of her body, in every heartbeat, with every breath. He was everything to her.

She pressed against him, needing the connection with him, welcoming the painful pleasure of his possession as he worked himself into her. She gloried in the sounds of his panting, his moaning, in an agony that was also ecstasy.

"You ensnare me as no other could," he said when he was fully seated, his cock throbbing in her dark depths to the rhythm of their racing hearts. His lips and tongue caressed the place he'd bitten. His hand returned to her breast while the other stroked her clit. "You are my world, Sophie, my life."

She shivered in reaction to his words and to the wealth of meaning they contained. "You're my life too, my world."

Severn began thrusting. Slow at first, careful not to hurt her. She was so tight, so hot, so human.

Her words were a song he'd carry in his heart until the day he died. Her body was a treasure he'd spend a lifetime savoring. She was his mate, the only one capable of humbling him even as she brought out the fiercest aspects of his dragon nature.

"Sophie," he growled as his thrusts became harder and his seed boiled with the need to escape from his testicles. The fingers on her clit became more aggressive, the ones on her nipple squeezed until her body tightened and she clamped down on his cock in savage ecstasy.

Severn saw flashes of red and dark blue as he jerked and shuddered in release. The spurs at his wrists slid into existence along with a shimmer of dragon scales as the last of his seed poured into her.

He was panting heavily, shuddering with pleasure as his chest lay across Sophie's back. His heart thundered not only as a result of fucking his mate, but at how close to becoming fully dragon he'd come.

He needed to get her to the dragon realm. He needed to make her fully his.

Her soft, sated body told him she'd been lost in passion and hadn't witnessed his loss of control. He was glad and yet at the same time he was impatient for her to see him in his other form.

With a kiss to her shoulder Severn forced himself away from her. He groaned as his cock left her tight depths. Sophie's whimper of abandonment fed his dragon satisfaction.

"Careful, my heartmate, or you'll tempt me into taking you again in that manner," he purred.

She laughed and straightened away from the wall. "Promises, promises," she teased as she turned and wrapped her arms around his neck before covering his mouth and giving him a playful kiss. When they broke away from each other they finished showering then shared the hairdryer until rich red locks had been brought under control and bound.

Sophie thought about the Dragon's Cup as she stepped into the bedroom wearing a sheer robe. She turned toward Severn and said, "What happened with VanDenbergh's girlfriend?"

He took her hand and led her to where several large cushions were scattered in front of the ornate chests he'd pointed out to her the day she'd agreed to stay with him. "She saw the thief leaving with the chalice and intended to blackmail him. Unfortunately he died before she could put her plan into effect. She told VanDenbergh's grandson, Carl VanDenbergh III. He has no idea of the chalice's whereabouts, of that I am sure."

Sophie laughed when Severn sprawled across the cushions like a sultan then pulled her down to him. She curled her knees under her and leaned her hip against his taut abdomen. "How can you be so sure he doesn't know something?" she asked as she traced the dragon tattoo.

"Because I have had my representatives speak with VanDenbergh III on numerous occasions. He has a gambling habit that requires a great deal of money to feed. If he'd ever gained possession of the chalice then I would have it now."

Sophie frowned. "You're positive?"

Severn brushed his thumb over her lips. "Positive. I've sent Xanthus to locate and question the grandson but I don't hope for anything other than confirmation of what the playmate told me."

"So what now?"

He grinned as his hand trailed downward to cup her breast. "I thought we'd explore the chests that are my gift to you."

Sophie glanced at the chests with their carved dragons. "Those are mine?"

"Yes. I took the liberty of unlocking them before joining you in the bathroom." He rose onto an elbow so he could tangle his hand in her hair and guide her mouth to his. "The contents of the chests are yours to do with as you please. They are the treasures I've collected over the years for my future mate." He gave her a quick, hard kiss. "Now open the chests, my heartmate, and tell me whether you find my offering suitable."

Sophie gasped as soon as she lifted the first lid. Necklaces and bracelets and rings glittered as they lay on a bed of loose stones that hinted at unexplored depths containing even greater riches. Tears gathered at the corner of her eyes. Her heart thundered in her chest. "These can't be for me," she said and immediately felt Severn's lips on her neck.

"And who else would they be for?" he murmured as he wrapped his hand around the heartmate necklace. "Didn't you claim only moments ago that I was your life, your world?" He sucked her earlobe into him mouth. "Your one true love?"

Her tumultuous emotions coalesced into acceptance and humor. "I don't remember saying you were my one true love," she teased.

Severn growled against her neck. His free hand parted her robe and swept from her breast to her bare mound. "Do you need for me to prove the truth of it?" he said as his fingers glided over her clit and slipped into her channel.

Sophie shivered. Her womb fluttered and her sheath clamped down tight and hard. No matter how many times it happened, it surprised her how quickly the need could rise, how fast play could turn into the fierce desire to feel his cock inside her.

"No," she panted, unable to stop herself from pitching forward, from pressing her chest to a thick cushion while her hips remained in the air, her knees spread, braced so he could take her from behind.

Severn jerked the flimsy gown upward. He'd intended to play, to relax, to enjoy the sight of her exploring the chests. Instead he mounted Sophie and fucked her in a wild taking that left them both sprawled across the cushions and panting.

"You're a distraction, my heartmate," Severn grumbled.

Sophie laughed. "I'm a distraction? You're the distraction. It's not every day I'm presented with jewelry and gems worth a fortune."

She pushed herself into a sitting position and lifted the lid of the second chest. It made her think of a pirate's chest filled with gold. She picked up a coin and blinked. "Is this a real doubloon?"

Severn chuckled and rose to sit next to her. "Of course. Most of the coins in this chest were recovered from shipwrecks or lost island caches."

Sophie picked up a handful of coins and let them sift through her fingers like sand. "Severn, just being with you is enough for me. You don't have to give me these chests."

Happiness and love made it impossible for him to speak immediately. He curled his arm around her waist as she picked up another handful of coins and let them drop through her fingers and back to the chest. "I know, my heartmate. But I want to give them to you. It pleases me."

Sophie blinked back the tears she'd fought earlier. He was everything she'd ever dreamed of in a man. Fierce, protective, dominant, loving, playful, intelligent, romantic—the list could go on and on.

She turned her head. Her eyes met his. "I do love you," she whispered before settling her mouth on his.

For long moments they kissed, lips rubbing and pressing in a gentle caress. Their tongues sliding and tangling in tribute and testament to emotions that transcended lust.

When they parted, Sophie turned her attention to the chest containing the jewels and loose gems. The sheer number of items made it seem unreal, a dream or a waking fantasy. As she pulled necklaces and bracelets from the trunk and put them on her neck and arms in glittering layers of blue, green, red and every shade in between, she felt like a little girl playing dress-up with her mother's costume jewelry. She continued putting on jewelry until eventually there was no room for more of it on her body. She laughed and turned toward Severn. The pleasure she saw on his face at her enjoyment made her own emotion blossom further and deepen.

He was leaning against the pillows, a sultan watching his favorite harem girl, or maybe a dragon appreciating all the glitter. Sophie grinned. He chuckled when she straddled him then fitted several sapphire necklaces on him. "Beautiful," she said. "They go with your eyes. Can I interest you in some matching earrings?"

Severn slid his hand underneath her parted dressing gown and stroked her side. "I'm glad you find my offering suitable."

Sophie nibbled at his mouth. "More than suitable. I'm blown away. But I'm also curious." She grabbed several loose rubies and diamonds from the chest. Those she placed in a line, forming a jeweled collar on the neck of the dragon tattooed on Severn's chest. He groaned when she bent down to inspect her work then detoured over to capture a tight nipple.

His cock was a hard presence between their lower bodies. Sophie was tempted to guide him into her. She ached with need—again—a state that was probably going to be a constant in her life for a long time. She held off, wanting to give him something more, something to remember the occasion by.

She kissed over to his other nipple and gave it the same attention. Feminine satisfaction filled her at the tightness of his body and the way he was already panting lightly. It was thrilling to know she held the same power over him that he held over her.

"What are you curious about, my heartmate?" he managed though she could tell he fought to get the words out.

She gave his nipple one last, long pull before lifting her head to meet Severn's gaze. Her finger traced the tattoo. "Do Hakon and Malik and Xanthus also have chests filled with treasures to present to prospective wives?"

Severn's eyes narrowed. His nostrils flared. "Why are you interested in what they have to offer?"

Sophie laughed and lay down on top of him so the necklaces she was wearing were trapped between them. "So I'd be correct in assuming this is part of the dragon fantasy, to drape your woman in priceless jewelry and then make love to her?" She bit his bottom lip. "In a minute you're probably going to insist we spread out the gold coins and use them for bedding."

The tension left Severn's body. Wicked amusement danced in his eyes. "And would you accommodate my fantasy?"

Sophie snickered. "Only if you're on the bottom."

Severn laughed, a deep, rich sound that made it impossible for Sophie not to laugh with him. When he finally quieted, he said. "You please me, Sophie."

"I intend to."

She gave him a brief kiss before rising to her hands and knees. The longer necklaces swept over his flesh as she gently bit and licked and sucked her way down his neck. She paused at the hard male nipples long enough to make him start panting again then she traced the dragon tattoo with her tongue.

His cock pulsed against her belly and strained as if guessing her intent. Its tip wet the underside of her breast in a kiss of greeting.

She slid lower. His penis glided through the channel of her cleavage, hard hot steel encased in smooth velvet. It throbbed with a heartbeat that matched her own. She reached for his cock but Severn's hand beat hers, his tortured, "No, Sophie," made her lift her head.

He wanted her mouth on him. It was written on his taut face, it glittered in his eyes and showed in the way his chest was heaving as if he was wrestling some demon for control of his body. "No, Sophie," he panted. "Not yet. We can't— Take me into you, my heartmate. Let me spill my seed in your tight sheath."

Sophie rose above him. She couldn't deny him, not when her need echoed his.

Severn groaned when Sophie impaled herself on him. Lust scorched through him, controlled and focused now that he was surrounded by the slick heat of her channel.

He wouldn't last, by The Great Shared Ancestor, he couldn't afford to. He'd very nearly shifted to dragon form when her intent to take him into her mouth had become clear.

He needed to finish bonding with her. Once she knew all of him then the magic wouldn't be challenged each time they made love.

Severn arched as her fingers found his nipples and she squeezed as she rode him. The pain-pleasure of it lanced straight to his cock and made the dragon ridges become more pronounced.

Sophie's moans grew more guttural as the ridges rubbed and stimulated her. Her head went back. The jewels at her throat and ears glittered and sparkled but they couldn't compete against the beauty Severn saw in his mate.

His hands went to her hips. His thrusts became faster, harder as he took control despite his position on the bottom. She cried out first, but her channel was a hungry mouth that clamped down on him. He jerked repeatedly until his sac was soft and relaxed between his thighs.

With a sigh Sophie draped herself over him again. Severn wrapped his arms around her and nuzzled her hair. She gave an inelegant grunt and said, "This jewelry is fun to play with, but it's not meant for sleeping on."

"We'll put your treasures up in a moment, once we've regained our strength."

He felt her smile against his neck. Her hand went to his arm and took the measure of his muscles. "I'm curious."

Severn laughed. "So soon? Dare I ask what you're curious about, my heartmate? Look where your last question led us."

Sophie squeezed his biceps in response. His own curiosity was stirred when he felt her cheek grow warm against his skin.

"How come we have to wait?"

In a heartbeat his cock threatened to fill. Severn's arms tightened around Sophie lest she try to slide down and take him in her mouth when his resistance was so low. "Only until we've finished bonding."

Her head lifted with a jerk. "We can have sex. You can spend long periods of very satisfying time with your face between my thighs, but we have to wait until we're married before I can put my mouth on you?"

Severn managed not to smile at the hint of outrage in his mate's voice. "An oddity of the culture I'm a part of," he said and hoped Sophie's curiosity would be satisfied and the conversation dropped.

His wish was answered by the ringing of her cell phone. Sophie rolled off him to answer it. A moment later she said, "Aislinn thinks she's created a ring that will help us find the Dragon's Cup."

Chapter Eighteen

ର

Sophie stared in awe at the ring lying on Aislinn's palm. It looked like an exact replica of the jewel-encrusted rim of the Dragon's Cup.

Photographs of the chalice littered Aislinn's workbench in the back room of Inner Magick. Strange script filled a tablet with a drawing of the ring on it.

"I'm not sure it'll work," Aislinn admitted. "But it's the only thing I could envision that might."

Sophie noted the deep tiredness in Aislinn's eyes and the way she seemed to sway with exhaustion. She gave her friend a hug. "I can't think of a single one of your creations that's been a failure." Aislinn returned the hug with a grateful smile.

Severn said, "I speak for Malik and Hakon, as well as myself. We are in your debt whether the cup is found or not. Your generosity with your gift is noted and appreciated. Should you need anything, you have only to ask and we will endeavor to meet your request."

Aislinn gave a slight nod then reached for Sophie's hand and turned it over before dropping the ring into her palm. Because of the number of tiny chips of stones required, the ring was as wide as a man's wedding band. Sophie assumed Severn would wear it, but Aislinn said, "This was as small as I could make it. Put it on your thumb. I think it'll fit."

Sophie slipped the ring on her left thumb. A shiver went up her spine at the sense of magic clicking into place. "Okay," she sighed. "I think we're good to go." She frowned as she looked down at the ring. "It's not going to juice me like a cattle prod if we get close to the chalice is it?"

Aislinn laughed. "It should warm and sparkle in proximity to the cup."

Sophie grinned. "Okay, I can live with that as long as skin doesn't start melting off." She gave Aislinn another hug and whispered, "Now get some sleep."

"Bed is definitely in my very near future," Aislinn said as the curtains behind Sophie parted aggressively and the room suddenly heated with cop-enhanced testosterone. "Let's go home, Aislinn. You're not spending any more time working," Trace Dilessio said.

Sophie turned to look at Aislinn's gorgeous, ultra-macho husband. "Nice to see you again too, Trace," she teased.

One side of Trace's mouth quirked up but Sophie was sure he only managed the small show of humor because Aislinn was in his arms and lifting her face for his kiss. Trace nodded at Severn before lowering his mouth and claiming his wife's. Sophie and Severn escaped to the main part of the shop where Xanthus and Marika appeared to be engaged in a standoff of their own.

"Love is in the air," Sophie quipped.

Severn laughed. "Apparently so, my heartmate." He took her hand and led her from the shop. They didn't speak again until they were in the mustard yellow sports car Sophie had selected for the outing.

"Let's start with Honey's place," Sophie said.

Severn grunted and pulled away from the curb. "A waste of time but we can go there if you wish it. My men searched her house and grounds thoroughly while she and I were having coffee."

Sophie's mouth opened in surprise, though in retrospect she didn't know *why* she was surprised. "Will it do any good to remind you that breaking and entering is against the law?"

Severn chuckled. He spared her a glance before turning his attention back to the road. "Are you going to be one of those females who feels duty-bound to reform their mate?"

Sophie snickered. "When it comes to some of his more dragon-like tendencies, I just might be."

"Then you have your work cut out for you, my heartmate."

Sophie laughed and curled her hand around his upper thigh. The band on her thumb warmed with his body heat. For the first time since seeing it she felt a touch of worry and doubt. What if she wasn't sensitive enough to notice the difference in temperature? What if they never got close enough to trigger the ring?

Severn's hand covered hers. As if sensing her fears he said, "In all the years of searching for the Chalice of Enos, I have never felt so sure about recovering it. We will find it, Sophie, and then we will finish bonding."

Sophie's eyebrows drew together. It was the second time he'd used the term bonding. She'd assumed bonding equaled marriage, but now a wriggle of uncertainty managed to work itself into her thoughts.

With a wry twist of her mouth she realized she seemed doomed to learn the same lesson over and over again when it came to Severn—mainly that it was a mistake to assume her meanings equaled his meanings. "What exactly do you mean when you say we'll finish bonding?"

"You will find it a pleasurable, reality-altering experience," he purred. "In fact you will be tempted to write about it but you shouldn't. It is a private matter between us, a welcoming of you fully into the culture I am part of."

Sophie couldn't keep from smiling. "In other words, I learn the secret password, the secret handshake, then you and I have wild dragon sex?"

His amusement filled the tiny sports car. "Something like that, my heartmate, though instead of a password or handshake you get a tattoo to match mine."

"You've got be kidding. In case you haven't noticed, my chest is not like your chest."

"Oh, I've noticed." His hand slipped between her thighs and upward, under her skirt. He didn't stop until his fingertips encountered her smooth, flushed and very wet cunt lips. "I've noticed all of our differences, Sophie."

She whimpered but still managed to warn, "That's not going to work this time, Severn. I'm not going to mindlessly agree to having a huge dragon tattooed on my chest because your fingers are pure magic."

Severn preened at her acknowledgement of his superior carnal skills. He stroked a silky petal of feminine flesh. She would be mentally ready to wake in the dragon realm and see him in his other form. She would accept the truths he would soon reveal and not be driven insane or terrified by them.

"Just a small dragon, Sophie." He found her clit and fondled it before coating her bare mound with arousal gathered from her slit. "Tell me where you wish to wear my symbol."

Mischief and desire made Sophie reach down and pull her skirt up in order to expose the parts he was driving her crazy by touching. His growl and the heat that filled the car were her reward. She positioned his hand near her left hipbone. "I'll wear your dragon right here."

He rubbed the spot as if making note of it then flipped her skirt back down. "You are a distraction. I believe I have said so more than once. Now behave yourself. We're almost there."

Sophie didn't bother pointing out that he was the one who'd started misbehaving in the first place. She already knew he was impossible, thoroughly irrepressible when it came to touching her.

They glided to a stop in front of Honey Mercante's home. Sophie blinked at the scattered lawn furniture and trashed landscape. It looked like a minor hurricane had blown through and affected only this one location. Next to her Severn growled a low curse before reaching for his cell phone.

Frustration raged through Severn. He had no doubt that the destruction in front of him was the work of Morgana or Neryssa throwing a temper tantrum because they couldn't get to VanDenbergh's playmate and question her. It angered him to have his steps in finding the chalice monitored so closely, but the task was too important to assign to others. By The Great Shared Ancestor he'd incinerate both of the fey from Otthilde's court if he could. Unfortunately they held an advantage in this realm. He was prohibited from taking his true form but it was against no law for them to be in their elemental states, water and air.

In dragon form he could see their essence. But in human form he could only sense their presence when they were very close. Only those dragons like Xanthus, whose blood held a hint of the fey, could reliably sense them at a greater distance. It was one of the reasons why he'd assigned Xanthus to guard Sophie.

The man assigned to watch Honey Mercante answered his phone.

"You are with the woman?" Severn asked.

"Yes."

"There was no disturbance at her house while you monitored her there?"

"No. There is a problem?"

"It looks as though a storm has blown through."

The man hissed and cursed. Severn hung up.

He glanced at Sophie and wondered if the locket Aislinn created would protect her against the fey. There'd been no opportunity to take Aislinn aside and ask her about it though he knew whatever stone was contained in the gold oyster-shaped locket was growing in power with each moment Sophie wore it.

"You've got someone watching Honey?" Sophie asked. The frown on her face made Severn want to lean over and kiss it away. He resisted. He knew all too well the danger of touching his mate and getting sidetracked.

"A precaution," he said. "Shall we see if the ring reacts?"

Sophie wiped suddenly sweaty palms on her skirt. She wanted to be successful in finding the chalice so badly that she was afraid she'd imagine the ring growing warm.

She did her best to clear her mind and settle the excitement in her chest before getting out of the car. Warm air and the smell of ocean water did a lot to calm her.

They walked side by side to the front door. The ring remained a comfortable presence on Sophie's thumb. "Nothing," she said, biting down on her bottom lip and wondering if she should suggest they revisit the idea of breaking-and-entering.

"My men have already thoroughly searched the house," Severn said. "Let's walk its perimeter before making a decision on how to proceed."

Sophie was happy to agree. They took the rocked path to the right of the house. The ring remained cool all the way around.

"I suggest we go to the VanDenbergh estate," Severn said. "We don't know how sensitive the ring is or how immediate the cup's presence needs to be. It's possible the ring will be sensitive enough to warm to a trail."

Sophie nodded. "Like following psychic particles or energy. That's how Aislinn has found missing people before, by touching something they own, something important to them, and following the connection to the person." Her gaze panned Honey's house and grounds again. Her thoughts were already on the possibility of tracking the cup from VanDenbergh's estate when she saw the dock. "There have been boats here. I saw them in several of the pictures I found on the Internet while you were with Honey."

Severn shrugged but took a step toward the path leading to the dock. Sophie felt a shiver of anticipation, the same dance of sensation that often accompanied one of her hunches. The ring tingled as they neared the water's edge. She bit her lip to keep from saying anything before she could be sure. But as soon as she stepped onto the wood of the dock she felt a definite warming where the ring touched her thumb.

"I think it was here," she whispered, caution urged her not to shout the news despite their being alone.

Severn moved to her side. He picked up her hand and took it to his mouth as if he was simply giving her a kiss. At the feel of the ring against his lips, she felt him tense. "I believe you are right, my heartmate." His voice was low, private. "It's a good thing you had the foresight to put your laptop in the car." He turned her hand over and sent heat spiraling through her with the touch of his teeth and tongue to the pulse point at her wrist.

They retreated to the car. "I don't think I'll have any trouble finding a signal, there are satellite dishes everywhere," Sophie said as Severn started the engine.

"Hakon's residence is not too far away. Wait until we get there."

He picked up his phone and called ahead. A short time later they were pulling through wrought iron gates with elaborate welded dragons taking up much of their centers. Sophie had to smile.

She expected to be greeted by a fantasyscape like the one that still took her breath away when they passed through the gates of Severn's estate. Instead she found a jungle of lush plants. There was no sign of a house.

Severn parked the car and they got out. The raucous call of birds filled the air along with the bellow of an alligator. Sophie laughed. "The last time I looked, we were still on the mainland and not on one of the islands. So why do I feel like I've left civilization?"

"I believe this is Hakon's attempt to discourage unwanted visitors, namely relatives who might drop in unannounced."

Severn took Sophie's hand and led her to a walkway lined with wide-leaved plants.

The jungle around them went quiet for an instant before once again filling with birds screeching and calling out an alarm. The canopy of plants above them blocked much of the light.

They walked for several minutes before coming to the house. This time Sophie's expectations were met. Hakon's home wasn't as large or elegant as Severn's, but it was breathtaking. Large sections of glass were set in stucco, smaller sections were stained with a stunning collection of dragons in flight. Low stucco walls were set above a sloping, shallow channel that made Sophie think of a moat when she noticed the path they were on became a suspended bridge.

A door opened and Hakon emerged. "Welcome to my home," he said, bounding toward them. They met on the suspended bridge just as Sophie noticed the alligators basking at water's edge. They were huge, bigger than any she'd seen outside of an alligator farm, and as far as she could tell, not confined in any way.

Hakon noticed the direction of her gaze. He waved a hand over the moat and the alligators. "Don't worry about them. They're distant cousins who mind their own business for the most part."

Sophie rolled her eyes and laughed. Dragons!

Hakon led them to a beautiful sitting room. The furniture was simple, made of light-colored wood and fitted with bright cushions. The large expanse of windows framing the lush landscape intensified the tropical effect, as did the platter of sliced fruit set out on a coffee table.

"Help yourself," Hakon said, waving a hand in the direction of the food.

Sophie's stomach rumbled in reaction. She reached for a plate only to have Hakon capture her hand. Severn's low growl freed it.

"You have news of the cup?" Hakon asked, his gaze still riveted on Sophie's ring.

Sophie handed Severn the plate of food she'd made for herself. She opened the laptop as Severn filled Hakon in on what they'd learned and why they'd come to his estate.

The links Sophie had followed when she researched Honey were still in her history file. It took only a few minutes to find the first society column article showing a boat tethered to the dock behind Honey's home. "Here's one of them," Sophie said. She turned the laptop so both Hakon and Severn could see the screen.

"*Fortune's Child,*" Hakon noted. "Who's the man with her?"

"Stuart Swain. The fourth," Sophie said.

Severn frowned. "That name sounds familiar."

Sophie clicked on several links before finding another with a picture of a boat docked at Honey's home. "This boat is *VanDenbergh's Folly,*" she said. "Want to guess who owns it?" She glanced at the date of the article. "The picture was taken before VanDenbergh Senior was murdered."

There was a third article, once again with *Fortune's Child* pictured in the background. Sophie glanced at Hakon and Severn. "There could have been a lot more boats tied to the dock. These are just the ones that ended up in the newspaper."

"Search on Stuart Swain," Hakon said. "The name is familiar to Severn."

Sophie typed it into the search engine. "Based on the number of hits he's a real party animal," she said.

Impulsively she narrowed the search further by linking his name to Honey Mercante's. There were only a few hits. She retyped, this time searching for a connection between Swain and VanDenbergh. Hakon whistled. "This is looking better and better. The grandson and Stuart Swain are frequent companions."

Severn abruptly set the plate of food on the table. "That's why the name sounded familiar. Stuart Swain is a drinking and gambling companion of VanDenbergh III."

"You're sure the grandson doesn't have the Dragon's Cup?" Hakon asked.

"I am fairly certain of it." Severn glanced at the ring on Sophie's thumb. "He's living on *VanDenbergh's Folly*. When Xanthus found him earlier today, the boat was docked in its usual spot. Sophie and I can double-check that the chalice is not onboard and never was while you and Malik search for the location of *Fortune's Child*."

"I contacted Malik as soon as you called," Hakon said. "He's waiting to hear back from me."

"Perhaps we could step into your office for a moment and place a conference call to him," Severn suggested. When Hakon nodded, Severn leaned forward and brushed a kiss across Sophie's forehead. "You're hungry. Take a few minutes to enjoy the fruit while Hakon and I speak with Malik."

Sophie closed the laptop and gratefully reached for a plate. "Take your time."

Severn chuckled. He stood and followed Hakon from the room.

"Your claiming a mate has been a coup for all of us," Hakon said as soon as they were settled in his office. "The elves have used their magic more often to enslave us than to help us."

"Aislinn has proved to be a friend. Unfortunately the fey from Otthilde's court are watching my movements closely. When we find the Dragon's Cup, we'll need to get it to Drake's Lair as soon as possible."

"You expect an attack?"

Severn shrugged. "I wouldn't dismiss the possibility, especially if *Fortune's Child* is at sea when we locate her. But I think you'll agree that we shouldn't waste time in determining if the chalice is onboard."

"I agree, as I'm sure Malik will. Let's hope *Fortune's Child* is safely berthed. If she's not then I have a speed boat here. We can be down the waterway and out to sea before the fey can gather their forces. Only Morgana and Neryssa might be powerful enough to follow us. Between the three of us, we should be able to keep them at bay."

"Four. Xanthus has a touch of the fey in his bloodlines. He will sense them before we do. The early warning would serve us well."

"It'll be a tight fit, especially with your mate along. I assume the ring must remain with her?"

"Yes." Severn glanced at the door. "I'll leave you to make the call to Malik while I collect Sophie and investigate *VanDenbergh's Folly*."

Hakon laughed. "No doubt you're counting the minutes until you can return to the dragon realm and seal the bond with your beautiful and resourceful mate. If the cup is recovered, the doorway between worlds will become heavily traveled with males carting their human females home."

"You included?"

"Perhaps. I am waiting to see just how enthralled and ensnared the great Severn Damek becomes before committing to such a course myself."

Severn chuckled but didn't deny the truth of what Hakon said. He *was* enthralled and ensnared by Sophie, and yet he'd never felt such utter contentment and satisfaction. It was a fate he'd wish on any male.

"Ready, my heartmate?" he asked as he stepped into the sitting room.

"Ready for a nap," she teased, stretching in a way that enflamed Severn. She glanced behind him to ensure they were alone before adding, "I think all the sex is finally catching up to me."

Visions of curling around her naked body had his cock filling with blood. When this was over and the cup safely ensconced at Drake's Lair...

She stood and smoothed her hands over her skirt. He followed the motion and thought about the bare cunt beneath the fabric.

"Ready?" Sophie asked. The amusement in her voice convinced Severn she knew what she was doing to him.

He took her in his arms. "I've warned you about playing with me, Sophie. Hakon would enjoy the sight of you bent over his furniture and screaming with pleasure as I fucked you." Not that he would ever allow another male to witness her ecstasy.

Severn gave her a punishing kiss. "Let's go."

Chapter Nineteen

ɞ

"It wasn't here," Sophie said as she paced the deck of *VanDenbergh's Folly.*

Severn shrugged. "Then we'll wait until we hear from Hakon or Malik about *Fortune's Child.* And if that lead becomes a dead end, then we'll dig deeper and find other boats to investigate." He snagged her hand as she passed.

"I feel like we're so close," Sophie said with a sigh.

"I feel the same. Come, we can find a coffee shop unless you'd rather return to the estate."

"No, a mocha sounds good." They climbed off the unattended boat and returned to the sports car. "My turn to drive?" Sophie asked.

Severn chuckled. "Not while you're with me. You can drive when Xanthus is accompanying you. He's required to obey any reasonable order you might give him."

"Do the words *male chauvinist* hold any significance for you?"

Severn's smile was quick to appear and slow to fade. "It's the nature of the beast."

Sophie rolled her eyes though she was smiling as she slipped into the passenger seat. "Back to the dragon thing again, I presume."

"Always, my heartmate." He picked up her hand and gave it a quick kiss before settling it on his thigh. His cellular phone rang just as he turned the key in the ignition. It was Hakon.

"Malik sent a helicopter into the air. *Fortune's Child* was spotted about five miles out. You're near the club where VanDenbergh's boat is berthed?"

"Yes. We were just leaving."

"Go to the guest pier instead. Malik is on his way to my home. Xanthus is already here. We'll pick you up and go directly to *Fortune's Child*. Malik's men remain in the sky to monitor it."

Severn turned off the ignition and closed his phone. "Coffee will have to wait, my heartmate." He picked up her hand again, this time brushing his lips over the ring.

"They've found the boat?"

"Yes, and will meet us at the guest pier."

Sophie leaned over and kissed him. "No violence, right? Just a flash of cash and the Dragon's Cup changes hand."

Severn turned his head slightly and deepened the kiss. For long moments he lost himself in the heat of his mate. If they were successful in recovering the cup then before the next sunrise he would be fully bonded to Sophie. If they both drank from the chalice she could soon be heavy with their young, though now that the possibility loomed as more than a fantasy, he found he wasn't ready to share her yet, even with his own offspring.

It didn't change his plan for the cup. In front of those at Drake's Lair he would still drink from it with Sophie. It didn't matter whether his mother and Audriss witnessed it or not, they'd soon learn of it. Hopefully it would end their plans of using him to form an alliance.

With a moan, Sophie snuggled into him. He couldn't stop himself from cupping her breast and savoring the feel of her tight nipple against his palm, from stroking down her side and thigh before changing direction and sliding his hand under the fabric of her skirt.

"They'll be here soon," she panted, flushed and breathless from his touch.

He wanted to cup her mound. He wanted to plunge his fingers into her slit and fuck her until she cried his name.

The car was filled with the scent of her arousal. The need to mate rode so close to the surface it took almost nothing to trigger.

Severn opened his door so the ocean air replaced the heady musk of his mate. "You are right." He gave her a quick kiss and got out of the car before he could fall into the trap of intoxicating femininity that was Sophie.

Sophie laughed. She tried to repair the damage to her hair and clothing—though after seeing her at the VanDenbergh estate looking thoroughly fucked, she didn't think Hakon and Malik would even blink at her current state of thoroughly kissed and thoroughly aroused.

When she'd done what she could about her appearance, she joined Severn and they strolled to the pier. Within minutes her hair was wind-tossed and ocean-sprayed as Hakon's speedboat raced toward open water.

"Is *Fortune's Child* anchored?" Severn asked.

"No," Malik said. "It's heading out but it doesn't seem to be moving fast. My men have spotted one person onboard so far, a man they believe is Swain."

"Let's hope he's amenable to being boarded," Severn said.

Hakon laughed. "I believe your name will get results. If Swain has the cup then he knows why you're hunting him down in open waters."

"If he knows I want it then why hasn't he contacted me?"

Hakon turned from the steering wheel with an eyebrow arched. "You're an easy man to find, especially if one wants to keep a low profile?" He looked at Malik. "Does my memory fail me, or is it only recently—with the acquisition of a mate—that Severn has shed the cloak of a recluse and come out to play?"

"I believe you make a valid point," Malik said.

Sophie grinned. Severn growled and tightened his arms around her. "Don't encourage them."

She started to say something but a sudden flash of heat where the band touched her thumb made her gasp. "The ring just reacted," she said an instant before Malik conveyed instructions from his men in the helicopter and Hakon altered their course sharply. The band warmed and grew warmer as they navigated through sailboats, fishing vessels and yachts, most heading toward land.

Xanthus lifted a pair of binoculars to his eyes. "*Fortune's Child* is straight ahead."

Hakon reduced their speed. Severn said, "Anything to be worried about, Xanthus?"

"No."

As they drew closer to *Fortune's Child*, Hakon reduced their speed further to minimize the wake that would soon hit the power yacht. Sophie said, "Look at the ring!" It was not only hot against her skin, but the gems sparkled in a way that couldn't be attributed to a sun close to setting.

She could feel excitement radiating through Severn's body. He tightened his arms around her waist and rubbed his cheek against her hair. "The cup is onboard *Fortune's Child*. I'd bet my fortune on it."

"Before we get any closer," Malik said, "I suggest we agree on what we will offer Swain for it." He glanced at Sophie, then Severn. "It is a given we won't leave without the chalice, but I imagine you've made concessions to your mate on how it's acquired."

Hakon chuckled. "Oh, how the mighty have fallen! And this is a fate you wish for yourself, Malik?" He turned his head slightly. "And you, Xanthus? Rumor has it your wings have been clipped as well."

His jibes appeared to aggravate all three of the other men. Sophie grinned. "If it's any consolation to you guys, one of my favorite sayings is, 'He who laughs last, laughs loudest'. It's followed by, 'What goes around, comes around'. I'll start racking my brain for someone to set Hakon up with. It might take me awhile, I'll have to find someone who deserves him — and I mean that in a *you poor woman* kind of way."

The men, including Hakon, laughed. Hakon said, "Your mate has sharp claws, my friend."

Severn nipped the side of Sophie's neck. "With any luck we'll be onboard *Fortune's Child* within minutes. Malik has a good point. I suggest our opening salvo be one million for the cup. That's the upper limit of what the insurance company would pay as a finder's fee."

"He'll want more," Malik said. "I'll match your offer if necessary."

"As will I," Hakon said. "But three should be our final offer. Any more and he loses the opportunity to negotiate with us. He has no right, either by law or custom, to the Dragon's Cup."

"Agreed," Severn said.

Malik nodded. "Agreed. Three million is a generous offer."

Hakon slowed the speedboat so the engine was a gurgle of sound as it drew within a few feet of the *Fortune's Child*. "Stuart Swain the illustrious fourth?" Hakon yelled.

"Who wants to know?" the man Sophie recognized from the society pages answered.

With a grand sweeping gesture, Hakon said, "Severn Damek and company, here to discuss a certain stolen artifact currently in your possession."

Stuart Swain threw back his head and laughed. "Your timing couldn't be more perfect. I'm in desperate need of an infusion of cash to fund my various vices. Let me cut the engine and drop the anchor."

It took only a few minutes for him to do it. The ocean was calm enough for Hakon to ease the speedboat alongside the platform at the back of the motor yacht. Between him and Stuart they quickly secured the boat.

"Ladies first," Stuart said as he offered his hand to Sophie. A low growl sounded in Severn's throat though he didn't prevent her taking the offered hand and stepping from the boat.

Stuart indicated she should climb the ladder up to the deck. Sophie's face flamed at the view she'd give him if she did. "I'll wait for Severn," she said.

Their host's eyebrows lifted in speculation. His gaze slid over her in an appreciative manner, lingering for a long moment on the short, thin skirt with its lack of panty lines. "You look familiar. Have we met partying?"

Severn joined them on the short platform. His hand curled possessively over Sophie's hip. He gave a meaningful look at the ladder. Stuart Swain took the hint with a laugh. He climbed to the deck. Hakon, Malik and Xanthus followed, though not without sharing glances with Severn.

If the ring on her finger wasn't burning and glittering, Sophie might have climbed back in the boat and buried her face against her knees in sheer embarrassment. "From now on I'm wearing panties when we're out in public," she whispered to Severn, letting him hear the determination in her voice.

His mouth found her earlobe. "Perhaps it would be best if you carried a pair in your purse—for emergencies. I find I don't like the thought of your starring in their fantasies. You're *my* fantasy."

Sophie didn't know whether to scream or laugh. It was nearly impossible to get mad at a man who could turn a blush of self-conscious mortification into one of feminine pride. "You go first," she said.

Severn chuckled. His hand slid around to her buttock. "Not a chance, my heartmate. I need to ensure your safety."

"Pervert. You just want a glimpse of my bare pussy."

"Always. Now go. The sooner we secure the chalice, the better."

Sophie grabbed the rung of the ladder, acutely aware of the view she was giving Severn. Her labia was swollen, flushed. She was ready for him again despite how often they'd made love. She prayed arousal wouldn't trail down her inner thighs and beyond the hem of her skirt before she could make it to the upper deck and sit down.

Xanthus offered a hand at the top. She accepted it gratefully since it allowed her to leave the ladder without flashing the men.

Stuart Swain and Malik were sitting on lounge chairs. Sophie claimed a deck chair next to Hakon. A moment later Severn sat next to her with Xanthus at his right.

"Let us cut to the chase," Severn said. "You are in possession of the cup that is erroneously known as the Chalice of Eros. My associates and I are prepared to offer one million dollars for it."

"It was insured for five million," Stuart said.

Severn casually picked Sophie's hand up and placed it on his thigh before covering it with his own and hiding the ring. "True. But its disappearance is connected to a very high-profile murder. With the thief and murderer both dead, the police and district attorney would no doubt like a conviction, even if it's only for possession of stolen property." Severn rubbed his thumb across Sophie's knuckles. "You learned of the cup's whereabouts from VanDenbergh's grandson?"

Stuart crossed his ankles. "Yes. We were lamenting the death of the old goat over a bottle of whisky, followed by a second, and perhaps even a third bottle. By then we'd moved on to considering which island to cruise to in order to gamble away V-Three's inheritance. Honey's name came up. One thing led to another and before I knew it V-Three was passed out in the stateroom of *VanDenbergh's Folly* and I was in possession of a very intriguing piece of information."

He lifted a beer bottle from the table next to his chair and took a swallow. "Can I get you one?" When no one answered in the affirmative, Stuart said, "It seemed wise to lay low and keep the thing hidden until things settled down. I intended to share whatever proceeds I got from the sale of the chalice with V-Three, of course. But once it was in my possession, it occurred to me that I was the one who'd taken all the risks in liberating it from the thief. And besides that, V-Three's prospects were vastly improved due to his inheritance." Stuart shrugged. "So here I sit, and here you sit. Five million would be a fair price. For that you get the chalice plus my silence—which is an important consideration given it's a stolen item and the police already know about your interest in it."

"Three million," Severn said.

Sophie heard the steel in his voice. She saw the flash of acceptance in Stuart's eyes though he didn't respond immediately. He took another pull from the beer bottle before setting it on the deck. "Once the money is placed in an offshore account, I'll give you the chalice."

Severn laughed. "We'll leave with the cup today."

"Do you think I'm crazy enough to keep it on *Fortune's Child*?"

Severn shrugged. "Crazy or clever or casual, it doesn't concern me. The cup is here and we will leave with it, peacefully or not. That's your choice." The words were spoken calmly, which made them more menacing.

"And my money?" Stuart didn't seem particularly frightened of Severn. Sophie wondered if perhaps he'd been gathering information about Severn in preparation for approaching him about the Dragon's Cup. It would explain how Stuart knew the police were familiar with Severn's interest in the chalice.

"Wired to an offshore account if that's what you prefer, though I would suggest an alternative," Severn said.

"What?"

"You've heard of Drake's Lair?"

Stuart snorted. "Who hasn't?"

"It would be a simple matter to place the three million in an account there," Severn said. "You would be allowed to come and go from the club as you please, taking out what money you want in a form that suits you—gold, gems, cash—until the account is empty."

Excitement burned in Stuart's eyes. He licked his lips. "Drake's Lair would serve only as a bank? Or would I be allowed to gamble there?"

"I offer access to the club, how you choose to use it is up to you."

"The money will be available this evening?"

"As soon as we reach land."

"Done." Stuart stood and disappeared below deck.

Sophie contained her smile though she wanted to shout with victory and celebrate Severn's cunning. She intended to hold him to his agreement to reimburse the insurance company, but at least now he wouldn't have to pay for the chalice twice. She doubted any part of the three million Stuart was getting would make it out of Drake's Lair. Probably a large portion of it would end up in Severn's coffers.

Out of the corner of her eye she saw Xanthus' head jerk to the side. Sophie followed his gaze but didn't see any sign of an approaching boat, nor were there any helicopters in the air, including the one piloted by Malik's men. Hakon and Malik rose and took up positions near the doorway Stuart had disappeared through.

Nerves danced along Sophie's spine. Her stomach tightened with a premonition of danger. She suddenly wondered if the men were afraid Stuart was going to come back shooting. But that didn't make sense. He'd seemed satisfied with the deal and Severn hadn't told her to take cover.

Sophie gasped and stood when the ring suddenly burned hotter against her skin. The stones shone like the sun as Stuart stepped through the door holding the Dragon's Cup. An instant later the ring cooled and dimmed to a comfortable level, as if having served its purpose, it no longer needed to call attention to the cup's presence.

The Chalice of Enos was much smaller than Sophie had imagined it. But even from a distance it resonated with magic.

The protection locket hummed against her chest. Even the heartmate necklace warmed where it rested between her beasts.

A sudden urge to take the cup gripped Sophie. She wanted to drink from it and then fuck. The assault on her senses was so fierce, so real, that she swayed. In a heartbeat it was easy to understand the rumors of orgy and sexual stamina that had evolved around the chalice.

Severn gripped her arm. "Soon, my heartmate," he murmured, his voice husky, as if he was being bombarded by the same hot need.

Xanthus positioned himself at Sophie's other side. Hakon's body tensed. Malik took possession of the chalice just as a sharp, ice-cold wind swept across the deck.

"Time to leave," Severn said. "Get down to Hakon's boat, Sophie. Xanthus, go with her."

Fortune's Child rose on a sudden, unexplainable swell. Sophie would have staggered across the deck if Xanthus and Severn hadn't been holding on to her.

"Go," Severn said. "Hurry." He released her hand and closed ranks with Hakon and Malik.

A small funnel cloud took shape on the deck and sent fear rushing through Sophie. She knew the ocean was treacherous but she'd never experienced anything to rival the strange wind and bizarre pitching in otherwise calm air and water.

She didn't resist when Xanthus guided her to the ladder. She tried desperately not to think about her skirt whipping and rising as she climbed down in a duet formation, Xanthus' arms parallel to her head, his chest inches away from her back.

Mayhem reined on the deck. Lounge chairs plunged to the water. Men cursed. The boat rose and fell and tipped.

Sophie hated not being able to see what was going on. Her heart sped up each time Hakon's smaller boat banged against *Fortune's Child*.

She breathed a small sigh of relief when Hakon appeared at the ladder. He started down. Malik followed, gripping the Dragon's Cup as he maneuvered on the ladder one-handed. Severn stood at the railing, waiting.

An icy gust came out of nowhere. It was timed perfectly with a violent pitch.

Malik slammed into *Fortune's Child* so forcefully that Sophie's stomach sickened with the sound of breaking bones. He went limp and the chalice was torn from his grasp. It didn't drop downward, into the waiting boat, but was caught by a spray of water that made Sophie think of a hand reaching up to capture it.

She dived into the water as the Dragon's Cup was carried under. Only the fact that she was closer and had acted so quickly enabled her to grab the chalice. She hugged it to her chest. A sense of elation and victory surged through her, but it was short-lived.

Cold water encased her, sucked her downward and away from the boat as she kicked and struggled. It reminded her of the strange, cold current that had pulled her under the water after she'd dipped the locket containing the fascination stone into the ocean.

She couldn't follow the thought further. Her lungs burned. Her eyes stung when she opened them to check the distance and direction to the surface. Air escaped in a whimper of pain. Panic threatened to seize her.

The water grew colder. She felt encased in an ice cube. Her legs and sides cramped. Her arms ached though she didn't release the cup even when a powerful current swirled around her as if trying to force it from her grip.

More air escaped. She could feel herself starting to black out and used the last of her strength to kick through the pain in her legs.

Sophie opened her eyes again and gasped at the sight of the two dragons descending on her. One was deep blue with traces of red, the other had shimmering scales of green and gold.

A wall of liquid fire burst from their mouths and rolled over her. She heard a woman scream. She thought it might have been her. The scorching heat struck her again and the last of her oxygen escaped even as her limbs stopped cramping and she felt herself moving toward the surface.

Too late, she thought, but as soon as she thought it, a mouth covered hers. Severn's breath became her breath.

She whimpered and felt his reassuring growl both in her throat and against her chest. Tears formed. She wanted to blink, to open her eyes but she resisted the urge until they'd broken the surface of the water.

"If you ever do anything so foolish again, Sophie, you will be unable to sit for a week," Severn said. "No treasure, nothing could make up for your loss." His mouth covered hers again, this time taking her breath away.

Hakon surfaced next to them. Severn ended the kiss. He took the Dragon's Cup from Sophie's unresisting hand and gave it to Hakon. "I'm serious, Sophie. Do not risk yourself again."

She looked around at the now-calm ocean. In the distance she saw *Fortune's Child*. Between it and them, Hakon's boat slowly approached the spot where they'd emerged and were treading water.

Xanthus drove. Malik held his arm to his chest. He sat at an awkward angle, one that suggested impending seasickness.

"Is Malik going to be okay?" Sophie asked, remembering the sound of bone breaking as he'd been slammed against the back of *Fortune's Child*.

"He'll be fine. He suffers from a concussion and some broken bones, nothing life-threatening."

Severn tightened his grip on her. Despite the calm water and their success at gaining and keeping the Dragon's Cup, Sophie could feel the way his heart thundered with turbulent emotion.

"I'm okay too." She touched her lips to his. "We can go back to your estate and take another shower together. If I remember correctly, you seemed to enjoy the one we took earlier today."

His eyes darkened. His nostrils flared. His hand found her bare buttock underneath the water. "We will accompany the cup to Drake's Lair and then we will finish bonding." His voice was a low, savage growl that dared her to deny him.

Sophie licked along the seam of his mouth in supplication. She had no desire to fight him. Whatever bonding entailed, she was more than ready to be fully part of his world, his life.

* * * * *

Severn sent a couple of his men to retrieve the sports car. Xanthus went to the estate for dry clothing. All of them arrived at Drake's Lair after a brief stop at Hakon's house.

Sophie grinned as she smoothed her hands over her shorts. Apparently Severn forgot to require a skirt, though lack of panties seemed to be a given when it came to male dragons.

Sophie's heartbeat quickened with thoughts of dragons. The shimmering images she'd seen in the water had seemed so real. The heat of their fire had unfrozen her limbs.

There was a rational explanation for it, of course. She'd been on the verge of passing out and even though she wouldn't have expected to suffer from delirium in the process of drowning, she did have a very active imagination. Her subconscious had recognized Severn and Hakon even if she was too far gone to actually see them. The dragons had been patterned on the tattoos they wore. The blast of heat that had freed her was merely an interpretation of why the strange, frigid anomaly in the ocean had disappeared as quickly as it'd arrived.

There you have it, everything boxed and bowed and neatly presented. Even Malik's miraculous recovery after a few minutes at Hakon's house could be attributed to powerful painkillers. So why couldn't she shake the overwhelming feeling that rational answers weren't the right answers?

Severn opened the passenger door and helped her from the sports car. "Just a little longer, my heartmate," he purred.

She laughed as she wrapped her hand around the heartmate necklace. Severn was the reason rational explanations didn't satisfy her. He was pure magic.

Any doubt about just how important the Chalice of Enos was would have been eradicated by the number of men who'd accompanied them to Drake's Lair. Besides Xanthus at least thirty bodyguards were present. Without visible tattoos Sophie couldn't tell at a glance which men were Hakon and Malik's and which were Severn's, but one thing was obvious— apparently there were no ugly male dragons.

A low growl redirected her attention back to the dragon at her side. She laughed and met his gaze. "You can't expect me to be in the presence of so much eye-candy and not look."

His lips pulled back in a hissing snarl that sent a shiver of erotic fear dancing down her spine and over her flushed cunt lips. He leaned in. The softness of his mouth against hers was an alluring contradiction to the hardness of his body. "Careful, my fiery mate, or your ass will soon burn from the punishment I will administer."

She resisted the urge to goad him. The lust that simmered between them was dangerously close to the surface, the same way it had been when Stuart stepped out on the deck with the

Dragon's Cup. She didn't trust Severn not to react with a kiss or touch that would send them both over the edge and into a very public demonstration of what they felt for each other.

"Very wise, my heartmate," he purred, guessing at her thoughts as he so often seemed to do.

One of the bodyguards opened the door to Drake's Lair. Overwhelming wealth and luxury, that was Sophie's impression before a cheer went up and men of all ages left tables littered with gold, jewels and scattered playing cards in order to crowd closer to the chalice.

The bodyguards fanned out, encircled the crowd, contained it—and in the process prevented Severn's mother and Audriss from nearing the chalice. Sophie's heart skipped a beat when she saw the two women. Severn's arm curled around her waist as he pulled her back to his front. "Dragon's Flame," he yelled, "for everyone who wishes it but especially for my mate."

Within seconds rounds of drinks were being served by uniformed waiters, all of whom had embroidered dragons tattooed on the collars of their shirts. "For you," Malik said, handing the Chalice of Enos to Severn before turning to the gathered crowd and lifting his glass. "May we all find the same good fortune as Severn has!"

The men raised their glasses and held them, waiting in silence, the excitement and anticipation so palpable Sophie's heart raced with it. A waiter poured the contents of a crystal glass into the Dragon's Cup. Severn swallowed from the chalice then placed its rim at Sophie's lips. "May you all find the same good fortune as I have found!"

A cheer went up as Sophie drank from the cup. The potent drink burned its way down her throat as the men in the room upended their own glasses and called for another round.

"Let's go," Severn said as he returned the Dragon's Cup to Malik's possession. It amazed and amused him how little he cared about the chalice despite having spent a lifetime pursuing it. Now all his thoughts centered on one thing, getting Sophie to the dragon realm and completing their bond.

By The Great Shared Ancestor his heart had very nearly ceased beating when she'd jumped from the boat and into Morgana's deadly, icy grip. Neryssa in the form of wind had kept both he and Hakon trapped for precious moments while Xanthus had struggled to get the boat untied from *Fortune's Child*.

He and Hakon had broken the covenant by shifting to dragon form in the mortal realm. They'd waited until they gained the water, but a second longer in the speedboat and Severn would have done it there, regardless of the consequences. Neryssa had joined Morgana by the time they got to Sophie. They'd dragged his mate deep in the water and yet she'd clung to the chalice and denied them their prize even as her life was being stolen.

Rage ripped through Severn at the memory of it. He hoped Neryssa and Morgana had died as dragon fire rolled over them. He didn't count on it. The fey were elemental, tied to the mortal world more strongly than either dragons or elves were. It would have to be enough that they'd been forced to retreat.

Severn guided Sophie through the males gathered around Hakon and Malik. When he cleared the ring of guards his mother was waiting for him. Her eyes flashed with fire. Her nostrils flared and she made a point of not acknowledging his mate.

Jory Strong

Chapter Twenty

Anger filled Severn. Instinct demanded he battle anyone who didn't treat his mate with the regard she deserved.

He met his mother's gaze in silent challenge. He would cut off all contact with her if necessary, though he didn't intend to delay their exit in order to fight with her now, not when he was so close to having what he most wanted, the dragon bond with Sophie.

"This is not settled," she said.

Severn shrugged. "If you are not gone from the estate when Sophie and I return from bonding then I will assume you are in possession of it and no longer consider me your heir. I will arrange for my treasures and furnishings to be removed. Sophie and I will make a home for ourselves and our future children elsewhere."

His mother stiffened. Heat rose around them as her temper spiked.

Her attention shifted to Sophie's belly as he knew it would. What she chose to do about his threat—the loss of her heir plus her grandchildren—was up to her.

She nodded curtly. "I will return to my home."

"With Audriss," Severn said.

His mother glanced around.

Severn's chest tightened with uneasiness when he saw no sign of the dragon female his mother had been intent on mating him with. He decided to take Sophie to the apartment his cousin Tielo maintained at Drake's Lair rather than to the estate. "I can not force Audriss to return with me," his mother said. "But I will ensure her things are removed from the estate and her invitation to enter is revoked."

Severn nodded and though it wasn't required, his time spent among the humans had taught him not to underestimate the power of courtesy and charm. "Thank you, Mother."

She blinked in surprise and tipped her head slightly in regal response. The small, telling gestures spoke of the possibility of finding a middle ground in which to deal with one another.

Severn said goodbye before the truce could be broken. He led Sophie through the club's restaurant and into Tielo's private office. He hesitated at the desk long enough to scribble *Do Not Disturb* on a piece of stationery then tape it to the door leading to Tielo's private quarters.

Sophie's gasp made him chuckle, as did the sign. In truth he'd only put it up for her benefit. He had little doubt that every male on the premises was aware of his location. How could it be otherwise? His mate was not only beautiful, but she would soon be a legend among his kind. He could well imagine the tales Hakon, Malik and Xanthus were weaving, tales he would expand upon when they returned from the dragon realm. His mate was responsible for finding the Dragon's Cup and saving it from once again becoming an orgy cup to be brought out for Queen Otthilde's amusement.

Severn opened the door to Tielo's apartment. He guided Sophie inside and locked the door behind them.

A wave of lust hit him with the sudden privacy. Need throbbed in his cock.

He'd come so close to losing her, but now she stood before him in fiery glory—his to claim, his to fuck—his to breed when the time was right for the both of them. "Strip," he growled, feeling the magic keeping him in human form pull taut against his senses.

Sophie's eyes widened with surprise first and then with sexual hunger. Her lips tilted upward. He braced himself for her refusal, for the dare she would send as a test of his will and his control.

She licked her lips instead. She made a show of slowly freeing the buttons of her shirt, then leaving it to hang open as she removed her sandals and set them aside.

"Sophie," he warned.

She responded with a laugh, by stepping into him and pressing her lush, nearly bared breasts against his chest. Her arms wrapped around his neck. Her leg curled around his as her pelvis rubbed against his cloth-covered erection and sent fire streaking up his spine.

Her aggression turned him on. Her disobedience heated his blood.

Severn cupped her ass. He ground his cock against her mound until she was panting lightly and flushed from the sensation. "Do you want another spanking?" he asked. "Is that why you're defying my order to strip?" His hand stroked a buttock. "I am more than happy to accommodate you. The sight of you jumping from the boat and risking your life is burned in my mind. The fear I experienced is a dark place on my soul."

Sophie's lips found his. Her kiss was one of supplication, reassurance, love. When it ended, he whispered, "I cannot lose you. You are everything to me."

"I'm safe now. You saved my life." She smiled against his mouth. "Those last seconds as I was about to black out I saw you as a fire-breathing dragon. You were magnificent, deep blue with traces of red, something straight out of a fantasy."

Severn's hands moved to trace the delicate line of Sophie's spine. If ever there was a moment to prepare her for the bonding, it was this one. "I would like to think I am your fantasy come true," he said.

She tilted her head back so she could meet his eyes. "You can't seriously believe you're not."

"I can be possessive, dominating. I've even been threatened with the label of male chauvinist." His heart flooded with emotion when his mate's eyes became limpid with the depth of her feelings for him.

"You're also protective, generous, incredibly sexy and very loving," Sophie said. She rubbed her cheek against his. "You know I adore everything about you. I can't imagine myself with anyone else. From the instant the heartmate stone responded to you, I've been swept into a world of magic and you're at its center. Aislinn told me once that the magic always requires that you give up something. I've given up my heart, my soul, the complete independence that was so important to me after living through the nightmare of my mother's murder. And I'd give up more if I had to. I can't even bear to think about life without you. I love you."

Severn cupped her face. Their lips met. For long, heartfelt moments they kissed as their hands sought skin and their bodies pressed tightly together.

When the kiss ended, Severn said, "I am both dragon and man, Sophie. In this realm I am forbidden from changing form though no threat of punishment would ever keep me from doing so—as I did today—if your life was in danger." He pressed his lips to hers again in order to keep her from speaking, from uttering a denial or making a joke. He wanted her to think about what he'd said, to mesh it with their teasing, with the things she already knew. She was clever, imaginative. She believed in magic. The heartmate necklace and protection locket, along with the vast collection of crystals were testament to it, as was her confession when they'd greeted the sunrise on the beach.

She would *not* flinch from him in terror. She would *not* be driven beyond sanity when he took her to the dragon realm.

Her heart pounded against his chest. Its beat quickened as what he'd said lodged deeper into her consciousness.

Severn lifted his mouth from hers. "Accept me, my heartmate. Know me in both forms. Bond with me."

Sophie's hands tangled in his thick locks of auburn hair. She met his sapphire gaze and felt nothing but excitement and love.

She believed him. She accepted him. How could she not? On some level she'd known all along he was more than he appeared to be. Call it instinct, hunch, the workings of her very active imagination. It didn't matter and she didn't intend to delve too deeply into it.

"I love you," she said, punctuating it with a brief kiss. "I accept you." She kissed him again. "I'll happily bond with you." A teasing smile formed on her lips. "Just tell me what I have to do."

Severn threw back his head and laughed. The sound was so full of happiness that Sophie's throat was choked with tears of emotion. But those tears were quickly burned away with searing lust when he set her aside and repeated his earlier command. "Strip."

She slid the already-opened blouse off her shoulders and let it fall to the floor. Her fingers toyed with the front clasp of her bra then abandoned it in favor of the top snap on her shorts. Severn's nostrils flared when her fingers found the zipper and slowly tugged it downward, revealing and mesmerizing him with a tantalizing glimpse of her smooth cunt.

"Your turn to take something off," she said, dipping her fingers into the opening of her shorts.

His breath came out in a sharp pant. His eyes darkened when she found her clit and moaned. Severn shed his shirt without argument, kicked off his shoes as her finger slid into her slick channel and she shivered as she imagined it was his tongue, his cock.

"Sophie," he growled.

She relented. She retreated.

She opened the clasp of her bra and shrugged the garment off. Her fingers found her nipples. She coated one areola with the arousal that still lingered from her cunt.

Severn's eyes blazed with lust. He removed his belt, his pants. "You test my patience," he said, his body taut with need, glistening with a thin sheen of sweat. "The rest of it, Sophie, or you will feel my hand on your backside."

With a sultry shimmy of her hips the shorts felt to the floor. She stepped into him, purred as she rubbed against him and felt his hard cock against her wet, wet pussy.

"Now what?" she whispered.

Severn fought for control as he'd never fought before. His provocative mate had no idea how hot the fire she was playing with truly was.

He tangled his fingers in her hair. He kissed her until they were both breathless and then he urged her downward.

Her mouth was wet and hot, decadent. He moaned when she took his nipples, sucking and laving and biting as he shivered in pleasure. Her tongue was a wicked delight, a sensory treat that had his abdomen clenching as she licked over it and dipped into his bellybutton in a shallow fuck.

Dragon fire burned through every cell. His cock strained and leaked and pulsed in anticipation. His heart skipped a beat when she looked up at him from beneath lowered eyelashes then turned her head slightly and nuzzled his shaft.

His buttocks clenched with the first brush of her lips against his penis. "Sophie," he moaned, granting her permission even as he was ready to beg her to take him into her mouth.

She kissed and laved, bit and suckled along the length of his erection until lust was a continuous thunder in his head. The magic slipped to reveal his true size.

Sophie's husky laugh was followed by an appreciative sigh, by fingers that measured the weight of his testicles and a hand that encircled his thick, rigid cock. "If you ever lose your fortune," she teased, "I think there's a place for you in the movies."

His lips curled in a smile though the breath was forced from his body when she took the tip of his penis in her hot, wet mouth. He bucked, instinct demanding that he drive himself deeper.

She tightened her grip on him. She punished him with the swipe of her tongue against the slit in his cock head. She sucked and licked and pleasured him until he was thrusting, pleading, no longer able to hide the dragon rings from her.

Severn cried out in protest when her mouth left him, when her hand slid downward so she could study the thick ridges beneath the head of his penis. "It's true," she murmured before ducking her head and exploring them with her tongue and lips, sending him into a tailspin of need that would only be satisfied with a lava-hot eruption of seed.

Sophie was enthralled, mesmerized. She'd known he was different, bigger than other men, but now she could measure those differences with her eyes, with her tongue.

Her cunt throbbed with need. Arousal rolled down her inner thighs. Her clit stiffened, waiting for attention.

She wanted him inside her but she wanted to pleasure him more. No wonder he'd denied her before. No wonder she'd felt stretched to the limit each time he'd filled her. No wonder each climax had been almost beyond enduring because of its intensity. He wasn't human.

Sophie took him in her mouth again. She took him deep, deep enough so her tongue could rub against the ridges underneath his tip. His moans were music to her ears. Each jerk of his hips was a validation of his need for her.

She reveled in his panting, in the way her name became a chant, a plea. She granted no mercy because he'd never shown her any when it came to passion, to pleasure.

"Listen to me, Sophie," he said, his voice strained, his hips thrusting in time to her sucking, her kneading of his heavy balls. "Look at me."

She forced her eyes open. A tremor of surprise moved through her when she saw the tiny claws at his wrists.

"I won't be able to keep from raking you with my spurs when I come," he said. "You'll pass out after the serum is injected. When you wake, you'll be in the dragon realm and we'll be bonded."

Realization dawned. Twice she'd passed out. Twice she'd woken in a different location with shallow scratches down her back.

He groaned when her mouth left his cock. She turned her head and surrounded the spur at his wrist with her lips and tongue. She explored it and found her lack of fear aroused him further.

His cock bobbed and leaked. It throbbed, hot and hard against her cheek. His breath grew shorter. The hands in her hair tightened and she knew she was only seconds away from being forced back to his erection.

Feminine power infused her. She released the spur and ducked her head to nuzzle his balls, to grasp the skin of his testicles between her lips and teeth, to burn them with the heat of her breath and passion.

Severn hunched over her. His fingernails scraped up and down her back and buttocks in warning. The sharp barb at the base of his wrists dragged along her spine without breaking the skin.

She took his cock in her mouth again, this time with the intent of hearing his shout of release. He thrust deep in her throat. He quivered as her tongue found every sensitive spot, as she explored the slitted head, the thick ridges. His hands went to her breasts. They cupped and pressed and stimulated her nipples. He bucked and jerked, fucked in and out of her mouth, gasped and panted and shivered only to pull away at the last minute and force her onto her hands and knees.

"Next time," he growled as he thrust into her channel. "Next time I'll let you swallow my seed."

Sophie whimpered as he stretched and burned her with his length and width. She canted her hips so she could take more of him. She widened her thighs and arched her back so he'd know how much she liked having him mount her.

"Mine," he growled, deepening his penetration. "Say it, Sophie," he demanded as his teeth gripped her shoulder.

"Yours," she panted, grabbing fistfuls of carpet and rocking backward, crying out as the thick ridges on his cock made her womb flutter and her sheath tighten like a fist.

He began moving, his strokes deep and hard, slow at first. But they were both too aroused to play any longer. They were both too needy, too ready to find ultimate fulfillment, to be joined permanently.

Her cries and whimpers filled the room. They were joined by harsh pants and guttural growls, by the sound of flesh slapping against flesh.

The air around her shimmered blue and red. Severn remained human, but only barely. His dragon form overlaid mortal flesh and bones. In a heartbeat Sophie was reminded of those moments in VanDenbergh's orgy room when she'd imagined him as a dragon.

She screamed as his thrusts became more forceful. All thought left her as he lay more heavily on her, as he became more dominant, more demanding—a male dragon demanding the complete submission of his human mate.

There was no fighting him. There was only the desire to yield, to accept. She softened, she cried out in pleasure, she came in a wash of ecstasy as his hot seed splashed into her womb and the spurs on his wrists raked down her sides.

Sophie woke on a bed of smooth, glittering stones. Diamonds, rubies, sapphires, emeralds, opals — those were just a few of the gems she recognized.

She scooped them up by the handfuls and laughed as she let them trickle through her fingers. Severn's arm tightened around her waist, his human body melded to her back. Familiar lips trailed kisses along her neck.

Sophie looked around and laughed again. She was in a cave, his *lair* no doubt. From the blue sky and white clouds visible through the opening, from the lack of tree tops or green of any color, she guessed she was high above the ground, very high. Her heart did a dancing stutter in her chest, her stomach lurched sideways.

"I think we need a safety railing if I'm going to spend much time here."

A chuckle sounded in her mind. A hand stroked over her stomach and cupped her mound. *If you fall, I will catch you.*

She startled at the sound of his voice. She tried to turn in his arms so she could look at his face. He held her tight. His fingers thrust into her slit. She grew wet and flushed in a heartbeat. She whimpered in protest when his fingers left her. They grazed over her clit and her hips jerked. She gasped when she saw the dragon tattoo near her left hip.

Severn traced the design. He painted it with the arousal he'd gathered from her cunt. *We are bonded now, my heartmate. Held together by magic as well as love. We are only a thought away from each other, regardless of my form or which realm we are in.*

This time when she attempted to turn in his arms he allowed it. His eyes were dark sapphire, his expression one of total satisfaction.

How did we get here? Sophie asked, finding it hard to keep her lips from moving.

We entered the dragon's realm through a common portal. He rubbed the spur at his wrist down her side. *And then I carried you to my lair in the usual way, held to my chest as I flew here.* His lips curled in amusement. *Based on your request for a guardrail, I suspect it was a good thing for both of us that you were unconscious.*

That's why you have claws?

In part.

In part?

The serum adapts your genetic makeup so you can have dragon offspring.

A moment of panic filled Sophie as she thought about them drinking from the Chalice of Enos before going to Tielo's apartment. She hadn't protested then because she hadn't actually believed the cup had anything to do with whether or not dragons could have children — despite the evidence, she hadn't *known* dragons existed. She wasn't ready to be pregnant! There was so much —

Easy, my heartmate, Severn said as he trailed a spur along her spine. *You are not pregnant. At a time of our choosing, the creation magic will alter the serum so you will conceive when we mate.*

Is that how the wizard's curse worked, it blocked the magic so the serum didn't change?

Severn's eyes sparkled. *Perhaps my beautiful and brilliant mate will solve that mystery too. The tale you're familiar with isn't entirely correct. Somehow Enos cast a spell and tied the creation magic of the dragons to the cup so male and female need to drink from it to ensure offspring — or so we were told. When we return to the human realm, we'll contact Malik and suggest he consult with those who are searching for a way to undo the spell. Maybe it is tied to the serum. Even between dragon pairs, injecting it is part of the mating act though we have always believed the serum evolved for the claiming of human mates.*

Sophie felt relief at hearing Severn say their children would arrive at a time of *their* choosing, not *his* choosing. But her curiosity was piqued, even if she wasn't sure she was ready to know the answer. *If our children will all be dragons...* Some of the images assailing her were straight out of a sci-fi movie.

Severn laughed. *They will be born human and in your realm they will remain that way. Even in this realm they won't be able to shift back and forth at will until they're older.*

Satisfied Sophie leaned back far enough to stroke the dragon tattooed on his chest. *Let me see you.*

A purring rumble went through him. She smiled, imagining him preening.

He leaned in and nipped her bottom lip. *Careful, my heartmate. Until you learn to shield your thoughts, you are an open book to me.*

She laughed, not in the least bit worried about what he might read in her mind. *Let me see you.*

He left the bed of gems. She rolled onto her back, surprised at just how comfortable the stones were. It was somewhat like lying on a beanbag chair. The gems yielded and molded to her frame. They were also warm, very nearly hot, as if they'd soaked in years of dragon heat.

She shivered in anticipation even as she admired Severn's human form. He was a living, breathing, very naked sexual fantasy.

His laughter filled the lair. His cock thrust upward in proud display.

Sophie licked her lips and pressed her thighs together. She wanted him.

You will have me.

A trace of erotic fear slid down her spine. Her cunt clenched at the purring promise in his voice. She wondered just *how* she'd have him as the air shimmered with red and blue, as man became magnificent beast.

She scrambled to her feet. Awe warred with trepidation. He was bigger, heavier than in human form and yet he wasn't terrifyingly huge.

Her gaze dropped to his nether regions. Her eyes widened at the sight of nothing but smooth scales of dark blue edged with red.

A long dragon tongue flicked out in a quick caress of her slit. *Do not worry, my heartmate. The cock that has already known the sweet bliss of your sheath is present in this form as well. When I mount you it will emerge and give you pleasure.*

His tongue flicked out again, this time lingering, tasting her, making her think of the figurine set he'd gifted her with, the human woman being tongue-fucked by her dragon lover.

It is a scene I intend to reenact many, many times, Severn said.

A loud, strident trumpeting made Sophie jump backward. The sound was followed by a wall of fire filling the opening of the lair.

Audriss! Severn hissed. His eyes flashed red. *Stay at the back of the lair,* he ordered before turning toward the entranceway. Fire roared from his open mouth as he launched himself through the dying wall of flame.

Heavy wings beat the air. Bodies collided in muffled thunder.

A deep voice trumpeted in rage. A higher voice answered with a call that sounded victorious to Sophie. She couldn't stand not being able to see what was going on. Despite his order, she inched forward.

The dragons were engaged in deadly combat—dark blue against scarlet red. Their talons, sharp and deadly, were locked together. Wings flapped furiously as they each tried to maneuver the other to the face of the cliff.

Terror filled Sophie when one of Audriss' claws managed to rake across Severn's chest. Blood gushed from the wound, coating his scales before falling toward the distant ground like red rain.

Sophie clutched her heartmate necklace out of habit and found the locket Aislinn gave her. She removed it from her neck and stepped closer to the edge, so close her toes curled over the ledge though she leaned away from the deadly precipice with the rest of her body. She prayed she was doing the right thing by interfering.

"Audriss!" she yelled, guessing the dragon female wouldn't be able to resist trying to incinerate her.

"Look!" she said, opening the locket to reveal the fascination stone before flinging it as far away from the lair as she could.

Before Sophie could draw a breath, the scarlet dragon was diving, its attention focused completely on the rapidly disappearing locket. "No, Severn!" Sophie screamed when he flew downward in pursuit of Audriss and the stone.

Horror washed over her when the scarlet dragon caught up with the locket. In a shimmer of red the beast became a woman falling to her death as she stared in fascination at what was in her hands.

Severn's claws wrapped around Audriss' upper arms. Sophie whimpered in fear as she envisioned him becoming human and freefalling the remaining distance to the ground.

For the first time she forced herself to look down. A moment of vertigo assailed her and she stepped back from the edge of the lair. She sat, afraid if she continued to stand she'd topple over.

The tightness in her chest eased when she saw Severn was still in dragon form. She watched in awe as he circled and glided and slowly became a dark shadow with occasional flashes of red when the sun struck him.

She remembered what he'd said about being only a thought away from each other. Without meaning to she'd put a shield between their minds when Audriss attacked—or maybe Severn had.

Sophie nibbled her bottom lip, hesitant to interfere, until her own inner voice chided, *As if you haven't already interfered, big time.* Despite her success in distracting Audriss she had a feeling Severn was going to be breathing fire when he returned to the lair.

Tentatively Sophie reached for him mentally. She tried to remain unobtrusive. But the moment they connected he growled, *I will deal with you shortly, my heartmate. I gave you fair warning about what would happen if you put yourself in danger again.*

She smiled despite being reminded of his threat to leave her unable to sit for a week. The fact he was making it told her the situation with Audriss was under control.

It was never out of control, he growled, clearly offended she might think it had been and he couldn't adequately defend them.

I trust you with my life, Severn. But I'm not helpless. I'm your mate even when you're in dragon form. She made you bleed. I used the weapons I had against her—her desire to hurt me and the fascination stone. Do you really want a mate who'll cower at the first sign of danger?

What I want is an obedient mate, he grumbled but Sophie could hear the thread of amusement in his voice.

Perhaps that's what you'll find when you return to the lair, Sophie said, infusing her mental voice with a husky tone. *What will you do with Audriss?*

I will reach an agreement with her. She owes me a life debt for not letting her tumble to her death. She can't break the stone's hold on her. Once she is deposited on the ground I will bathe the blood off and return to you. Now get away from the edge of the lair before you attract trouble.

Sophie laughed and gladly abandoned her position. She let the mental link close though it seemed to take forever before her dark blue dragon filled the entranceway. She greeted him with a sultry smile. She leaned back so she was resting on her elbows with her thighs splayed. She let the image of the erotic figurine set fill her mind. "Now where were we when Audriss so rudely interrupted?"

Severn's nostril's flared. His sensual purr filled the lair as he closed the distance between them. *I believe I was just beginning to demonstrate what it means to be mated to a male dragon.* His long, very agile tongue wrapped around her thigh before the tip of it found her entrance. *I love you, my heartmate.*

Dragon or man, I love you too, Severn.

Why an electronic book?

We live in the Information Age — an exciting time in the history of human civilization, in which technology rules supreme and continues to progress in leaps and bounds every minute of every day. For a multitude of reasons, more and more avid literary fans are opting to purchase e-books instead of paper books. The question from those not yet initiated into the world of electronic reading is simply: *Why?*

1. ***Price.*** An electronic title at Ellora's Cave Publishing and Cerridwen Press runs anywhere from 40% to 75% less than the cover price of the exact same title in paperback format. Why? Basic mathematics and cost. It is less expensive to publish an e-book (no paper and printing, no warehousing and shipping) than it is to publish a paperback, so the savings are passed along to the consumer.

2. ***Space.*** Running out of room in your house for your books? That is one worry you will never have with electronic books. For a low one-time cost, you can purchase a handheld device specifically designed for e-reading. Many e-readers have large, convenient screens for viewing. Better yet, hundreds of titles can be stored within your new library — on a single microchip. There are a variety of e-readers from different manufacturers. You can also read e-books on your PC or laptop computer. (Please note that Ellora's Cave does not endorse any specific brands.

You can check our websites at www.ellorascave.com or www.cerridwenpress.com for information we make available to new consumers.)

3. **Mobility.** Because your new e-library consists of only a microchip within a small, easily transportable e-reader, your entire cache of books can be taken with you wherever you go.

4. **Personal Viewing Preferences.** Are the words you are currently reading too small? Too large? Too... ANNOYING? Paperback books cannot be modified according to personal preferences, but e-books can.

5. **Instant Gratification.** Is it the middle of the night and all the bookstores near you are closed? Are you tired of waiting days, sometimes weeks, for bookstores to ship the novels you bought? Ellora's Cave Publishing sells instantaneous downloads twenty-four hours a day, seven days a week, every day of the year. Our webstore is never closed. Our e-book delivery system is 100% automated, meaning your order is filled as soon as you pay for it.

Those are a few of the top reasons why electronic books are replacing paperbacks for many avid readers.

As always, Ellora's Cave and Cerridwen Press welcome your questions and comments. We invite you to email us at Comments@ellorascave.com or write to us directly at Ellora's Cave Publishing Inc., 1056 Home Avenue, Akron, OH 44310-3502.

erridwen, the Celtic Goddess of wisdom, was the muse who brought inspiration to story-tellers and those in the creative arts. Cerridwen Press encompasses the best and most innovative stories in all genres of today's fiction. Visit our site and discover the newest titles by talented authors who still get inspired - much like the ancient storytellers did, once upon a time.

CERRIDWEN PRESS
www.cerridwenpress.com

Discover for yourself why readers can't get enough of the multiple award-winning publisher

Ellora's Cave.

Whether you prefer e-books or paperbacks,

be sure to visit EC on the web at
www.ellorascave.com

for an erotic reading experience that will leave you breathless.

763557

Printed in Great Britain by
Amazon.co.uk, Ltd.,
Marston Gate.